Mazed

by

J L Wilson

*A Remembered Classics Romance,
Book 7*

Mazed

Cover Art by *Kim Mendoza*

The Wild Rose Press, Inc.
PO Box 708
Adams Basin, NY 14410-0708
Visit us at www.thewildrosepress.com

Publishing History
First Crimson Rose Edition, 2020
Trade Paperback ISBN 978-1-5092-3261-1
Digital ISBN 978-1-5092-3262-8

A Remembered Classics Romance, Book 7
Published in the United States of America

"I'm not telling her. You tell her."

I threw up my hands. "What?"

"I'm supposed to be your bodyguard," Dillan muttered behind me.

I turned slowly to stare at Dillan. "My what?"

He met my eyes, his face still flushed. "Bodyguard," he enunciated.

I counted to five, then I wheeled around to face Pop. "You hired a bodyguard?"

"I hired a guy to work in the garden, and he can also be a bodyguard." Pop put his hands on the edge of the bed and stood.

I took his arm, holding him steady. "I still say you need to go to the doctor."

"I will. Or I'll call," he amended.

"I'll call and you'll see him." I got on Pop's right side and helped him walk to the door. "Let's go sit and try to talk about this like rational people."

"I can help," Dillan said, moving forward.

"You can get the hell away from me," I snapped. "I've had a shitty day starting with you scaring the crap out of me at the crack of dawn and ending with a psychotic bitch scaring the crap out of me an hour ago. I'm going to make a drink, sit down, and try to make sense out of my life. You can join me or not, but you will move, do you hear me?" I shot him a glare that would have eviscerated him if my eyes were lasers.

Dedication

I created a fictional support group for the survivor in my book, but several excellent organizations do exist in the world for those people who are victims of acid attacks (vitriolage).

The Acid Survivors Trust International works to improve the lives of victims and to prevent the root cause of acid attacks, which usually have women and children as its targets.

My victim in this story is, indeed, one of the lucky ones. Women in developing countries who suffer such attacks have an extremely difficult life ahead of them, both medically and psychologically. Re-entry into society is frequently barred to them, and they end their lives in poverty and disgrace even though they are the victim, not the perpetrator, of the crime.

When I began writing this story, I was simply looking for a convenient disfigurement for my heroine, the "Beast" of my "Beauty and the Beast." While researching this topic, I uncovered the horrific crimes which occur every day. It opened my eyes, just as it did for my heroine. And, like her, I've discovered a world that I didn't know existed.

Chapter One

I opened the door, expecting to see the landscape guy I hired to work on my garden. Instead I got a nightmare.

Blake Kelleher glared at me. "Hello, Lilith. I need to talk to you."

I was so stunned, I stared at him for a second. It was twenty-five years since I'd seen him. He'd gone from brusque, arrogant middle age to brusque, arrogant old age. His black hair was changed to white and he was a bit stooped, but he was still an imposing man even at age seventy-five.

"What do you want?" I clung to the door for support. Kelleher Senior always had that effect on me.

"To talk to you." His imperious brown eyes swept over me, taking in my crinkled neck and hand, the obvious results of the attack. It felt like he had x-ray vision and saw beneath my loose pants and long-sleeved cotton shirt to evaluate the other injuries.

"About what?"

"I'd prefer to talk inside." He moved forward, but I moved, too, blocking his way.

"I'd prefer you talk outside." I didn't want him in my house. Irrational though it might be, I thought he'd taint the premises if he set foot inside.

His fists clenched. He wore a tailored dark suit,

incongruous against the backdrop of my wildflower garden, a thorn among my tea roses. "I came to see how you're doing."

Years of pretending in front of other people had schooled me how to hide my reactions. "Why?"

My bluntness appeared to surprise him. "I-I wondered if you—I thought that I should—" He drew in a deep breath, and his steely exterior returned. "I may not be able to continue paying your allowance."

It was odd. I'd been expecting this since the attack on me at his house, twenty-five years ago. I was always surprised that the money continued to be deposited into my checking account every month. But hearing it now from him somehow shocked me. I managed to say, "The stipulation of our agreement is that you will provide me with an allowance until my death. In the event of your death, it will be continued by..." I swallowed, "...by your heirs."

"My heirs." He snarled the words. "Don't talk to me about my heirs. It's because of my heirs that I had to come out of retirement."

Come out of retirement? From what I read in the Business section of the newspaper, he had refused to relinquish control of any of his business holdings to his son, who was waiting to step into a leadership role. That didn't surprise me. Blake Kelleher had an iron fist when it came to his family, and I could well imagine that he would hold on to his control of his companies just as tightly. "That isn't my problem," I said. "Are you saying you're unable to come up with the money? I find that hard to believe, given the lifestyle you and your family live."

His thin lips thinned even more. "You are in no

position to judge my lifestyle. It's none of your business."

"You're right." I clung to the door, trembling with anger. This man had almost been my father-in-law. Good Lord, what would that have been like? I pushed the thought aside. "I've held up my part of our agreement." Even though inflation has taken its toll, I longed to say. The miserly pittance he gave me barely covered my additional medical expenses and the physical therapy I required three times a week.

"Did you ever tell your father about the other part of our agreement? Does he know how your mother's gambling debts were paid off so quickly?" The sly insinuation in his voice made my anger double.

"Don't you dare. That was a private arrangement between you and me." I felt like I was in a bad movie, and I didn't know the plot. "Don't try to renege on our agreement." I glimpsed the garden worker coming up the path between my flower beds behind Kellcher. He didn't appear like he was dressed to work. He wore a polo shirt and khaki pants, not the uniform of a man who would be digging in the dirt. Damn it, I needed somebody to get my landscape into shape. What was the deal?

"I will do everything I can to maintain my part of the bargain, but if I can't, I don't want you doing anything rash." For an instant, his features seemed to crumple with grief. "Promise me."

"What do you mean? Promise you what? What are you talking about?"

He pointed a finger at me, and I raised an arm to fend off his blow. I must have caught him unaware because he stumbled back off the concrete step, teetering when he tried to catch his balance. The worker saw us and strode up the path in time to catch the old man before he fell completely.

"Oh, thank you," Kelleher wheezed.

"Get out of here," I snapped. "And don't come back. If you insist on welching on our deal, I'll have my lawyers contact you." My lawyer, an elderly gentleman who collected baseballs and did family law, wouldn't be up to the task of litigating with any high-powered attorney Kelleher hired, but it was the best threat I could come up with on the spur of the moment.

Kelleher cringed, clinging to the beefy young man who shot me a disbelieving glance, an expression that changed to one of puzzlement then pity when he saw my scarred neck. "Oh, leave." I transferred my glare to the worker. "You're late."

He released Kelleher's arm but stayed near the old man, who swayed as though he might fall. It was act, I was sure. Blake Kelleher was like an oak tree—tough, solid, and impossible to dislodge. "I stopped by to tell you that we don't have time in the schedule. We'll try to get you in rotation in July." The man walked away.

"Wait a minute, you promised!" I started down the steps, but my bum right leg chose that moment to give out, almost tipping me forward. I grabbed the iron rail to keep myself upright.

"We'll have time in July." The man walked with Kelleher, giving the old man a solicitous hand. "What happened to her?" The man looked over his shoulder at me. When he saw me watching, he ducked his head as though dodging my wrath.

"A vitriol attack years ago. I suppose it soured her disposition." Kelleher and the worker moved out of earshot, and I was left to stare at my garden, which so badly needed tending.

I returned to the foyer. My father peeked at me from the dining room. "Who was that?"

I longed to tell him about the whole encounter, but why upset him? Blake Kelleher was a part of my unpleasant past, one that I successfully put behind me until today. "The garden workers we hired. They said they don't have time to help us until July." I went past Pop to the kitchen at the back of the house.

"What?" He followed me, setting his coffee mug on the counter near the doorway. "You just wait, I'll tell them what they can and can't do."

"No, Pop. Let it go. I sure wish Terry hadn't moved." My previous garden helper had recently married and moved to the next state over, Nebraska.

"They're doing this, aren't they?" Pop stalked to the kitchen island, five-foot-six of angry old man. "Those damn sisters."

I followed him and took a seat on a stool at the island. The Three Sisters was a rival landscaping company in the nearby town of Beaumont, with more money and more connections than I as an individual consultant could command. They were my rivals in the upcoming Garden Showcase competition. It was imperative that my garden be in its best possible shape for the judging taking place in a week and for the public viewing that followed.

I fought the panic that thought invoked. A week. I had a week to try to force my garden into a semblance of controlled beauty. Pruning, mulching, staking, weeding. I also had tentatively planned on moving a few large shrubs from one spot to another. I leaned my elbows on the faux marble countertop and took in a deep breath. "We'll figure something out."

"I'm sorry, honey. I wish I could contribute more." Pop covered my left hand with his right and gave me a companionable squeeze.

"We'll manage. Don't worry." I said it absently. I was mentally adding up the contents of my checking account and savings account. Good help was pricey, and we needed good help and lots of it. I knew a lot of landscape companies, but this was the busy time of year and there weren't any experienced crews to spare.

The doorbell rang again and I slid off the stool. If Blake Kelleher came back for another round, I was prepared to deck him this time. I flung open the door and my physical therapist, Swann Yeh, brushed past me into the house. He was a slender Asian-American man with steel gray hair and hands like iron. He'd been working on my broken body for almost ten years and knew his way around my house.

"Who was that grumpy old man I saw?" he asked, bustling past me, his 'medicine bag' in hand. "He was getting into a black sedan down at the road."

"Wrong number." I glanced at the kitchen. "Swann and I are in therapy, Pop."

"Okay," he called back. "I think I'll go putter around with Mazie."

"It's Labbie," I corrected. "A labyrinth." This was a long-standing joke between us.

"Maze, labyrinth, what's the difference?"

"A maze can have multiple entries and exits. A labyrinth has only one way in and out, as you well know. Cover yourself with bug juice," I cautioned. "They're fierce. And don't stay out too long. It's hot."

"Hmm."

I knew what that meant. He would probably overdo it and end up crashing on the couch tonight. Pops was the same age as Kelleher and as different as night from day. But age was slowing both him and me and we couldn't do as much of the garden work anymore.

I followed Swann through the living room to my PT space at the rear of the house. When I bought this small bungalow twenty years ago, I had part of the living room walled off, giving me a private nook that opened into the mud room and abutted the first-floor powder room. My treadmill was there and I used part of the space for the yoga I did daily. In addition, I had a waist-high massage table and a small side table where Swanny unloaded his gear.

"Are you going to tell me about the grumpy old man, or do I have to pry it out of you?"

"Nothing to tell." I peeled off my long-sleeved shirt, leaving me in a pale pink camisole. Next, I shucked off my jeans and pulled on the gym shorts hanging from a hook near the doorway. I kicked off my clogs and slipped on a headband to push my short shaggy gray hair away from my forehead.

"I know you, Lily. You're hiding something. What is it?" Swann helped me onto the table where I stretched out, my injured leg not quite straightening because of the scars. "Deep breaths," he instructed. "Calming breaths." Swann pressed my leg down, massaging lotion into the burn scars puckering my right side. "Who was it?"

"Blake Kelleher," I mumbled.

He massaged, pressed, and tugged. "He's the father of the guy, right?"

The guy. "Yes," I said. "He's Shaw's father." Swann knew about the attack. It was in my medical records. Acid thrown at me by an angry ex-girlfriend of the man I was supposed to marry, Shaw Kelleher. I was lucky. The attack happened at the Kelleher house, and we were standing by the swimming pool. I was so shocked I fell backward into the pool, which probably saved my life.

It didn't prevent disfiguring burns—my neck, shoulder, my right leg, right arm and hand, and chest. Still, I was alive, I had my eyesight and hearing, and I didn't inhale any of the acid. Yes, I was one of the lucky ones.

"I still say the guy's a jerk because he didn't stay with you after it happened."

Swann didn't know the whole story, of course. No one did except my father, Blake Kelleher, and me. And my father only knew half the tale. "I don't blame him." I struggled to relax when Swann lifted my leg and rhythmically flexed it inward then out. I knew the puckered flesh wouldn't tear, but it always felt like I was only one more leg move away from another hospital stay. "The Kelleher family paid for my medical expenses and it's because of him I can have you come here three times a week."

"Yeah, maybe. But the son still should have stood by you." Swann kept his eyes on my face while he flexed my leg, gauging the extent of my pain.

He didn't stay by me because I told him not to, I wanted to say. I didn't want to see him watching me in the hospital when the nurses changed the bandages on my raw and seeping wounds. I didn't want to see the expression in his eyes when he saw my naked body, no longer supple and beautiful.

I took the money his father offered and told Shaw to never see me again. One part of me secretly wished Shaw would have ignored me and sought me out. But the rational part knew it was best that he didn't.

"It was a tragedy for everyone," I managed to say.

"That little bitch got off easy. Move to your side." Swann helped me slide onto my left. "Five years in a mental hospital, if you can call it a hospital. From what I've read, it's more like a spa for celebrities."

Tanya Sidero pled diminished capacity due to pain-killers and spent five years chatting with doctors and painting pictures at a posh hospital in Switzerland, paid for by her wealthy parents. She returned to Beaumont to become the business manager of the family company, which was now my competition in the flower show.

"I'm amazed you haven't run into her. You're both in the same business."

"Not really." I struggled to relax while Swann maneuvered my right leg upright, stretching the tortured flesh. "I'm a consultant to hospitals and nursing homes. They do commercial landscaping."

"But you're both in gardening."

"That's like saying you should know Jackie Chan because you're Asian. We don't run in the same circles. Besides, they're in Beaumont and I'm in Le Prince. We're miles and miles apart." That wasn't strictly true. Le Prince, pronounced "Lee Prince," abutted Beaumont, the larger town. I was on the far west edge of Le Prince and Beaumont was on the east, so it was more like six miles distance.

"Well, I guess you're lucky." Swann began massaging my leg, working in the cocoa butter that kept the skin somewhat flexible. "It would be hard to see her after what you went through."

"I doubt that will happen." I didn't mention the restraining order, which dictated that Tanya stay at least fifty yards away from me. As soon as I knew she was released from custody and returning here, I had a judge issue the order. I wasn't taking any chances. I renewed the order every year for the past twenty years even though I had never been in the same room with her or with Shaw.

Swann worked in silence for a time, his fingers digging into my sensitive flesh. It was twenty-five years since the attack. It still hurt, although not at all like what I went through when it first happened. I still had nightmares about that hell.

While he massaged my fingers and arm, I thought about the visit from Blake Kelleher. My check came from his attorney, who handled the business transactions for the past twenty-five years. The amount hadn't changed even though the cost of medical treatment rose. I knew better than to ask for more, however. Kelleher was a tough, uncompromising businessman. We made a bargain, and I would stick to it.

One part of the bargain was private between Kelleher and me, and that had me worried. My mother, who died of a stroke five months before the attack, racked up an impressive amount of gambling debt at the nearby casino, a debt that would have eaten up my father's meager retirement account and equally thin savings account. Part of the deal with Kelleher was that he paid off her notes.

Pop thought an anonymous donor came to his

rescue. He always suspected it was a pool of money from the guys at the auto shop where he worked. I didn't want to wound his pride by telling him Blake Kelleher saved his butt.

"I wish you were distracted every day," Swann said. "You barely made a peep while I worked."

"I guess it pays to be worried after all," I admitted. "I hardly noticed."

Swann rolled up his towel, tucking it into his carryall. "I'll be back on Tuesday, like we planned, since the Fourth is on Wednesday. Are you sure you want to do only two sessions next week?"

I would need every free minute to work in the garden if I couldn't get any help. "Sure, Tuesday and Friday. I'll be fine."

"Keep applying the lotion and do your exercises," he chided while fitting tubes and equipment into his bag. "I know you don't like to ask him but have your father work with you on the stretches."

I slid off the massage table and stood upright for a second, trying to get my balance before moving. "It's just one missed session. I'll be fine." I reached for my shirt, slipping it on but not buttoning it. We didn't expect any visitors this late in the day, so I wasn't too concerned about covering up.

"Physical therapy is critical, and you know it. Take care of yourself." Swann gave my left arm a squeeze. "You're one of my success stories. Don't screw it up for me now." His normally stoic demeanor shifted to that of a mischievous child.

"I wouldn't dream of it." I walked with him to the front door, moving stiffly. These sessions always left me a bit drained of energy and today was no exception.

Combine that with the moist heat of a June afternoon, and I was ready to relax.

I watched Swann make his way down the front path, navigating the five stone platform steps to the street level. The sloping front garden was in relatively decent shape and I wasn't too worried about it. It was the back garden, Labbie, and the side arbor that needed the most work.

It was too hot for me to do anything now, though. My injuries meant I didn't sweat as much as I needed to and unless I slathered myself with sunscreen, my fragile skin burned easily. Heat stroke was my constant fear. Consequently, I limited my activities to early morning or late evenings.

I went to my office, which faced north, opposite the dining room at the front of the house. I spent an hour going over my finances. The house was paid for, part of the deal with Kelleher, a lump sum negotiated when I was in an induced coma. Pop told me that Shaw insisted on making sure I had a home and the allowance. My poor father was in no shape to argue. His wife had recently died and now his only child was in the hospital, fighting for her life.

I had money coming in from my consulting business, designing therapeutic garden areas for the disabled and elderly. I squirreled that money away to use on my garden research. My disability check, Pop's social security and his pension paid the upkeep on the house and our basic living expenses. The Kelleher allowance paid for my ongoing physical therapy and medical expenses with a bit left over for savings.

I also got a speaker's fee for talking at several different conferences every year, conferences centered around survivors of tragic accidents or attacks. I was scheduled to talk next week on Thursday evening at the yearly conference of Vitriolage Victims, whose annual meeting was being held in St. Louis, a two-hour drive for me.

I didn't charge a great deal for my fee. Most organizations operated on a shoestring budget and had little money to spare. Besides, I was one of the lucky ones. My injuries weren't life-threatening, only disfiguring.

I stared out the window at our quiet street. Our house was the last one at the bottom of a steep hill, a dense stand of trees marking the drop-off beyond the street. A circular patch of pavement for turning around was west of us, downslope. No one lived across the street due to the steep hill there, so my nearest neighbor was up-slope, to the east, separated from us by dense shrubs and trees.

The front garden was small, a third of it occupied by the huge stone steps leading from the street to our front porch. If I went out early in the morning, I could get the garden whipped into shape. That would leave the back and the sides to do. The main reason I entered the competition was to show off my roses, which were interspersed within Labbie in the back. I had several varieties of climbers as well as shrub roses alternating with the yews that formed the high walls of the labyrinth.

The crowning glory were the roses growing in the center of the labyrinth and twining up and over the top of the walls. These were an odd dark-blue color with a rosy pink center, the product of more than fifteen years of selective breeding. I had hopes of selling it to one of the big growers. If that happened, I wouldn't need to worry about money for a while.

I heard Pop come in the back, through the mudroom. I went to join him, putting my worries aside for a time while I tossed together a light supper. As I expected, he was exhausted from his 'puttering' and he slumped in front of the television until I prodded him to go to bed.

I stayed up, savoring a glass of wine before popping one of the Good Pills I kept for the Monday, Wednesday, and Friday evenings of Swann's visits. I rationed myself to only three a week, knowing it would be far too easy to disappear into a pill bottle. Whenever I was tempted to deviate from my pattern, I recalled my stay at the hospital after the attack. *That* was true pain and it always served to put today's pain into perspective.

I climbed the stairs, pausing by Pop's bedroom to listen for his snores. Then I went into my bathroom and attached closet and changed, slipping on the sleeveless T-shirt that hung just past my butt. Winter and summer, that's how I slept, with as little fabric as possible touching me. I went into my bedroom from the bathroom and crossed the room to peer out on the backyard.

My neighbor up the hill was hidden from me by the slope of the street and the landscaping between our properties. I had no neighbors downhill or behind me. I was the last house on the street, which paralleled a deep ravine and my property ended in a precipitous drop-off beyond where Labbie sat.

The rose arbors alternated with yews to form the walls of the labyrinth. I began the project years ago as a way to keep pain and memory at bay. Walking the labyrinth forced me to concentrate, pushing thoughts of the attack and my recovery to the side. I originally designed it to be a maze, but it was too hard to maintain. There were still thin spots in the yew walls where once I had a maze pathway.

I started with a simple layout, but that soon wasn't challenging enough for me. Within a few years, I switched it to a more complex model, the path inlaid with stones. The yew hedge was now six inches taller than me and the arbors that filled in the formerly thin spots were thickly grown with vines that were almost as dense as the shrubs.

The path was broad enough not to feel claustrophobic, but two people couldn't easily walk side-by-side. Anyone taller and broader shouldered than me might be cramped. I only hoped the garden judges would appreciate it and not be unsettled. Groups of judges were coming at various times of the morning. In the afternoon, we would open the garden to the public. The prizes would be awarded on Sunday morning at the Beaumont County Fair.

I leaned against the casement window, the woodwork cool from the air conditioning vent below it. The awning over the back stoop was below me, hiding the steps leading from the mudroom. The moon was bright but that wasn't what caught my attention. The motion light near Labbie was on. Someone was moving around out there. I glimpsed light and shadow inside, playing through the latticework of the rose arbors.

How could that be? The gates to my side gardens were locked and fences separated me from my side neighbor. There was no access through the rear of my yard because of the dense trees bordering the drop-off. I straightened, prepared to go outside to check when I saw the telltale stripe of a racoon tail. Those damn varmints loved trundling around the yard, usually foraging near the bird feeders on the borders of my property.

I had a brief rush of concern for my precious roses, then reasoned that the coons wouldn't bother with them. They were more apt to knock over a bird feeder than desecrate a rose bush. Whatever it was, it would have to wait. My pill was kicking in and I knew sweet sleep was only a few yawns away. I'd deal with it later, whatever it was.

But later I didn't have to deal with a coon. I had to deal with a body I found in the middle of the labyrinth, sightless eyes staring at my rose bush.

Chapter Two

The next day, I went out the back door into the damp morning, clad in my usual working gear of lightweight long-sleeved shirt over a camisole, long linen pants, and a garden hat with netting draped around my face to protect against biting gnats and mosquitoes.

It was cool but humid, promising another scorcher. Labbie was ahead of me and slightly to the right, the path leading into it at an angle to the house. I went to the right, passing the low flowerbeds bordering the house and the attached garage. I opened the shed next to the garage and got out my basket of garden tools.

The sun was a smudge out beyond the back edge of my property. At this time of year, it was light enough to work outside by five o'clock. I seldom slept more than five or six hours a night, so that meant I could get in four or five hours before the heat of the day and the sun drove me back inside. On my non-Swann days, I could come out again at seven-thirty or eight at night and get in another hour of work as the sun set.

I decided to work in the back, which faced south. The only time I worked there comfortably was early morning. By afternoon, it was too warm. I tackled the raised flower beds curving around the east and west side of the labyrinth structure. As I weeded and mulched, I thought through my address to the conference next week. Acid attacks were horribly common in many third-world countries and many of the attendees would be officials and medical personnel who tried to help the victims. The conference organizers had forwarded details to me about some of the more prominent people attending, so I would tailor my talk to them.

I worked for an hour, taking a break when I began to get warm. I went into the house and sipped my ice water, returning as the sun peeked through the trees at the back of my yard. I surveyed the yews and the seven-foot lattice arbors that formed Labbie. I would need to get out the ladder to handle those. My previous garden helper, Terry, was a tall man and he managed the trimming with a stepstool, but I was only five-five. Pop was only a tiny bit taller than me and too wobbly to be climbing up on a ladder. I resolved to tackle that chore later, perhaps some other morning when he was asleep and wouldn't know what I was doing. It needed attention to be ready for next week's judging.

I moved on to the short trees that hid my yard from the neighbor up the hill on the west. Pop and I raked out debris earlier in the spring, but now it was time to work on the weeds steadily creeping in. I was finishing up when Pop came out of the house.

"What's that in the middle of Labbie?" he asked, his travel coffee mug in hand. " I thought I saw something out the upstairs window when I came down this morning."

I couldn't see much through the dense growth of roses on the arbors. "Is it that damn cat again?" I fumed. "I wish people wouldn't dump their pets out here."

"You know how assholes are," Pop said. "They figure a cat can take care of himself out in the woods. I've lost track of how many we've trapped and turned in." He sipped his coffee, eyeing the trees I tidied. "What do you want me to work on today?"

"Nothing," I said firmly. "It's Saturday and your day to meet your buddies." Pop always spent Wednesdays and Saturdays hanging out with his friends at the Jean Marie Senior Center in town, affectionately known as Jean's Place. They frequently ended up at the bowling alley, the golf course, or a coffee shop, shooting the breeze.

"Nope, not today. We've got a bunch of stuff to do and—"

I shook a finger at him. "You go and meet your friends. I'll do some touch-up paint on the chairs and tables in front." We had four metal armchairs in front, vintage pieces with white arms and dark green bodies with a stylized floral design inlaid on the backs. They were a pretty contrast with the pale green house. The white metal tables were badly in need of a fresh coat of paint. I stowed my tools in the basket and went with Pop to the garage.

"You know, I think I'll ask the guys if they know of anybody who might be able to give us some garden muscle."

I doubted any seniors would know of landscaping help who might be available, but if it made him feel better about taking the day off, that worked for me. "Thanks, Pop. That would be great."

He kissed my cheek. "Anything to help my girl." He winked then went into the garage through the back door. We got out my painting supplies, and he helped me muscle the chairs into the garage once he backed out his small truck, parked next to my ancient Ford sedan.

I dragged over a stool and settled down to paint as he drove off. It took more than an hour to get the chairs lightly sanded and painted, but they looked great when I finished. I'd give them a second coat of paint tomorrow and they'd be ready.

I took another break for water, standing on the back step as I sipped, surveying the yard. That reminded me I needed to check about the cat who might be sniffing around. I picked up my favorite offset pruning shears and wended my way into Labbie, studying the rose arbors and pausing to prune any thorny protuberances that might annoy a garden judge.

The path was composed of flat, irregularly shaped pavers treated with a luminescent paint visible only at night, when it had a faint glow. They were inset into a bed of thyme, which released fragrance as I strolled, mingling with the heady rose aroma. The arbors were spaced every six feet and occupied three feet of space, so it felt roomy and yet closed in at the same time. There were no decision points in the space. That was the purpose of a labyrinth, to remove the need to choose one direction or the other. All a person needed to do was focus on the path and follow it to reach the center.

In the center of mine was a grouping of four chairs and a small metal firepit bowl. Two of the chairs had cushions that unfolded to form two single beds. They were foam and not very comfortable, but good enough for the occasional night out. When the bugs permitted, I sometimes came out at night when I couldn't sleep and lay on my back, staring at the stars above me. I always felt protected and secure, surrounded by the roses and the greenery.

I paced along the path, trimming and snipping whatever I could reach. The structure was laid out so that the final turns were several rows away from the center, hiding it completely until you rounded a corner and saw it ahead of you. I kept my attention on the yews and the roses but then I remembered Pop's comment about the cat and I lifted my head. I'd seen a big tabby cat prowling around the yard for the last week, but I couldn't get close enough to see it clearly, much less hope to trap and transport it.

I spied a dark shape on the ground near the black outline of the firepit. The surrounding chairs were pale faux rattan with red cushions and the area at the center was laid with white and gray rock, so the shape was immediately noticeable. At first, I wasn't sure what I was seeing, but when I got closer, I knew.

It was a leg in dark pants. I stopped, unbelieving. How could someone be in the center? It made no sense. I was paralyzed by surprise. The firepit was tipped over and the leg lay in the ashes scattered around the center.

A rustling in the nearby yews made me jump so high I almost crashed backward into an arbor. The tabby cat slunk away from the shrubbery, ran in front of me to the center, and vanished again like some Cheshire cat of old. That emboldened me. I crept forward, pruning shears in hand.

When I cleared the confines of the row, I had a better view. It was a man, stretched out on the gravel behind the firepit, between two of the chairs. He lay on his back, his body twisted and his sightless eyes staring at me.

It was Blake Kelleher.

His face was mottled and puffy. He wore the same clothes I saw him in the day before—dark trousers, a white dress shirt, and a suit coat, now in disarray and tangled around him. I stared at him, knowing I should approach to see what was wrong and knowing I wouldn't because it didn't matter. He was dead. I was sure of it.

I dropped my shears and fled, taking 'my' shortcut by squeezing between the yews in certain spots where they were thin. That brought me out of the structure in record time, panting, sweating, and dizzy.

I had a panicked moment as I considered what to do. Then common sense kicked in and I did the only thing possible. I went into the house and dialed 9-1-1. I babbled something somewhat intelligible to the calm dispatcher then I went outside to wait.

Sad to say, the first thing I thought when I saw Blake Kelleher's body in the middle of Labbie was— This is going to screw up my entire day completely.

I was right.

****

I stood outside the labyrinth, watching anxiously as the officials maneuvered their gurney into the first row. I tagged along behind, wincing whenever they snagged on an arbor or a yew. They had gone through about half of the paths when they noticed me behind them. I was escorted back the way we came with a stern admonition to stay out of the way.

I meandered back to the start, eyeing the side walls gloomily. The structure would require extensive grooming. I suppose that was an uncharitable thought, but it was better than thinking the other thoughts that lurked at the back of my mind:

Why was he even in Labbie?

How long had he been there?

How did he die?

It gave me chills to think that I was sleeping in the house while the old man might have been out there, dying. I was hoping I'd find out he somehow stumbled inside, fell down, and had a heart attack. But that still left the biggest question unanswered:

Why?

It took them almost two hours to photograph, examine, and finally extract Blake Kelleher. While they were doing that, I sat on the side porch and watched, wincing every time someone's clumsy foot scraped my path and imperiled the thyme growing there. One more thing to mend before Saturday's judging. I felt curiously removed from the tragedy of a dead man in my yard. I suppose I was in shock, or maybe just disbelieving.

When they brought out the body, encased in a black plastic shroud, I shuddered. I didn't like Blake Kelleher, but it was sad to think of him dying alone like that. Of course, he had alienated almost everyone in his family, so I suppose it didn't matter where he died, here or at home. No matter where he died, he'd be alone.

I was escorted to the police station in a nondescript blue sedan. "We need to take your statement and get your fingerprints, so we can eliminate them at the scene," a fresh-faced young officer said reassuringly. "All routine."

"I suppose you'll want to talk to my father," I said. "He lives at the house. He's not here today, but he'll be back later."

"Sure, we'll talk to him, too. Where is he?"

"He likes to meet friends on Saturday at the Jean Marie Senior Center. They might be bowling or playing cards."

"We'll see if we can find him. I'm sure you'd like to have him with you." The kid kept glancing at me as he drove as though assessing my responses.

I didn't reply. I wished they'd leave Pop out of this mess, at least for a while, but they would probably track him down no matter what I said.

We entered the police station, which was different than I expected. I suppose I was anticipating something from *Law and Order* or *Blue Bloods*, but this was a bright and airy open space with several desks and offices lining the side of the spacious room. I vaguely remember a vote on a bond issue several years earlier, with the funds going to update our local police station. It was good to see that the funds were used appropriately.

I was taken to an office where another police officer sat. This one was older, with a careworn expression, thinning brown hair, and startling blue eyes. He introduced himself as Detective Hunter and handed me a business card, which I tucked into my purse. He gestured me to a chair in front of his desk, which was full of piles of paper files stacked at least a foot high. A small clear space among the piles allowed him to regard me, his hands clasped in front of him.

We began with some routine back and forth. Verification of my pertinent data: Lilith Griffin, home at Palisade Road. Yes, it was my property. No, it's not a maze, it's a labyrinth, with only one way in and out. I hesitated before saying that because of my shortcuts, but no one else knew about those, so I didn't bother muddying the water.

Yes, I knew the victim. No, I didn't know how he got there, in the middle of my labyrinth. Yes, I regularly visited the center. No, I hadn't visited it until this morning. The last time I was there was at least a day earlier, if not more. Yes, my father lived with me, but he was gone for the day. I'm not sure when he was last in the center. Yes, perhaps yesterday. I followed my usual routine the previous evening. I read a bit before bed, I answered email and checked the online support forum where I volunteered, then I went to bed.

"Online forums?"

"There are support forums for people who are victims of attacks like the one on me. I'm one of the monitors. We provide information for victims and help them adjust to their injuries."

"That must be hard on you. It probably reminds you of what happened."

I raised my hand. "I'm always reminded, Detective. If I can help others, I'm glad to do it. I'm sorry, but nothing last night was unusual. I didn't hear anything, and I didn't see anything."

The man was polite but insistent. "Are you sure? I'm surprised."

I met the cop's gaze. "I take pain medication at night."

His eyes flickered over my neck and my hand. "What about your father?"

"His room is at the other end of the house, facing the street. I sometimes wake at night, but I don't remember what I see. My medication is—" I hesitated, lest he think me an opioid addict or something.

"Strong?" Hunter supplied.

"Yes. I take the medication on Monday, Wednesday, and Friday. I have physical therapy on those days and I'm often somewhat sore." I had many nights pacing the house, unable to sleep, but I refused to become dependent. "I keep the side gates locked. We have no need for protection in the back because of the slope and the ravine there."

"Did you check the locks before going to bed?"

I started to nod then stopped. "I don't think so. The lock seemed latched, so I didn't bother to check."

"The one on the west side is broken. It appears in place, but it isn't." He examined his small spiral notebook, sitting on the desk.

The west side of the house. It was downslope, on the other side of the garage. I hadn't checked that lock in days because I seldom used that entryway.

"You don't have any security."

"I didn't know I needed any." My voice was sharp, and I was immediately regretful, but I was tired and in pain, a combination that wreaked havoc with my patience. I needed to walk in order to keep my muscles from stiffening, and I'd been inactive far too long. "We're one house among a several on the street. Our neighbors are as private as we are. I doubt if anyone even knows we're here, much less a target for a robbery."

"A robbery? Is that what you think this is?"

"I have no idea what this is," I snapped. "How did he die? Was he attacked?"

"We won't know for certain until we get the results of the autopsy." He regarded me impassively. His name, Hunter, was appropriate for a police officer, I suppose. He was like a hunter, with his sharp eyes and craggy face.

"I told you, I had no idea he was there."

"You and Mr. Kelleher have a history together." He stated it flatly, his voice curiously non-accusing.

"I know him," I conceded.

"You were engaged to marry his son."

"A long time ago."

"It was when you were attacked." His gaze went to my hand, resting on my lap. "We don't see many acid attacks around here. Thank God."

"It's appallingly common in other parts of the world."

"Mr. Kelleher was paying you as reparation for your injury." Hunter's cool blue eyes were fixed on me.

"Yes, he was. A stipend every month."

"And he paid for your house as part of a lump sum payment at the time of the injury."

"You're well informed."

"Most of this is a matter of public record."

I had a sense where this was headed, but his next question still surprised me. "Why did Mr. Kelleher come to see you yesterday?"

"Who says he did?" I was pleased I sounded merely curious and not defensive.

"His son. Your ex-fiancé."

I struggled to keep my face still. "You've spoken with Shaw?"

"He's the next of kin. He has to identify the body."

Poor Shaw. He and his father didn't get along, but it was still a lot to ask a son to identify his father's body. "Shaw knew his father came to see me?" I asked.

"His father told him about his conversation with

you when he returned to his home last evening. His son said that they met after dinner to discuss business. Shaw Kelleher was under the impression that you and his father argued."

"We didn't argue. Mr. Kelleher told me that he might not be able to pay the stipend we agreed on."

"Really?" Hunter tapped his desk with a pen. "What did he say?"

I'd relegated my previous conversation with Kelleher to the back of my mind, labeling it *not worth worrying about*. Now I dredged up the few words he and I exchanged and recited them for the police officer.

"Why did he come to see you? Do you have any ideas?" he asked when I finished.

"No, I don't. I haven't communicated with anyone in his family since the attack and the subsequent agreement we signed."

Hunter regarded me with a thoughtful, evaluating stare. I returned it without flinching. People have stared at me for twenty-five years and I had long ago left embarrassment or annoyance behind me.

"Have you spoken with Tanya Sidero since she was released from the psychiatric hospital?"

"As I'm sure you know, there is a restraining order against her. So, no, I haven't spoken with her."

"Not by phone, perhaps?"

"Why do you ask? What does that have to do with Blake Kelleher's death? She was released more than a decade ago. Why would I talk to her now?"

He eyed me, his gaze reflecting nothing of his thoughts. "Do you have any enemies?"

I blinked in surprise. "I beg your pardon?"

"Enemies. Someone who would want to do you

28

harm."

"I know what an enemy is," I snapped, my patience stretched. "I don't believe I have any."

"Good. That means no one would try to implicate you in Blake Kelleher's death, would they?"

I sighed, my patience strained far past its normal breaking point. "I have no idea, Detective. Why would someone want to do that? I live a quiet life and I have a negligible impact on anyone."

"That's an interesting way to phrase it."

"I don't know how else to phrase it. I assume people gather enemies because they've affected other people. To my knowledge, I haven't negatively affected anyone."

"Except Tanya Sidero."

It took a second for me to gather the shreds of my patience to say, "She is responsible for her own actions. I'm not."

"But she might feel you are responsible."

"She might be crazy, too, but there's nothing I can do about that." I stood with difficulty, staggering when my leg began to cramp. "I'm not leaving. I just need to stretch my muscles. It's one of the aftereffects." I circled behind the chair, using it to keep my balance while I worked out the pain.

"Do you blame Blake Kelleher for what happened to you?"

I turned in surprise. "Why would I blame him? Tanya Sidero was the attacker."

"He's a wealthy man. He could have done far more to support you."

I resumed walking. "He didn't have to do anything."

"You seem remarkably forgiving for what was a horrible event that changed the course of your life."

I paused, leaning on the chair to gently stretch my sore back muscles. "I had a good social worker when I was recovering in the hospital. She was assigned by the police department to help me. She always said that assigning blame was a losing game and I think she's right."

"Maybe I know her." Hunter watched me, his eyes flickering to my neck.

"She's retired."

"I still may know her. I've been around a long time." He smiled, but it wasn't reassuring. The man's eyes never reflected any warmth.

"Olivia Meredith." I remembered Olivia's motherly, kind face as she sat by my hospital bed, reading to me. "She taught me not to be a victim."

"Not a victim?"

"Let me rephrase that. Not to be a continual victim. Yes, I was attacked, but I don't have to carry the bitterness forward. If I do that, it means Tanya wins. And I won't let her win." I met Hunter's incredulous gaze. "I decided to make the best life I could and put my past behind me." I slowly flexed my hand, narrowing my eyes when the stinging sensation began. "Sometimes I even succeed. Olivia taught me not to let the hatred and anger taint what might be happiness in life."

"That sounds like something she'd do. I worked with her a few times. She had a tough life of it, but she always managed to make the best of things."

"You mean her son?" I remembered Olivia talking about her only child, a product of her first marriage which ended in an acrimonious divorce. She remarried but the boy didn't get along with his stepfather or his stepsister. He ended up in trouble with the law somewhere on the West Coast. I had spoken with her recently because she would be in St. Louis at the same time I was giving my talk, and she thought she might attend. I made a mental note to call her and give her the details about the place and time.

"Yeah. He was a disappointment to her husband, I think," Hunter said. "Of course, her husband was a stickler for discipline, so I guess it's not surprising the kid acted out. His daughter is an attorney in a suburb near St. Louis or Kansas City. I can't remember which."

Olivia didn't talk much about the stepdaughter. I always had the feeling she didn't like the girl, but Olivia was far too polite to say as much. "I'm glad she's done well," I murmured. "I'm sure Olivia's husband is pleased." From the way she described him, I thought her husband sounded like a bossy dictator, but I had never met the man, so I didn't know.

"I think he is. And I think he and Olivia's son have finally made peace."

"Good." I reached for my small purse. "Are you done with me? I'd like to go home and rest if I can."

"Sure. You'll be around if we want to ask you some more questions, right?"

I slipped the purse strap over my shoulder. "Are you telling me I can't leave town?" I didn't wait for his answer. "That's okay. I have no plans to leave until Thursday, when I'm giving a talk at a conference in St. Louis."

He jotted a note on the pad then stood to walk me

to the door. "I'm curious." He paused with his hand on the doorknob. "What did you do before the attack?"

"Oh, a bit of this and that. I worked for several years for Lerner Software as a technical writer. I always wanted to act, though. I did community theater and had many starring roles. I got an audition for some parts in Chicago, but then the attack happened and—" I looked away, seeing but not seeing his cluttered office. "Then I got detoured."

"What do you do now?"

"Olivia got me started with gardening. I took a few classes and finally got a degree in Landscape Horticulture with a major in Therapeutic Gardening. It took me almost ten years to do it. I did most of my work online because I was still recovering and had quite a few setbacks."

"And that's what you do now? You build gardens?"

"No, I design them. I don't have a crew. I work with some of the companies in the area and freelance when a special garden design is needed." That was why the upcoming Garden Showcase was so important. Not only the judges but the public would be viewing my landscape and my business cards would be sitting there, waiting for eager clients to take. It was essential that my grounds were their absolute best.

"Quite a change of pace from what you did before."

"Yes. Like I said, I got detoured from acting. I never took it up again."

"That's too bad. I have the feeling you're a very good actress." He smiled but his eyes remained cool.

I don't think he meant it as a compliment.

Chapter Three

It was after two in the afternoon before I got home. I made myself half a sandwich and ate it standing up, then I went to the backyard, steeling myself for what I'd see. I thanked God that I had no lawn to speak of. We had installed patio stone interspersed with moss or thyme throughout almost the entire back yard wherever there wasn't gravel or mulch. If I had grass, it would be torn up by now. As it was, the open areas of the back were trampled and sad-looking where dozens of heavy-footed people had trod.

Well, if we had a good rain that would perk things up. I'd tuck in some new thyme here and there to make up for what was gouged out by gurneys and wheeled dollies. I went into Labbie, inspecting the path and the walls while I paced. It wasn't as bad as I feared, but it still needed work. Crushed branches were underfoot and there were spots were the roses were shoved out of the way, probably to make room.

I made a mental vow to come out early in the morning and get a start on reparations. I still needed to get another coat of paint on the chairs, paint the side gates, finish prepping the flower beds in back, plus work on what needed doing in the front. Six days to get the work done. If I worked late into the evening and got up early, I could do it. I had to do it.

I stopped outside the center of the labyrinth. The chairs were shoved here and there, pushed into the surrounding yews and arbors. I resisted the urge to start straightening things out. It was too hot and airless here in the center. I was already warm and if I kept working, I was sure to harm myself. I went back the way I came but stopped when I saw the tipped firepit and ashes on the ground. Damn it, that would be a major mess to clean up. The ash would kill everything there unless I swept it up quickly, before the heat of the day set in with a vengeance.

I hurried back through my shortcut, grabbed a dustpan and brush, and returned to the center. Thirty minutes later it was relatively clear of debris. I took the long way out of Labbie following the path, balancing the ashy pile in the dustpan. By the time I got to the house, I was sweat-streaked with ash and irritated.

I went inside to blessed air conditioning, but I had no sooner taken a sip of water than the doorbell rang. I debated answering it. I wasn't expecting anyone, but on the other hand, it might be the police again. I pulled open the door and found six people on my front porch, one with a camera aimed at me.

"Miss Griffin, can you tell us about Blake Kelleher's death? When did you find the body? How did he die?"

The questions were tossed at me like grenades. I instinctively stepped back, away from the onslaught.

"Why was he here? Did he stay overnight here? You were once engaged to his son. Does Shaw Kelleher know that his father's body was found at your house?"

I glimpsed Pop's truck, pulling into our driveway then I heard the garage door open. "Please leave. I have

34

nothing to say and—"

The lead person, a young woman with bright blonde hair, pushed forward. "Have you talked to Shaw Kelleher? What was his reaction when he heard that his father was found here?"

"I don't want to talk to you about—"

"Have you spoken with Tanya Sidero? Did you know that she and Shaw Kelleher have been seen together at several charity functions?"

That stunned me. I occasionally saw Shaw's picture in the papers, usually in a business setting. Our local newspaper didn't have a Society section, so I didn't see any pictures of him in his role as wealthy trendsetter. "I don't know what you mean. It's irrelevant who he's seeing." That sounded wimpy even to my ears.

"But she was the one who attacked you. Does Shaw Kelleher blame you for breaking off the engagement?" The woman's gaze was traveling over my exposed neck, faint repugnance showing in her baby blue eyes. "Did you resume your relationship with him? Was his father upset about that?"

I tried to close the door but somehow the man holding the camera had moved forward and I couldn't get past his foot, which blocked my way. "Leave now. I have nothing to say."

"Why not? Surely you have some idea why Blake Kelleher was here. Does it have something to do with the attack on you years ago? Have you seen—"

"You can leave." Pop pulled me back and shoved the young man with a sharp jab at the guy's shoulder. The man stumbled backward, slamming into one of our porch columns.

"You don't need to be hostile," the reporter woman snapped. "There's no reason for you to—"

Pop slammed the door. "Assholes." He regarded me. "What happened to you?"

I swiped at my stained and filthy clothes. "The police were here. I found Blake Kelleher's body in Labbie."

He gently pulled me to him. "I know. One of my buddies at the Center listens in on the police band radio and I heard about it. I went to the station, but you were already gone. I'm sorry, sweetie. I should have been there to help you."

I leaned into his solid warmth. Pop was like me, small-boned and short. His once firm muscles weren't quite as firm as they used to be, but he was still a bolster of strength when I needed it. "I don't know why Kelleher was here. How did he get in the middle of Labbie? And why was he here?"

"The police will sort it out. Have you eaten anything? Come on, let's go sit and have some iced tea and hash it over."

I let him lead me into the kitchen and watched while he poured tall glasses from the jar of sun tea we kept refilling all summer. We went out to the screened-in side porch, accessed via French doors off the kitchen and settled on the wicker furniture. Dense shrubs and trees shielded us from the neighbors on one side. Another side faced the front side garden full of day lilies and the last side faced the back yard.

I took my favorite chair, set into a corner opposite the doorway and giving me a view of Labbie and the path leading to it, bordered by purple and white alyssum. As I sat, I noticed the front gate. "Damn, I forgot. That detective said the lock on the garage gate was broken or something. I'll check it."

"I'll check it in a minute. You rest. It's been a long day for you."

I didn't argue. I was exhausted, as much mentally as physically. "The body was in the center of Labbie. It's a mess, Pop. Somebody knocked over the firepit and ash got everywhere." I ran my hand over my sooty linen shirt. "I hope this cleans up."

"That's an ugly chore to handle."

"No kidding. I got most of it swept away, but I'll need to replace the thyme in there. It's trampled and torn."

"Will the police let you?"

I hadn't even considered that. "Nobody told me it was a crime scene. I mean, if I wasn't supposed to do anything, somebody would have said, wouldn't they?"

"I'm sure they would have. Nobody said anything to me when I was at the police station."

I leaned into the soft cushion, a damp but cool breeze wafting past me. "Good. I'd hate to get in trouble with the cops."

We talked and re-talked and came to no useful conclusions. Pop went out to the inspect the gate and I went upstairs to shower and change. Somehow, before I knew it, night had fallen. I went into my office and my computer, checking the support forum and my email.

Half an hour later I went upstairs, looking out the window at the garden, highlighted by the luminescent paint on the pavers. A thunderstorm was moving in and lightning streaked the sky. I thought I saw movement and sure enough, I glimpsed that tabby cat skulking around the raised beds. I considered going out and chasing him away but then the rain began, and he took off at a run.

I'd deal with him in the morning, I decided.

****

The doorbell rang at eight o'clock the next morning. Too damn early for a Sunday, as far as I was concerned. I opened the door, ready to tear a strip of skin off any reporter standing there.

It wasn't reporters. It was a man, tall and lean with short gray-and-white flecked hair and a clipped beard framing his mouth and chin and running along his jaw line. He took a step back when I slammed open the door. "I'm here about the job," he said.

"What job?"

"Yard work?"

Pop came to the door behind me. "Who are you?"

"I came about the job that was advertised."

"We didn't advertise any job." I started to close the door.

"I advertised." Pop slipped in front of me. "Down at Jean's Place. I called Mark and asked him to post a sign."

"What?"

"A sign. Help Wanted." Pop faced the man, who was at least a foot taller than him. "What's your name?"

"Dylan Lyle." The man extended a hand. "Mark Eames suggested I drop by."

Pop shook the hand. "I'm Merchant Griffin. My friends call me Grif. That's my daughter, Lilith. Do you have any gardening experience?"

I tugged Pop's T-shirt. "You posted a sign? And you told people to come here?" I glanced at Lyle, who watched us, his oval face showing nothing of his thoughts. I'm good at reading most people, but he was good at hiding whatever reaction he had to my scarred neck and burned hand. "Excuse us. I need to chat with my father." I grabbed a fistful of fabric and dragged Pop away from the door. "Just give us a minute."

"Sure." The man stepped back and went to the right, where the steps met my front walkway.

I closed the door. "Are you crazy? We can't hire some guy who walks up and asks for a job."

Pop went into my office to peer through the window. "I'll bet he can do the work."

I followed him to peer at the man standing near my porch. "We don't know anything about him. We need references and—"

"We need a strong guy for a week."

"Pop, think about it. If we hire from a landscape company, they've done background checks and all that stuff. We're at least somewhat sure we won't get a serial killer or something equally gross."

"He doesn't look like a serial killer."

"How do we know what a serial killer looks like?" I peered out the window. The man stood with his back to us. He was tall and slender but muscular. That much was obvious because his black knit shirt strained against his biceps. "We can't just hire anybody off the street."

"Mark Eames recommended him. Mark's a retired cop. I used to work on his car. Mark had a sweet Impala that he modified, and I did his engine work. If Mark says he's okay, he's okay." Pop crossed his arms in that *I'm laying down the law and that's that* way he had.

"How do we know this man even knows Mr. Eames? Honestly, Pop. You're too trusting."

"And you aren't trusting enough."

Well, true enough. Stalemate. What to do? The man appeared strong and Pop was right, we needed the help, but I wasn't comfortable letting a total stranger hang out at my house. "I'm going to call that detective from yesterday. Maybe he can do a background check or something."

"It's Sunday. He's probably not there."

"He's a cop," I countered. "Aren't they always on the job?"

Pop shrugged. "You do that. In the meantime, I'll talk wages with him. We won't pay an arm and a leg because we're desperate." Pop went to the door.

"Pop, wait a second. Let me—" But it was too late. He was already stepping out to the front porch.

I found my purse and dug out the business card the detective gave me the day before. I dialed the number, expecting to be routed to a secretary or an answering machine, but to my surprise, Hunter answered. I identified myself then said, "I'm sorry to disturb your Sunday. I wasn't sure who to call, so I hope you can tell me who to ask about this."

"We don't worry about weekends when we're working a case. What's up?"

"I'm trying to hire a man to help us with our garden. We're preparing for the big Garden Showcase this weekend and I'm afraid your people made a bit of a mess." Oh, damn. That sounded prissy. "I mean, they were tramping around the labyrinth and the grounds and I need to—"

"Yeah, we tend to not worry too much about shrubbery when we're dealing with a possible crime scene."

That made me pause. "What are you saying? I thought he had a heart attack or—"

"I can't discuss that now. Anyway, I'm sure you didn't call to find out Blake Kelleher's cause of death." Pause. "Did you?"

"No, no. Of course not." I don't know why I felt so apologetic. "No, I'm calling because we're trying to hire garden help and a man came to our house in response to an ad. I know this isn't in your purview, but I don't know who else to ask." I hesitated. "Given what happened with Mr. Kelleher, I don't feel comfortable allowing a stranger to work closely with me and my father without doing at least some checking."

"It's a smart move." I imagined Hunter's blue eyes, faintly amused. "What's the guy's name?"

"I think he said it's Dylan Lyle. I talked to him briefly. That's an odd name. Perhaps it won't be too hard to find out something about him." Long pause. "Hello? Are you still there?"

"What? Oh, yeah. I'm here. Uh, where did you say you found this guy?"

"He was recommended by one of my father's friends from Jean's Place. I mean, the Jean Marie Senior Center. A Mr. Eames vouched for him, I believe."

Another pause, then, "What's Mr. Eame's first name?"

I struggled to remember. I was still a bit rattled to think that Labbie might be a crime scene. "I think it's Mark."

"O…kay." Hunter dragged out the word in a doubting voice. "I see."

"Is there a problem?"

"No, no. Hang on a minute. Let me do some checking."

"Oh, you don't have to do it now. I was hoping—"

"No, that's fine. It'll only take a minute." The line went silent with that odd hum that tells you that you're on hold.

I meandered closer to the window to view Mr. Lyle, standing next to Pop, who was pointing at plants in the garden and talking a mile a minute. Lyle had his hands in the back pockets of his black jeans, nodding now and again. Nothing about him spoke "strong" and yet I had a sense of strength emanating from him. Perhaps it was the confident way he spoke. Or maybe it was how little he spoke. Most people filled any conversational void with chatter. He didn't appear to feel the need to do so. Or maybe there wasn't any void given Pop's volubility.

Lyle was attractive in an unusual way, I decided. His face was long and narrow and not conventionally handsome. Nose slightly crooked, goatee and mustache liberally flecked with gray, and clipped hair equally gray. It was hard to guess his age, but I think it was somewhere near mine, in his fifties. When he shifted position, his golf shirt strained against his back, showing taut muscles. Perhaps I was wrong about the strength.

"Okay, you should be fine to hire this guy. I thought you could, because if Mark Eames okayed him, I was sure he was legit, but I wanted to check to be sure." Detective Hunter startled me from my covert evaluation. I drew away from the window at the same moment Lyle glanced over his shoulder. I'm not sure if he saw me or not. "I know Mark and you can take his recommendation to the bank."

"Do you mean he has no criminal record?"

"Nothing wrong that I can see." Hunter cleared his throat. "And just so you know, the guy's name is spelled kind of odd. It's Dillan with an 'I' and his last name is spelled Ly-all. That made it easy to find him in the system."

That was alarming. "He's in the system? In what way?"

Another pause. "Well, everybody's in the system." Hunter gave a curt laugh, which sounded more like a wheeze than a real chuckle. "You're in the system. You've got a driver's license, right?"

"I suppose," I conceded. "Thank you. I have to admit, I'm relieved. We have only a few days to get ready for the Showcase and we need all the hands we can get."

"I'm sure he'll be fine. By the way, I'm glad you called. I meant to call you to let you know that Kelleher's body has been released to his family. His son was here earlier today and made arrangements to have it moved."

"Oh. Well, good. Does that mean you're done with the investigation?"

"No, not quite. We have a few loose ends to tie up."

"Can you tell me how he died?"

There was another hesitation on the other end of the phone. "I'd rather not discuss it. It's nothing contagious or anything like that, if you're worried about it."

The thought hadn't even crossed my mind. "That's good to know," I said faintly. "I meant to call you yesterday but—" *Better to ask forgiveness than permission*, a little voice whispered in my head. "I tidied up in the labyrinth. Some ashes were spilled and it was important to get those cleaned up before the thyme died. Ash can be caustic if left too long on a plant, especially overnight. I hope that's okay. If you wanted me to stay out, you would have stretched that yellow tape around if it, right?" I waited hopefully.

"That's fine. We took plenty of pictures and as you said, what with last night's rain, any evidence would have washed away anyway. Besides, we've determined cause of death and it's nothing to do with your plants."

"I beg your pardon? I thought you said you hadn't determined cause of death."

"No, I said I wasn't prepared to discuss it. But I suppose it won't hurt to tell you. He was poisoned."

"What do you mean? Was he ill? Did he take medication or—"

"We believe he was poisoned and that caused his disorientation. He was forced into your maze where he died."

I sucked in a deep breath. "Poisoned? You mean he was murdered?"

Yet another pause. "Yes, he was murdered, but technically, not murdered there. He ingested poison and the medical examiner thinks it was done several hours before his death. He may have been barely conscious when he was put into the maze."

I staggered back, barely landing in my office chair which, thank God, was behind me. "But—but—"

"Don't discuss this with anyone. The fewer people who know the details, the better." He hesitated. "You can mention it to your father, of course, but not anyone else. Not yet, at least."

"I don't understand. Is the autopsy done? Is that how you know—"

"I need to go now. I think Mr. Lyall will be a useful addition to your garden staff. It was good talking with you."

I replaced the phone. Poisoning? Good heavens, why would someone poison that nasty old man? How could they do it? I mean, I suppose poison was readily available, but still…

I shook my head. I had other problems to deal with. I thought about Hunter's words. 'My garden staff' was me and my seventy-seven-year-old father. Well, I was in a jam and I guess I couldn't look a gift worker in the mouth. I went outside, grabbing my hat from the hook near the front door.

"I was filling him on what needs done," Pop said. "I'll let you take over now. I want to see if I have a padlock we can use on that gate." He headed for the garage. "Oh, and I told him if those damn reporters come by, he should shoot them."

I sighed. "Freedom of speech, Pop. First Amendment and all that."

"Yeah, well, defense of private property and all that." He stomped off, muttering.

I tilted my hat, shading me from the encroaching sun. "Ignore him, Mr. Lyall. Mornings are not his best time of the day. Are you sure you don't mind starting work on a Sunday?"

He frowned. "Nope. Not a problem."

"Okay, then let me show you where the tools are kept. I trust my father discussed wages, working hours and other details with you."

"Yes, he did. You can call me Dillan. Where do you want me to start?"

"You can call me Lilith." I held out my hand. After a brief hesitation, he shook it gently. I pushed up the sleeves of my long-sleeved linen shirt. "Let's start in the front, I think. We have mulch that needs to be spread. Pull any weeds as you go." I pointed to the bags stacked near the retaining wall but his eyes were fixed on the scars on my right arm.

"Fire?" he asked.

"Acid attack." His gray eyes widened. "You must not be from around here. It made the newspapers." I entered the garden, following the steppingstones set throughout the plants.

"I moved away a while ago. I came back around Christmas."

"What brought you back?" I covertly checked his passage behind me. He was picking his way carefully, stepping where I stepped. I silently approved his caution. The garden was chock full of plants and a foot in the wrong place would crush something.

"My stepfather had a heart attack."

"I'm sorry. Is he—did he recover?" I continued downward to the concrete wall, where I balanced for a second before jumping down next to the stack of bags.

"Yeah, it'll take more than a heart attack to kill that old buzzard." Lyall stood on the wall above me. "Where do you want me to put it?"

"I'll move the bags. You split them and spread the mulch."

His gaze went from me to the dozen or so forty-pound bags. "I can move them. Show me where."

I considered his proposition. I confess, I wasn't

looking forward to hauling the bags into the garden. I couldn't use a wheelbarrow because of the narrow space, so I usually ended up clutching them or dragging them where I wanted. It was hard physical labor and the day was already turning warm. "I'll mark the spots with landscape paint. Thank you."

"That's what I'm here for." He landed next to me, lifted a bag, and slung it over his shoulder.

I envied him his strength and flexibility. I went to the metal mailbox affixed to a post near the driveway. "I keep tools and gloves in mailboxes throughout the garden here and in the back. It minimizes walking. The heavier tools are in the shed behind the garage, in the back."

"What about pesticides and stuff like that?"

"I use it sparingly. I use companion plantings and integrated pest management."

"How's that work?"

"It's a long story. I don't like to use chemicals." The smell of some of them made me ill, reminding me too much of my lengthy hospital stays. "Let me get the spots marked for you. Did you bring gloves?"

"Yep."

I eyed his dark shirt and pants. "You might get dirty."

"I expect I will." He walked to the steps and moved upward, the bag balanced on his shoulder.

I got the fluorescent landscape paint and followed him, going among the plants and spraying spots where mulch would be needed. He dropped a bag then went back for more. When I finished, I stood at the top, sweating from even that small amount of exertion. "I'll set out a cooler of water for you," I called to him.

"Make sure to stay hydrated. If you need a hat, there's one in the box."

He glanced up from his place in the middle of the garden. "Thanks."

I went inside and made a beeline for the kitchen, where I added ice to a 10-gallon cooler. Then I moved the table I painted the day before back to the porch from the garage and put the cooler on it. I filled several gallon jugs with water and topped up the cooler, setting plastic cups nearby for his use.

The garden already looked better. Dillan had moved the bags and was at work on emptying them, bending over and examining vegetation as he moved. I had my plants marked, so hopefully he wouldn't mistake one for a weed.

I went back inside and cooled off with some lemonade. I would work in the garage today, I decided, and get a second coat of paint on those chairs. I would also make some calls and get the thyme I needed for filler.

I went to the kitchen window overlooking the front and glimpsed a group of people climbing the steps. Damn, it was those reporters again. Or maybe not the same ones, but someone of that ilk because I saw the polo shirts with logos, camera equipment, and an airbrushed young blonde ready to get a sound bite.

I headed for the front door but stopped when Dillan moved to block their movement. "Can I help you?" I heard him ask.

"We're here to see Lilith Griffin." This came from the man carrying the bulky camera.

"She's occupied at the moment. Come back later."

The cameraman shifted position but Lyall moved,

too, somehow managing to block the entire step.

"Who are you?" the blonde demanded. She raked him up and down with a dismissive gaze that changed to something more speculative when he met her eyes.

"I'm a family friend. She's busy and can't be bothered."

"Do you know a man was murdered here yesterday?" The woman thrust a microphone at his face. "What's your name? What's your connection with the family? Did you know Blake Kelleher?"

Lyall took her microphone. It happened so fast I don't know how he did it, but he somehow ended up with the microphone and one hand on her arm. "Why don't you leave now? Miss Griffin is extremely busy getting ready for the Garden Showcase. You know about that, don't you?" He maneuvered her back toward the steps.

"That's next week, right? People walk around and stare at plants." She may as well have said *Idiots stare at boring plants, how stupid* from the way she spoke.

"Ah, but it's not only that. It's a chance to get a glimpse into the mind of a landscape designer and you know that is..." Their voices faded when they moved out of sight.

"He might prove useful." Pop's voice behind me made me jump.

"You sneaky old man." I set my glass in the sink. "I'm going out to see how much vegetation I need to replace. I'll get that ordered today."

"Don't be out too long. It's getting brutal hot."

I made a mental note to refill the cooler on the front porch. "I'll be careful." I went out through the mudroom, into the backyard. Pop was right. It was hot and humid, with a faint moist breeze moving. I took my time, though, stepping around the entire yard and making notes on the clipboard I carried about what would be needed.

I went into Labbie and stepped off distances, noting what needed trimming, straightening or filling. I got to the center and slowly turned around, taking in the entire space. That's when I saw it. That's when I realized.

My blue roses were gone.

I screamed.

Chapter Four

They were gone. The beautiful blooms that I nurtured through the cold May spring and the unseasonably hot June were gone. The plant was there, but the big blossoms were absent. Only a handful of buds remained on each plant.

"God damn it!" I threw my head back and shook my fist at the sky. "Damn it!" It was a long time since I allowed my anger to show and I let it all out now. "Damn it all, when do I get a break!" I screamed.

"Lilith? Are you okay?" I heard Pop's concerned shout.

"Damn it!" I threw the clipboard into the lawn chair as hard as I could. The webbed chair bounced and hit the metal firepit with a resounding clatter, everything tipping over and clattering even more. "Damn it to hell!"

"Lilith?!" I didn't recognize that shout. Was it Lyall?

"Somebody cut my roses," I called out. "If I find out who did, I'll kill them!" I leaned closer to one of the arbors, praying I might find a mature blossom tucked away among the foliage.

No such luck. The long, vining stems didn't hide anything but buds, some of them close to blooming, but probably not for at least a week, or maybe longer.

Probably not soon enough for the Showcase. "Damn it," I muttered. "Who did this?" I moved to one of the other three arbors, poking and peering into the variegated leaves.

"What is it? What's wrong?"

I whirled. Dillan raced into the center of the labyrinth, a weed digger clutched in his fist like a weapon. He stopped suddenly, falling over one of the chairs, but he righted himself so fast I wasn't even sure he'd fallen. The man had the reflexes of a cat.

"Someone cut my roses," I fumed. I went to the next arbor, muttering a silent plea that I might find a rose there. "Damn it, I can't believe it."

Pop came trotting into the center, gasping for breath. "What happened? Are—you—okay?" he stammered, clutching the back of one chair while he struggled to breathe. His face, normally pink, was red with exertion and his hand trembled visibly when he reached for the chair.

"Oh, you silly old man." I started to go to him, but Dillan was there first, putting an arm around Pop's shoulders and leading him to one of the chairs.

"I'm fine," Pop muttered. "I'm fine. Don't fuss."

"I'm not fussing. I'm rusty with CPR and I don't want to have you collapse in here." One corner of Dillan's mouth twitched in what might have been a smile as he helped Pop into a chair. "I'd hate to show what a lousy CPR tech I am."

"Pop, are you okay?" I moved next to him, leaning over to peer into his face.

He waved a hand. "Just winded, that's all. What happened?"

He did seem better. His red cheeks had calmed, and

his breathing was slowing. I threw my hands up, gesturing to the arbors nestled among the yews. "Look."

Pop saw right away. "Blazing Buddha in a bucket," he muttered. "Who the hell did that?"

Dillan pivoted. "What's the problem?"

"What's the problem? There aren't any roses!" I shook my fist at one of the arbors.

Dillan frowned. "There are some. They're just little."

"But they're not blooming. I need them to be blooming. I need some in bloom by Saturday." I sagged wearily against one of the yews, my frenzied anger draining me.

"Can't you do something? You know, give them some fertilizer or something?" He snapped his fingers. "Oh, wait. That's right. You don't do chemicals, so no fertilizer."

"Of course, I use fertilizer," I snapped. "Organic fertilizer. That won't help." Something in his words nagged at the back of my mind.

Dillan leaned over to examine one of the rose bushes. "At least they didn't take the whole plant. They only took a few flowers."

"A few flowers? Do you know how long it took me to breed those?" My outrage was returning, infusing me with new energy.

He straightened. "You know what I mean. What's special about that rose?"

"It's bred from seeds I got from my grandmother. It's an heirloom rose with smaller, more open petals. It's more useful for bees than the newer, fussy roses. It's easier for them to gather pollen from than those double-and-triple petaled varieties. And it's blue. Well, sort of blue. There aren't any blue roses."

"I've seen blue roses."

"You've seen roses that are painted blue."

"Oh. Bees?" Dillan glanced around. "In here?"

"There's a hive or two out beyond the edge of the property." Pop heaved himself to his feet. "Some of them drop in now and then for a taste." He went to the nearest arbor and peered at the buds. "Can you force 'em? Maybe figure out a way to accelerate the growth. Some of these are close to blooming."

I didn't want to consider that now. I wanted to focus on my anger. "I'm going to call that detective," I fumed. "His men must have cut them or something while they were doing that crime scene stuff."

"Detective?" Dillan asked. He didn't sound worried, just curious. "Why was a detective in your maze?"

"It's a labyrinth," I corrected automatically.

"Lilith found a body in here yesterday morning. Blake Kelleher."

Dillan's eyebrows rose. "Kelleher? Kelleher Motors? Kelleher Real Estate? Kelleher Bank and Trust? Kelleher Holdings?"

"Yeah. That Kelleher."

"What was he doing here?"

Oddly enough, he didn't seem alarmed at the idea of a dead body laying where he was standing. I think I might have been a bit disturbed by the thought, but Dillan appeared to be taking it in stride.

"I have no idea." I sighed at the sight of my denuded rose bushes. "Maybe he was stealing my heirloom roses."

"Damn it to hell. I thought—with him dead, what about—" Pop stared at me, his eyes huge.

"The allowance? I don't know." Weariness once again made me sag, this time against one of the chairs that had remained upright during my tirade.

"Allowance?" Dillan looked from me to Pop.

"I get an allowance from Kelleher because the attack happened on his property." I raised my right hand to show my crinkled skin. "The acid attack. I was engaged to his son, Shaw, when it happened. I think Shaw talked the old man into helping us out. I never threatened to sue or anything, but Kelleher probably thought I might. He got enough bad publicity from it, I'm sure."

"But if he's dead, then what happens to your allowance?" Pop seemed so worried I went to him, putting a hand on his shoulder in commiseration.

"The agreement said his heirs are supposed to honor it."

"His heirs?" Pop shook his head. "That means that Shaw has to honor it. Will he?"

"He has to. It's part of the agreement."

"You said you were engaged. Did the son break it off when you were hurt?" I heard a faint hint of reproach in Dillan's voice.

"It was a mutual decision, decades ago." I surveyed my arbors, the empty arbors. "I have more pressing problems now. I need roses blooming for Saturday's judging and Sunday's open house. Those police people must have taken them."

Dillan stood at the south rose arbor, staring downward. "They didn't do it." He squatted near the base of the plant. "They wouldn't disturb a crime scene like that. But they might know who did it."

"What?" I moved close to him, leaning over to peer at whatever he was examining. I tripped on an uneven paver and put a hand on his shoulder to catch myself. "What is it?"

Dillan wrapped his fingers around my wrist and tugged. I winced. "That hurts."

He immediately released his grip. "I'm sorry." He pointed downward.

I couldn't squat on my heels the way he did. Scarred flesh wouldn't allow it. Instead I got to my hands and knees. "What am I looking for?"

Dillan gently removed my hat and peered into my eyes. "There. Below the fencing stuff."

I leaned forward, examining the base of the rose bush where the metal arbor was sunk into the earth. I had eight rose bushes in four spots around this center circle, all of them with metal arbors that allowed the stems to vine upward. They were planted years before and the undergrowth was dense.

Under this one I saw an indentation in the soil. "Is that a—" I turned my head to my right and saw Dillan was inches away, leaned forward like I was, staring downward.

"It's a footprint. I'll bet the police got a cast of it."

"A cast?" My knees began to hurt so I twisted, landing on my butt in the gravel.

"They'd pour plastic into the print and lift it out. That doesn't take long to do."

"I thought they used plaster of Paris," Pop said behind me. "I saw that in a TV show once."

"They used to, but now there's fast-set polymers that do the job." Dillan swung to his right and crab-walked to the next rose bush. "There isn't one here. Check the other bushes."

I started to rise, but Pop waved me away. "I'll check it." He picked up the weed digger that Dillan had dropped and poked into the bottom of the east rose bush. "Nothing here. Maybe they were careless in one spot."

"That means that we didn't only have a rose thief last night," I said. "We had a murderer, too."

"What?" That came from Pop. "Did that detective say it was—" He stopped and peeked at Dillan.

I tossed up my hands. "I guess we have no secrets. He said Kelleher wasn't killed here. He was killed elsewhere, and the body was moved here. I suppose they have ways to do determine that." I looked at Dillan. "How do you know about fast-set polymers and footprints?" I dragged myself to my feet, using one of the chairs to aid me.

He shrugged. "I guess we have no secrets. I'm in the Criminal Justice department at the community college. I teach a couple of classes. That's why I'm free this summer. No classes."

I hadn't even considered *why* he applied for a job here. He certainly didn't seem like a menial laborer, but I suppose it made sense that he had free time so why not pick up some extra money? I knew a few other teachers who did part-time jobs to supplement their meager salaries.

"Maybe you can talk to the police and find out where he was killed," Pop suggested.

"Why do we care where he was killed? He was dumped in my labyrinth and now everything's screwed up." I stared at the rose bushes, hands on my hips. The center of the labyrinth was cool and shady. It wouldn't get direct sunlight until mid-morning, when sun rose above the trees in the south.

The thought triggered a half-baked idea in my overactive brain. "I wonder if I can trim the yews around the roses so that they get more sun—no, that won't work. I'll put grow lights in here. That's what I'll do." I nodded emphatically, putting together a plan in my head. "And I'll sleep in here for the next week. I'm not letting anybody getting near these roses."

"Uh, you can't sleep here." Dillan turned slowly around the center. "I mean, the bugs will kill you. You'd need to set up a tent."

"I can sleep on the porch," I said, thinking out loud. "It's close enough that I can keep an eye on the entrance."

Dillan appeared skeptical but didn't comment. "Do you have exterior extension cords?" He gestured to the densely packed yew and rose vines. "Can you even get an extension in here?"

"I know my way through every inch of this space. I'm sure I can do it." I sank onto one of the chairs, working out calculations in my head. "At this time of year, the sun doesn't crest the yews on the east until—"

Pop sighed. "She'll be at this for a while. Let's go find those extension cords. They're in with the Christmas stuff in the garage. We'll have to figure out how to work them through the yews."

"This thing is really disorienting," Dillan said. "I couldn't tell front from back when I got in here."

"That's the point," Pop said. "You gotta focus on the path not your problems." Their voices faded when they went out of sight.

I stood, pacing around the area and counting off my steps. I might need to buy more cords, but we could do it, I was sure of it. Now to find my grow lights. I headed after the men, a woman on a mission.

It took an hour and a bunch of crawling around, but in the end, I had enough grow lights and extension cords. I sent Dillan back to work in the front and by the time he finished there it was almost noon. He took off on a motorcycle parked at the curb, promising to be back in an hour.

I checked his work after he left. He did a good job, the mulch evenly spread, and the spent bags tidily bundled into a stack and put near the trash cans. If he proved to be reliable, maybe we might be ready for the Showcase after all.

I fiddled with the timers for the grow lights for another hour, eating a bowl of cereal for lunch while Pop ran to the nursery and got the thyme I needed. When Dillan returned early in the afternoon, I showed him how to dig out and replace the herb. "Take plenty of breaks," I warned. "It's a heat stroke kind of day."

He had changed into a pair of brown work boots, khaki shorts and a pale blue T-shirt, attire that was probably much cooler than his earlier wardrobe. "Don't worry," he said, giving me a mock salute. "I'm well aware of Iowa summers." He lifted a flat of the thyme and headed for the far side of the yard.

I went to the garage and put a second coat of paint on the lawn furniture. By then it was mid-afternoon, and the heat drove me inside. I peeked out on the porch and spied Pop, dozing with the Sunday newspaper scattered on the floor and the Sports section on his chest. Reassured that he wasn't trying to help with the yardwork, I went to the dining room to survey the backyard.

Dillon had made remarkable progress, but it only made the sad parts seem even sadder. I was encouraged, though. I might have a presentable garden in time.

As I watched, he took a break, going to the steps leading from the mud room and taking a seat under the awning. Dillan took a drink from the cooler then got up, pouring the remains from his cup into a disposable aluminum pan, probably one of the ones I kept for paint in the garage. He carried the water to the arborvitae that formed the border on the west side of the yard and crouched down, sliding the pan forward.

Intrigued, I went to the mud room and stepped outside. He heard me and turned. "Is that your cat?"

I spied the hulking tabby monster, crouched under the big shrub. "No. He's been hanging out around here for the past week. Some people think that because there are woods here, they can toss out their pets and expect them to live." I frowned at the cat who glowered at me. It had a torn ear, a puffy jaw, and a bunched shoulder, giving it a Hunchback of Notre Dame appearance. "I feed them when I can, but the coons get the food as much as they do, I think."

"He's big." Dillan squatted and held out his hand. The cat glowered at him malevolently, an implacable expression of disdain on his lopsided face.

"It looks like his jaw is screwed up," I said.

"He might need some dental help."

"He's not mine."

"Hmm." Dillan poured more water into the dish and backed up.

"I have a live trap," I offered. "People dump

animals out here all the time." I frowned at the creature, who regarded me with a world-weary expression. "I suppose we can try to catch him and get him to the Humane Society. We might end up catching a racoon, though."

"Are you really going to sleep on your back porch tonight?" he asked.

"Of course. I'm not letting anybody get at those roses."

"Hmm. Well, if you sleep out there, you can keep an eye on the trap and scare away any coons that come sniffing around."

"I'll do no such thing," I replied. "When I sleep out there, I plan to keep an eye on my labyrinth. If you want to trap that animal, it's your business. You'll have to care for him once you trap him."

"I can't. I have an apartment. Pets aren't allowed."

"I don't want a cat."

"We can talk about it after I catch him." Dillan went to the garage. "I saw the traps in there. I'll get it set up then I'll get back to work. I should be able to finish that side bit today. What time do you want me here tomorrow?"

"I start early, while it's cool. If you want to come early then take a break in mid-day, that's fine." I glanced at the spot where he put the pan. "This isn't negotiable. I don't want a cat."

"I probably can't catch him anyway."

"I mean it," I said. "I've caught my share of them, and I turn them over to a rescue group to handle. But I don't know if they'll take one that's so bad-tempered."

"We'll see." He walked away.

"I mean it," I called after him. "This isn't

negotiable."

"I understand." He waved a hand and disappeared into the garage.

I glared at the door then returned to the house, where I spent the rest of the afternoon in my office, answering email and working with other counselors in the online support forum. I heard Dillan's motorcycle leave a little before five o'clock. I went outside and he had indeed finished his work in the side yard. I didn't see a live trap, so perhaps he gave up on that idea.

"You're sleeping out here?" Pop asked after supper while we enjoyed a cup of coffee on the porch.

"You bet I am. If somebody is coming in the yard, I want to know about it." I considered my sleeping options. If I dragged the couch a bit away from the side, I would have a reasonable view into the back yard. The extension cords going into Labbie weren't very visible, so I hoped if someone did indeed try to come in, they'd trip and make noise.

"What will you do if you find somebody?" he asked.

"Make so much fuss I'll scare them away." He shot me a skeptical glance. "I don't know what I'll do. I do know that I'll feel better if I'm doing something to protect my roses."

"You know, I was talking to Mark, the retired cop I know from the community center."

"Hmm." I was eyeing the location of the labyrinth in relation to the couch, trying to estimate the best way to angle it.

"He thinks we might need a bodyguard."

I almost dropped my coffee mug. "What? A bodyguard? Why?"

"You found a dead body on our property, Lilith. That's pretty serious."

"I told you what that detective said. He said Kelleher wasn't killed here."

"But somebody went to the trouble to break the lock and drag that body into our labyrinth. That means somebody wants to cause us problems. And when they find out that we're off the hook for that, they might do something worse."

I suppose he had a point. I could tell how worried he was—he didn't call it a maze. Pop always teased me about my 'maze'. I gave his words some thought. "Even if I wanted a bodyguard, where would I find one? In the Yellow Pages? On Google?"

"The cops can probably recommend somebody," he said promptly. In fact, it was so prompt I suspect he was coached.

"I'm sure they could, but I don't think it's necessary."

"I think we should consider it. You know, I don't like the idea of you sleeping out here. I'm pretty far away if anything happens." He brightened, smiling broadly. "Tell you what. I'll sleep in the living room. If you hear anything, you holler, and I'll come running."

I wanted to protest that it didn't make sense for both of us to have a lousy night's sleep, but he was so excited by the prospect, I didn't. What the heck. He often fell asleep in his recliner anyway. Instead of waking him to go to bed, I'd let him sleep.

That evening I did some work on my Thursday speech and put the finishing touches on a presentation I needed to make the following day. Then I changed into a long T-shirt and grabbed a pillow and a sheet.

I switched off the air conditioning and switched on the overhead fan in the living room where Pop dozed in front of the television. I tossed a lightweight afghan over his lap then I went out to the back porch, leaving the French doors open behind me.

I lay on my back on the wicker couch, the only position even relatively comfortable. The cushions were not made for long-term seating, much less sleeping, but I hoped the two glasses of wine and the over-the-counter sleep aid would do the trick.

My mind roamed as I tried to relax. Where would I find a bodyguard? What would a bodyguard even do? The idea was laughable.

My appointment tomorrow had me a bit worried. I was working on a design for a healing garden at a nearby public healthcare facility for terminally ill welfare patients. A local Boy Scout troop wanted to work with me as a community project. Tomorrow would be our first face-to-face meeting. Everything prior to this was done via phone or email. How would they handle working with someone like me? I'd had little interaction with children in my life. What would they do?

Well, I couldn't worry about that now. I would handle them the way I handled anyone new—answer questions that came up and ignore the rude stares.

The trees around me stirred in the breeze, casting shadows on the screens that were like people engaged in some kind of odd dance. The peep frogs were noisy at the edge of the property and I heard the other usual night sounds. Then I heard it—a grunting, wheezing noise.

I sat up, choking on fear. It sounded like someone

struggling to get through the gate a dozen or so feet away from me. I moved slowly, slipping off the couch to the worn area rug in the center of the porch. I crept toward the screen, inching my way in between furniture. I heard something outside, footsteps or scurrying on the gravel of the path. Someone was out there.

I had no weapon with me. Weapon? Who was I kidding? I didn't own a gun and I would never harm someone, anyway. Why didn't I keep a golf club nearby? Even if I didn't use it, I might threaten someone with it.

I reached the knee wall, white slatted wood that let in air through the floor-to-ceiling screens, but which kept the rain out. I peeked up over the top and that's when I saw the racoon, a foot away, standing on his hind legs and peering in at me.

I dropped back on the floor, trembling with fear, anger, and finally, laughter. I got to my feet and that was enough to startle the creature into running back into the trees. I returned to my couch.

The gate was open.

Damn. We hardly ever used that gate. We used the one by the garage because it was usually handier. Why would that gate be open? I pulled on the flip-flops I'd kicked off and went out the porch door, moving quickly over the pavers, praying no coon poop was there to sully my walk.

I got to the gate and drew it shut, sliding the bolt on the lock until I heard a solid thunk. I hurried back to the porch, resisting the urge to peek back over my shoulder every step of the way. I got inside and flung myself on the couch, kicking off my sandals and pulling the sheet up to cover me. *If the boogieman can't see you, he can't get you,* my mother used to say. I slipped into a fitful doze, waking and peering around whenever I heard an odd noise.

I awoke at first light, stiff from sleeping on the not-made-for-sleeping porch couch. I stumbled into the house and started coffee in the kitchen, then I went through the dining room to the living room. Pop was snoring in his recliner, the afghan tugged up around his chest. His breathless episode yesterday had me worried. I made a mental note to nag him into a visit to the doctor. I closed the pocket doors so my moving about wouldn't wake him.

I went upstairs and considered my appearance in the bathroom mirror. I decided to postpone showering until later in the morning. By then I'd be sweaty anyway. I tamped down my bed-head hair with some spritzes from the water bottle on the bathroom vanity. I had thick, coarse, straight hair and it only took a few swipes with the brush and I was presentable enough for a morning of yardwork.

I dressed in loose-weave pants and a blouse over a camisole. Twenty minutes later I was back downstairs. I slipped outside and checked off items on my clipboard list, editing my thoughts about what we might accomplish. Trimming, mulching, weeding, and ground cover replacement. A lot to do in a few days. I wouldn't be able to help this afternoon, and Thursday afternoon would be lost, too, because I needed to drive to the conference. I assumed Dillan wouldn't work on Wednesday because of the Fourth of July holiday, so that left today, Tuesday, half-Thursday, and Friday to get almost everything done.

I sucked in a steadying breath and examined my list. We simply couldn't get everything done. Transplanting that serviceberry shrub, moving the viburnum, and putting in the annuals would have to drop off the list. I drew a thin line through them and tried to push my worry to the back of my mind.

I went into Labbie and confirmed the grow lights were on, giving me three extra hours of daylight in the morning and two hours more at night. I settled in one of the chairs and made notations on my list, considering ways to work around the items I knew we couldn't do.

I emerged from Labbie and stopped. A man was coming around the side of the garage, heading for the arborvitae. He was in the shadows, and I couldn't see his face. I didn't even pause to consider my actions. I raced across the yard and hit him as hard as I could with my clipboard where he was bent over, peering into the shrubbery.

Chapter Five

The man pitched forward, face-first, into the dirt and mulch. I ran to the garage, reached inside, and grabbed my offset hoe from the rack near the door. I whirled, prepared to defend myself.

"What the hell?" the man croaked, backing out from the shrubbery. He twisted, sprawling on the ground with his knees up and his arms protecting his head.

"Oh, shit." I let the hoe drop. "How did you get in?"

Dillan rubbed his head, wincing. "What did you hit me with?" He glimpsed the hoe, lying at my feet. "Holy God, did you hit me with that? I'm lucky I'm not dead."

I picked up my clipboard, which I dropped by the garage. "This."

"Why did you hit me?" He checked his hand. "I'm surprised you didn't draw blood. I think I have a bump, though."

"How did you get in?" I repeated.

"What are you doing up this early?"

"I asked you first," I countered.

Dillan got to his feet, staggering. His khaki shorts were grass-stained, and dirt covered the front of his dark green T-shirt. "Your father gave me the padlock code. I figured I'd get started early. And I wanted to check—yep, there he is." Dillan plunged back into the shrubbery.

"What are you doing?" I dropped the clipboard on the back steps and hurried to where Dillan vanished. As I got there, he backed out, live trap in hand.

"I wanted to check and see if we got him. I didn't want him trapped and panicked when it gets hot."

I bent over to peer at the trap. The huge tabby cat hissed at me, lunging against the side of the cage. Dillan juggled it, almost dropping the cage until he got it righted again. "Calm down, buddy," he said, setting the cage on the grass.

The cat snarled at him and pressed against the wire sides, fur raised, and teeth bared. Well, sort of bared. One side of his face was swollen, giving him a squinty, pirate-ish sort of demeanor.

"I'll take him to the vet," Dillan volunteered. "I know a vet who opens at six and she said if I trapped the cat, I could bring him in."

The cat hissed again, but without much energy. It turned, showing a chunk of pink flesh on its flank and what might have been a broken tail. "Good Lord, what happened to the poor creature?"

Dillan circled the cage. The cat wasn't sure who was worse, me or Dillan, so it continued to crouch and hiss and growl at the world in general. "Probably was in a fight or maybe he got burned or got into chemicals or something."

I sighed. "Okay. We'll take him to the vet. But I told you, I don't need a cat, so you'll have to take care of him."

"Why don't you want a cat? He'll handle your mouse problem." Dillan returned to stand with me and regard the cat, who huddled as far as possible from us in the cage. "I can't believe you hit me." He touched his head again.

"Well, I'm sorry, but you snuck into my yard. I don't have a mouse problem."

"I didn't sneak. I was invited. And you don't have a mouse problem because you have a cat," Dillan said with exaggerated patience. "I'll pay for it."

"Why?"

"Why what?"

"Why adopt a feral cat?"

Dillan lifted the cage. The cat appeared enormous, but Dillan made handling him seem effortless. He peered at the monster. "Everybody needs a place. Maybe this is his." He set the cat back on the grass. "Don't worry. I'll handle it."

"Did you bring a car today? You can't strap him to a motorcycle, you know." Dillan looked so surprised I knew the answer. "Oh, for heaven's sake. I'll go with you. Put him on the back porch for now. It's still cool there." I glanced at my watch. "The vet doesn't open for a few minutes. Do you want some coffee?" I headed for the porch.

I got my clipboard and went inside, holding the door for Dillan to maneuver the bulky cage. He set the cat off to one side then followed me in. I poured us both a mug of coffee then I gestured to the stools at the kitchen island. "Do you need ice for your head?"

He rubbed the back of his skull. "It's okay. I may ask you for some aspirin if the headache doesn't go away."

"I'm sorry. You startled me."

He stared at the porch where my pillow and folded

sheet rested on the couch. "You slept out there last night?"

"Yep. No disturbances, either, except a wandering racoon and an open gate which I would have sworn was locked."

"What? Open gate?"

"I'll check the lock later on. We hardly ever use that entryway, so I'm not sure why it was open." I eyed the cat through the open French doors. "I'll bet he was abused and tossed away. People do that kind of shit all the time."

Dillan pulled over the clipboard I dropped on the counter. "Is this the to-do list?"

"Yep."

"How come you crossed out some stuff?"

"I doubt we can get to them. Those are big landscaping jobs. It takes more than one person to do them and I'm not sure I'll have time to help." I tugged the clipboard away. "And I don't want Pop helping, okay?"

"I'm happy to hear you say that." Dillan sipped his coffee, peering at the cat. "He's not very attractive," he admitted. "He's kind of beat up."

"He'll fit right in here, then. Pop and I are kind of beat up." I waggled a finger at Dillan when he started to speak. "But that doesn't mean I'll adopt him."

"Hmm." Dillan regarded me. "Why do you always wear long sleeves and pants?"

"It keeps me from getting scratched," I lied.

"I've seen your arm. It won't bother me." He continued staring at me.

"That's what they all say," I said lightly.

"Yeah, but I mean it." He slipped off the stool. "I'll

show you mine if you'll show me yours." One corner of his mouth twitched in that half-smile of his.

"What are you talking about?"

He reached down and peeled off his T-shirt. The first thing I noticed was his tanned chest and solid abdomen. Then I saw it. An oblong puckered scar on his left side, stretching from his armpit to his waist. He moved to the left, revealing white scar tissue bisecting his right shoulder, looping around it like an epaulet.

He twisted, and I gasped at the red scar running diagonally from his left shoulder to his right buttock. It was tight, the skin bunched around it.

"Holy moly," I muttered. "What happened to you? The military?"

"I fell in with some bad people." He turned to regard me. "Then I was a cop on some mean streets." He jerked the T-shirt on, tousling his hair so it stood up in little licks. "I got out before I died. Trust me. It won't bother me."

"I'm glad."

He tilted his head to one side, staring at my neck. "It's not that bad."

"Six surgeries for my neck and chest," I said, pressing my hand against my breastbone. "Five on my leg and arm. Four on my hand. The acid was bad, but I got some infections afterward that screwed up my recovery." I flexed my hand. "Almost normal."

"I hate hospitals," he murmured.

"You and me both." I moved away to the window, wondering if he saw me trembling.

"You don't seem bitter about it." He spoke from behind me.

"I decided long ago that I wouldn't let the scars

define who I was. I had to let go of the hatred in order to do that." I looked at Labbie. "I walked the path more times than I can count before I finally figured it out."

"I don't know if I ever figured it out." He joined me at the window. "Maybe I need to do some walking."

"You're welcome to try."

We were silent for a minute then he said, "My wife left me six years ago."

"What? Because of a few scars?"

"Because I was a cop. Because of the scars. Because she didn't want to hang out at the hospital. You choose."

I wasn't sure what to say, so I settled for a complacency. "It can be hard seeing somebody you love in pain."

His mouth twitched again. "That's assuming love was involved. Anyway, I've got some other scars, but I don't show them to everybody."

"How come?"

"Well, they're in a place I don't show to everybody. If you know what I mean."

"Oh." My face flared with heat. I brushed by him and put my mug on the counter. "I guess we can go now."

"You're the driver. Whatever you say." He put his mug next to mine then went to get the cage.

"Follow me." I grabbed my purse from the hook near the door and we left by the back through the mudroom and my PT space, which opened into the garage.

He settled the critter in the back of my small Chevy SUV, putting the cage next to the box of hardscape samples I carried to client sites. I backed out of the garage. "Which way?"

"Beauty and the Beast Vet Clinic. It's west of here, off of—"

"I know where it is. That's where I take the ones I find." I drove up the hill, the neighborhood quiet in the early morning. "Do you always go around taking off your shirt for strange women?"

"It's going to get hot today. I figured I might want a dousing with the hose and I didn't want you to faint if you saw my war wounds."

"It'll take more than that to make me faint." I drove out to the main road and soon we were turning in to the parking lot at the vet's office, a storefront in a strip mall a few blocks from my house.

"Hello again," the vet said when she saw me. "Dillan didn't mention it was your cat." She led the way into an exam room with a big metal table and a small sink inset into a counter in the corner.

"It's not mine. Somebody dumped it. Again." Dillan set the cat cage on the shiny examining table. "You two know each other?"

"I know his sister," the vet said.

"Stepsister," Dillan snapped.

The vet raised an eyebrow. She was a tall woman with dark hair pulled back in a ponytail and a porcelain complexion. "That's right. I keep forgetting." She drew on a pair of long leather gloves which nearly reached to her armpits. "Let's see what we have here."

"He's mean," I warned. "You might want to—" Before I completed the sentence the vet had opened the cage, dragged out the monster, and had him in a hammer lock, hissing but not moving. "Wow. You know your stuff."

"I do this all the time." The vet poked and prodded then called in an assistant to hold the critter while she examined his mouth. "Abscessed tooth," she said. "Those other wounds are healed burns and his tail was probably smashed. I should amputate so it doesn't keep getting infected."

"Assholes," I muttered.

"And he's declawed. His front paws. That's what most people do. At least they had him neutered. They did one smart thing."

"Declawed?" Dillan shook his head. "What kind of asshole tosses out a wounded, declawed animal to live in the woods?"

"Heartless, uncaring assholes," the vet said. "I'll need to keep him here today. I want to do some bloodwork first. If that comes back okay, we'll do surgery this afternoon for the tooth and the tail. I'd like to keep him overnight to monitor how he reacts to the anesthesia."

Ka-ching, I thought. This will be pricey.

"Sounds good. It's on my tab," Dillan said. "I'll pick him up tomorrow.

"Wait a minute. I thought you said that—" The vet glanced at me.

Dillan put a hand under my elbow. "Let's go, Boss. We have a garden to prep." He nodded to the vet. "If there's any problems, call my cell phone. You've got the number, right?"

The vet checked the sheaf of papers on the clipboard near the sink. "Put him in quarantine until we get test results," she told the assistant. The guy manhandled the monster back into the cage and vanished out the door, the cat hissing and snarling all the way. "Your number didn't change since the last time, right?" the vet asked Dillan.

"Still the same. Thanks."

"The last time?" I asked him as we left the office.

"My mom adopts strays. I'm the designated vet-dropper-offer and picker-upper."

While I drove back to the house we talked about the day's work. "Make sure you take plenty of breaks and if you need to, come in the house to cool down."

"This Showcase thing is important to you, isn't it? I mean, you might get some work because of it?"

"Yes, but it isn't important enough to compromise your health." I drove down the hill to my house. "Oh, now what?" I fumed when I saw the dark sedan parked in front. A man got out when I turned into the drive.

"He doesn't look like a reporter," Dillan said.

I slowed, eyeing the man climbing the steps to the front porch. He was still handsome even with his thick, dark hair now gray. "It's Shaw."

"Shaw?"

"Shaw Kelleher."

"The dead guy's son?"

I nodded. "And my ex-fiancé."

"What's he doing here?" Dillan asked while I drove into the garage.

"I have no idea. I guess I'll find out." I parked the car and got out, taking my purse from the backseat where I'd dropped it.

"You want some backup?" He joined me at the back of the SUV.

What a sweet gesture. "No, thanks. I can handle it."

"Call if you need me." Dillan and I left through the open garage door. I went right to meet Shaw, who followed the path to join us. Dillan hesitated before heading left, around the garage to the side gate.

I clutched the purse slung over my shoulder, using that to still my shaking hands. "Hello, Shaw." I stopped in front of him.

Shaw Kelleher was stop-and-stare handsome, with rugged features, thick hair, and an oval face. In his youth, he was a dead ringer for a young George Clooney and he'd aged well, his skin still smooth with only distinguished-looking crow's feet around his pale blue eyes. His suit was a dark charcoal gray, which exactly matched his hair. The crisp pale gray shirt he wore appeared cool even in the morning's building heat. He was the picture of the successful businessman from the top of his brushed and coifed head to the tips of his black wing-tip shoes.

"You're still beautiful," he said with that charming, wide smile I remembered.

"And you're still a liar." I said it lightly, dismissively.

He leaned forward and touched my chin. His pale blue eyes moved to the bunched skin of my neck, and his hand moved away. "I've thought about you so much."

So much that you couldn't get in touch with me? A small, niggling voice spoke bitterly in the back of my mind. "I'm sorry about your father." I stepped back, away from his hand. "I hope you know that I had nothing to do with his death."

My cool words seemed to shake him away from whatever trance kept him staring at me. He stepped back, too. "I know that, Lilith."

"I read about your mother's death last year. I know

how close you were to her." I didn't say I was sorry. His mother was harridan, a nasty, sharp-tongued witch who adored Tanya and blamed me for the break-up between Tanya and Shaw.

I used to be tortured by memories of my time with him. Beach parties, trips to New York, outings on the boat the family kept at Lake Michigan. The Kelleher family was Rich with a capital R and Shaw had no qualms about living the High Life and sharing it with me. We met, partied, and fell in love, all within six months. He proposed to me in Cancun, on a long, drunken holiday weekend there. His family hated me, and I always wondered if they were relieved when the attack happened.

I had relegated those memories to a dusty corner of my mind and now here they were, coming back to kick me in the face. "What do you want?" I asked. "It's not even eight in the morning. You're not a morning person. Or you weren't."

"I wanted to see you before anyone else was around. I was afraid reporters might be here." He looked past me, to where Dillan stood a moment before. "Who's that man with you?"

Something in his tone of voice irked me. Perhaps I was annoyed that he showed up out of the blue. Maybe I was nervous. "He's helping me with my garden. I have a large event coming up to prepare for." I must have sounded critical because Shaw immediately apologized.

"I read about that. You're a garden designer, aren't you? I'm sorry, I must be in the way. I wanted to see you and talk to you. I won't take up much of your time. Please. Can we go somewhere and talk?"

He seemed so anxious. "Come inside." I led the way into the garage and we entered the house through my PT space at the back.

"What's this?" Shaw asked while we crossed the room to the mud room. "Exercise room? It's working, that's for sure. You're as slender and fit as ever. You've stayed in great shape, Lilith."

"Physical therapy," I said. "I need regular sessions to stay flexible." His eyes skimmed over my hand.

Pop was in the kitchen, reading the morning paper at the island. When he saw who was with me, he almost dropped his coffee mug. "Shaw—what are you doing here?"

"Hello, Merchant. I came to talk to Lilith. I didn't know you lived here, too."

"After the attack, I needed help. Pop and I decided the best thing to do was pool our resources and live together. Do you want some coffee, Shaw?"

"No, thanks. Are you retired now?" Shaw asked Pop.

"Yep. I quit working at the shop about ten years ago or more." Pop met my eyes where I stood in the doorway.

I shrugged. *No, I don't know why he's here.* "We can sit on the porch if you'd like," I suggested. "It's still cool out there." I didn't wait for a reply, but went to the French doors, opened to let in the morning breeze.

"I hope we can get caught up sometime, Merchant," I heard him say to Pop.

"Sure," Pop replied doubtfully. "That would be fine."

I knew what was going through Pop's mind. It was

the same thing going through mine. *Why bother with us after twenty-five years? Why was he here?* I gathered my pillow and folded sheet, putting them on a chair, then I gestured to the couch. "What's going on, Shaw?" I sank into my chair, facing the back yard.

"You always did get right to the point." He said it with a smile, his old charm on display.

"It saves time." Beyond him, I saw Dillan working about six feet from the porch. He was bent over, perched on his knees, weeding. A wire cord was draped over his back connecting his earbuds to whatever gadget he had in his back pocket. I wasn't sure if he even knew we were there.

Instead of sitting on the couch, Shaw took the wicker hassock positioned in front of my chair, a foot or so away from me. He sat, unbuttoning his suit coat and smoothing down his gray-and-black striped tie. Our knees touched, and I sat up straighter, pushing back in my seat. "I want you to go to my father's funeral with me. It's scheduled for Thursday."

I stared at him. The words made no sense to me.

"Well?" He leaned forward to put his hand on mine where it rested on the arm of the chair. I managed not to gasp, but it hurt when he squeezed it.

"Why?" I asked in an almost normal voice.

"I'd like your support. It will be tough." His expression changed from hopeful to woeful in the blink of an eye.

"Why me? It's more than twenty years since you've even seen me. Why do you want me there?"

His hand tightened on mine. I slipped it out from under his and shifted back in my chair, afraid he might put a hand on my leg next.

"Lilith, there's never been anyone like you in my life. I've never forgotten what we had together. Oh, sure, there have been women in my life, but no one like you. Father wouldn't let me contact you. He was a tyrant. He terrorized Mother and me. He railroaded me into that sham of a marriage. Thank God it only lasted six years."

You're an adult. Grow a spine. You're slinging bullshit. The words were on the tip of my tongue. The news of Shaw's wedding five years after the attack had thrown me into a depression that I struggled to get past. But I did get past it. Why the hell was he here now, raking it up again? "I know your father wasn't happy about our relationship. But that doesn't explain why—"

Shaw gave a mirthless laugh. "Not happy? He threatened to cut me off without a penny if I married you."

This was news to me. I knew his father had hoped for a more advantageous match for Shaw, but to disinherit him? "I didn't know that."

Shaw stared me, his luminous eyes beseeching. "I know there isn't anyone in your life. I mean, well, I mean I don't think there's anyone, is there? I'm sure, since the attack, that it's been—I mean—you know what I mean." He had the grace to appear slightly ashamed.

Only slightly. I don't know what pissed me off more, that he assumed—rightly—that I had no man in my life, that I even needed a man in my life, or that I would jump at the chance to take up with him again. I didn't know what to say. I loved Shaw when I was twenty-nine and I was fifty-five now. I had spent almost my entire adult life alone. I never allowed myself to think about a 'normal' life. I lived the life I had and never looked back, at least not after the first few years. The life I had with him belonged to someone else, someone twenty-five years in the past. Why would he think I'd want to go back to that? Why would he think I could?

Instead of saying what I thought, I resorted to polite dissembling. "Shaw, I'm sorry. But I don't think you know what you're asking. Your father's body was found at my house. How would it seem if I went to the funeral?"

"Why did Father come to see you?" He scooted forward, separating his legs so I couldn't move without hitting one of his thighs. "What did you talk about?"

"He threatened to cut off my allowance," I said flatly.

"What?" Pop jumped to his feet from his spot in the dining room. He came to the doorway. "You never told me that."

"I didn't want to bother you," I said.

"That bastard." Pop glanced at Shaw. "I'm sorry, but if he was cutting off Lilith, then he was a bastard."

"You'll get no argument from me." Shaw twisted on the hassock to peer at Pop over his shoulder. "Of course, I'll do everything I can to continue it, but our business has suffered since he came out of retirement. It might be difficult."

Wait a minute. Old man Kelleher said he left retirement to save the business. Now Shaw was saying that his father ruined the business. Who was telling the truth?

"I won't lie. I need that money," I said. "We can get by without it, but it makes my life easier."

"I'll see what I can do. If the family lawyer calls you, don't talk to him. He'll probably try to convince you to sign a new agreement." Shaw touched my hand again. "I wish you'd reconsider coming to the funeral. It would show everyone that I have full confidence in you and that I know you had nothing to do with it."

Pop began to speak, but I got in first. "I don't have to prove anything to anyone."

"But—now that Father is gone—you don't understand. I was hoping we could—"

"Hey, Boss." Dillan peered at us through the screens. "Sorry to interrupt, but can I get some aspirin for my headache?" He pulled off his floppy hat and touched his head.

"Sure." I leaned forward. Shaw took the hint, moving to one side so I could get to my feet without bumping into him.

"I should be going," Shaw said, standing. "I need to make a quick trip to Minneapolis on business."

"I'll walk you out." I went to the porch door and held it for him to precede me. "Dillan, come with us. I have aspirin in my office up front." I was happy to have someone else nearby.

Dillan went ahead of us to the side gate, unlatching the lock and pushing it open. He dodged to one side then walked into the front yard.

Shaw and I followed. A bee came zipping toward us and Shaw swatted at it.

"That's a bumblebee," I said. "He won't sting you."

Shaw glared at the unoffending bee. "Tell that to it. I hate them."

"Why? They don't harm people."

"They do if you're allergic." He dodged the bee when it meandered back toward us. I imagined it humming a tune while it perambulated here and there.

"Are you allergic?" Dillan asked from in front of us.

"I was stung once and my hand swelled."

"That doesn't mean you're allergic. Bee stings have venom and that's a natural reaction. You're allergic if you go into anaphylactic shock." He turned to peer past Shaw to me. "That reminds me. My epi-pen is in the saddlebag on my cycle, in the cooler."

"What? Are you allergic to bees?" Shaw stared at him, mouth agape.

"Yep."

"And you're working in a garden?" I asked incredulously.

"Like you said. They won't bother me."

His words finally soaked in. "Cooler? Is it like insulin? Do you need to keep it cold?"

"Not cold. Just cooler than sitting uncovered in a motorcycle bag on a July day in Iowa."

"For heaven's sake, bring it inside and leave it on the counter or something."

"Nah. It's okay."

I put my hands on my hips. "I don't want to be responsible for your medication. Bring it inside."

Dillan gave me a snappy salute. "Aye, aye." He dashed down the stone steps.

"He's insolent," Shaw commented. "Where'd you find him?"

"A friend of a friend." I stopped on the top step. "It was good to see you, Shaw."

"I want to see you again, Lilith." He gave my arm a

squeeze. I winced and drew back. "I'm sorry. It's been such—"

"You need to get through the funeral and all that first," I said firmly. "Then we'll see what's possible."

"I suppose you're right." He bent over and kissed me on the cheek before carefully navigating the steps, passing Dillan when he came back up.

"Well, ain't he pretty," Dillan muttered, shooting a dirty look at Shaw's back. "You were engaged to that asshole?"

"I was a different person twenty-five years ago."

"You'd have to be a completely different person to want to be with him."

I watched Shaw drive away. Something about his visit bothered me, besides the obvious fact that he contacted me at all.

Why didn't I trust him?

Chapter Six

Dillan came inside carrying a bulky syringe. "Here's my pen."

"I'll put it in on the island in the kitchen. You can get to it through the porch if you need it. We don't lock those French doors unless we're leaving." I got the aspirin from my desk drawer and handed him the bottle, exchanging it for the pen.

I had a large-scale garden plan for the Showcase on an easel in the corner. He stood in front of it, head tilted to one side. "You want to move that little tree over there, right?" He pointed at the drawing. "Then put that tree where the other one was?"

"It's not a tree, but a big shrub. Yes, that's the idea. The viburnum isn't getting enough sunlight where it is. The serviceberry will do well in its spot. They've been in place a long time, so the roots are deep. I meant to switch them earlier in the spring, but time got away from me." I stood next to him, envisioning the changes in my mind. "I didn't count on the maple getting so tall so fast." I pointed to the tree on the map. "It's beautiful in the fall so I don't want to trim it back."

"There's a lot to think about when you design a garden. I guess I never considered what goes into it."

"Most people don't. They figure you put in a few plants and you're done. I like to plan for the long term and that means making decisions that might not take effect for years. I'm lucky—I don't have to contend with near neighbors, so I can make my own choices. Sometimes choices are made for you."

"Shit happens. Like what happened to you."

"I suppose that's one way to look at it."

"How did it happen? Didn't anybody know what she planned to do?" I hesitated. This was a day for raking up memories, apparently. "Hey, I'm sorry. None of my business."

"No, it's okay. I suppose it's a shock to anyone who wasn't around here when it happened. Acid attacks aren't that common in the States, thank God." I considered how to answer. "I don't think anybody guessed. She didn't seem that upset when Shaw broke up with her."

That wasn't strictly true. Tanya was bitter and angry at first, but after a month, she seemed to shrug it off and was once again a regular at Shaw's parties. She and he attended the same private schools and ran in the same crowd most of their lives. It seemed natural that she'd rejoin the group.

"Where did she get the acid?"

"Her family runs a landscape business. She probably stole it from their stock. Some companies use it in their own special mixes of insecticides."

"Wow. I didn't think—I mean, I didn't know it was that easy to get."

"Licensed landscapers have access to many chemicals. I never did find out exactly where she got it." I moved away from the plans, taking his insulated sack and going past the front door to the dining room.

"How did she do it?" He took one last look at the

easel then came with me.

"It was a pool party at the Kelleher house. In July. We partied all the time." Booze and drugs flowed freely around Shaw. Back then he was into cocaine and vodka. I stuck with wine because someone had to be a responsible adult. I never liked doing drugs. I hated that out-of-control feeling they gave me.

I went to the kitchen and put the pen on the kitchen island. Then I jotted *Leave here for Dillan* on a sticky note in case I forgot to tell Pop about it. Dillan came in behind me. "It's hard to believe nobody knew what she was planning."

"She might have told one of her friends that she would get back at me. From what Pop told me after it happened, everybody swore that they were surprised and had no idea what she would do." I had played and replayed that moment in my mind for decades. "I was wearing a bikini and talking to Shaw. Tanya gestured for me to join her. I moved toward her and she tossed what I thought was a glass of wine at me."

Dillan flinched. "She was that close?"

"She was two, three feet away from me. I was so stunned I didn't move until I felt the burns. Then I instinctively ran for the swimming pool." I ran my left hand lightly over my right arm. "That's why it wasn't so bad. The water washed off most of the acid."

"But you were wearing a bikini, so you got it on your exposed skin." I heard the anger simmering in his voice.

His gray eyes seemed to snap with some kind of inner fire. "I was one of the lucky ones," I said softly. "I work with victim groups. Believe me. It could have been worse. It might have gone in my eyes or I might have swallowed some. As it was, I did okay. Most of the scars are from reconstructive surgery. One of those got infected and that set back my recovery by weeks."

"What happened to her?"

"A stay in a psychiatric hospital then probation at home. Her family runs the Three Sisters Landscape business."

"She's in town, here?" His eyes widened.

"She's in Beaumont." I peeked at the porch, but Pop wasn't there. "If you see Pop outside, make sure he doesn't overdo it."

"Sure." He hesitated, touching the insulated bag. "I didn't mean to pry."

"That's okay. Scars like mine—or yours—aren't normal. People are always curious."

"Yeah. No kidding. Thanks for leaving the pen inside. You never know when I might need it." He left the house through the porch, picking up the hat that he'd dropped on the coffee table.

I watched him go out into the yard. He must have done his research. I hadn't mentioned any particulars about the attack, but he asked about 'her'. Oh, well. A simple Internet search would bring up a dozen newspaper articles from the last twenty-five years.

I inspected the pen on the counter, making sure I knew how to use it in case I had to. It appeared straightforward. Twist off the blue thingy and jab. No measuring or anything. That was reassuring. I filled a mug with coffee and went on the porch. Shaw, back in my life. I closed that door a long time ago. I refused to dwell on the past, but now and then I wondered what would have happened if—

If Shaw's ex-girlfriend didn't throw acid on me.

If Shaw defied his father and came after me.

If my mother didn't gamble.

If my father had better control of his money.

Why in God's name would Shaw want me to go to the funeral with him? Why would he want me back in his life?

I had no answers to those central questions. I gave up trying to figure it out. I had to do trimming in the front, prepare for my afternoon appointment, and put the finishing touches on the signage for Sunday's open house. I didn't have time for Shaw.

Dillan disappeared at noontime and hadn't returned by the time I needed to leave after lunch. I stripped off my work clothes, leaving them on the chair in my bedroom, and changed into my usual professional attire, an ankle-length lightweight skirt and a blouse with elastic at the waist. Pop called it my Gypsy Queen disguise. I suppose he was right, but it was non-restrictive, comfortable and pretty. I went out to the garage to leave instructions for Dillan.

"Why are you dressed up? Where are you going?" Pop was puttering around, working on a 'sculpture' of his made from found objects. This was his latest hobby, along with watercolor painting and Mahjongg.

"I have an afternoon appointment. You remember—the Boy Scouts?"

"That's tomorrow."

"No, it's today," I corrected.

"But—you need to wait for Dillan to get back. You have to tell him what to work on next."

"I'm telling you. Have him finish cleaning out under the trees out back and if there's time, mulch around them."

"But—I thought—you need to wait until he gets back to—"

"Weird seeing Shaw again, wasn't it?" I said to divert him from whatever worry he had about giving Dillan work to do. "I have no idea why he stopped by. Just like I have no idea why his father came to see me. Neither of them make much sense, especially after all this time."

"It sounded like Shaw might want to pick up where he left off." Pop focused on polishing a broken garden shear welded to a metal frame, shooting me little interrogatory glances while he worked.

"Not going to happen," I said immediately. "He's had twenty-five years to pick up where we left off. It's too late."

Pop straightened. "I'm glad to hear you say that. I never liked that son of a bitch."

"You hid it well."

"Your mother thought he was a great catch. I hated to argue with her." Pop sighed. "You know how she got."

Yeah, I did know. Mom used any disagreement with Pop as a chance to leave the house, which we later discovered meant "go to the casino and lose a bunch of money." Of course, Mom used any excuse to gamble. Her addiction almost cost Pop their house when she went to loan sharks for financing because she was sure she could win it back at the blackjack tables.

It still amazed me how oblivious Pop and I were to her gambling. She became increasingly irritable and angry when we questioned her, but we wrote it off to menopause and didn't think twice about it. Neither of us had any idea that she was in for two-hundred-thousand dollars at twenty-percent interest. Pop found out when Mom died, around the time Shaw and I began dating.

"Nothing to worry about," I assured him. "Shaw Kelleher isn't back in my life."

"Good. I was wondering about the mulch you want to use in back. Do you want the shredded bark? I thought the hardwood would look better."

I checked my watch. "I don't have time to decide now. You and Dillan talk it over and decide what's best."

"But—"

"I have to go or I'll be late. See you later." I tucked the tube of design plans in the back of my SUV next to my samples and left. Pop watched me with the same worried expression as I drove away. What was his problem today? Normally he didn't even notice if I was there or gone. I suppose the body in the labyrinth had him worried.

It had me worried, too. If he was killed elsewhere and put in my backyard, that meant somebody wanted to draw attention to me and to the murder. I watched enough crime dramas to know that most killers tried to hide their crime, not flaunt it.

It made no sense to me. I decided to focus on something that did make sense—the upcoming meeting. I drove to the care facility on the outskirts of town, where farm met the city, enjoying the sight of the verdant fields stretching away as far as the eye could see. The corn in the fields was more than knee-high and I spied a familiar sign in the parking lot at the drugstore when I passed. *Sweet Corn Here!* Yep. July in Iowa.

I went into the lobby, pausing at the reception desk

then proceeding to the conference room attached to the director's office. Four boys in Scout uniforms sat on one side of the table with a man introduced as Scoutmaster Barnett.

The director of the facility came in with the chaplain, both men I had worked with before. After exchanging a few pleasantries, I unrolled the plan I designed for the garden to be built in a now-overgrown weedy area south of the main building. I stood over the design, stretching over the table to describe the plan.

"We can hire a crew to do the initial cleanup," I said. "There are several basswood and ash trees there that need to be removed, but there's one oak I want to keep if we can. Once they've cleared the ground, the Scouts can come in and help amend the soil and we'll work on laying out the flower beds and the paths."

I covered the base plan on the bottom sheet with the tracing paper overlay of the paths. "I've designed several outdoor rooms. The paths lead here and here." I pointed to the places I meant. One of the little boys nudged his companion when he spied the crinkled flesh on my wrist. "In each space I want a patio area that's surrounded by the beds and the trees to give privacy."

I slipped over the third overlay, the one for the flower beds. "We'll probably need to get some help building the raised beds."

"My dad can help," one of the kids piped up. "He's in construction."

"That would be great." I regarded the Director. "If we time it right, we can get most of our planting materials at cost from nurseries, who will use it as a charitable donation. We'll want to set up fund-raising for materials or ask for donations from the community.

And we might want to do fund-raising for the tools the residents will use to work in the gardens. They'll need adaptive tools. I know of ways to modify regular tools, so we might be able to get donations and handle it that way."

"You want the residents to manage the garden?" the scoutmaster asked.

"It's a healing garden. Working outside can be therapeutic. They'll have direction, of course. Some of the local Master Gardeners have volunteered to act as mentors."

One of the boys, older than the others, asked, "Do you have a garden?" His gaze was on my hand, resting on the table a foot away from him.

"Yes, I do." I pushed up my sleeve and his eyes widened.

"Were you burned?" This came from a younger boy with short dark hair and freckles.

The scoutmaster shot him a reproving shake of the head. "That isn't polite. It's none of your business."

"No, that's okay," I said. "I don't mind discussing it. I'm the victim of an acid attack. A woman threw acid on me."

The boys stared at me in stunned surprise. "Why? When?"

"Twenty-five years ago. In the summertime." I looked at the scoutmaster. "You might remember it. It happened at the Kelleher house."

"I do remember. It was horrific. You almost died, didn't you?"

"Yes. That kind of attack can be lethal. It was touch and go for a while. I was kept in an induced coma for several weeks because of infections."

"Does it hurt?" the boy asked, staring at my puckered arm.

The scoutmaster seemed shocked and started to reprimand the kid, but I broke in. "I don't mind. It does hurt, sometimes. It kind of burns. The skin is hypersensitive because the nerves are screwed up. I need to be careful how I shower, dress, and everything."

"Why did she do it?"

I wasn't sure how to describe what happened. How old were these kids? What did they understand? I decided not to worry about it. "I think she was afraid. I was engaged to be married to a man she loved. She was jealous, I suppose, and angry."

"Wow. Did you get married, then?"

I turned away from the child's perceptive blue eyes. "No. It didn't quite work out. Instead I design gardens now and try to help other people who are in pain."

"Does that mean you're disabled?" the young one asked.

"Not really. I think of myself as limited because I don't need to use special tools like a wheelchair for somebody who's paralyzed or a cane for a blind person. This garden has to serve people who are limited and people who are disabled, so we need to keep that in mind as we work."

The boys nodded enthusiastically. I'm sure they were imagining merit badges in their heads. This was a big project and I suspected they'd get a lot of kudos if we pulled it off successfully.

We discussed how to proceed and the timing. "We should clear the land in the fall and do passive kill-off for the weeds." All eyes turned to me with questions in them. "We'll clear-cut the lot, mow it as low as we can, then spread clear plastic over everything we want to kill. Next year, when we plant, most of the weeds will be dead. We'll pull up the plastic, drop newspaper over the whole area and start working on top of it." I regarded the boys. "Spread the word. Everybody saves their newspapers all winter."

Four heads bobbed happily.

"That gives us a year to do fund-raising," the chaplain said. "I wonder if we can get some Girl Scouts involved in that."

I rolled up the plans, which I would continue to refine over the coming months. "There's no reason they can't be involved in everything. There's enough work to go around." I smiled at the boys. "Girls can certainly do some heavy lifting as well as boys."

"No kidding," one boy said morosely. "My sister beats my butt at arm wrestling all the time."

We set a date and time for another meeting to discuss how to proceed in more detail, then we left, the boys walking ahead and the Scoutmaster walking with me.

"Thanks for talking so frankly with them," he said. "Kids are smarter than most people give them credit for. They're naturally curious, too, and don't mean any disrespect. They haven't had much opportunity to be around people who have physical limitations."

I slung the design tube over my left shoulder by its strap. "I don't mind talking to a receptive audience. Many people think that because I don't have a prosthetic device I'm not handicapped. It's important to understand that there are limits that affect people. It's not only serious issues that are a problem."

"What happened to you is serious enough," he said gently.

"I'm mobile, I have my sight and my speech intact, and I don't have any major respiratory problems. Believe me, I've learned about acid attack victims and I know I'm one of the lucky ones."

"What a world we live in. We'll see you in a few weeks." He hurried to meet the Director, who waited at a junction of hallways ahead.

One of the boys who hadn't spoken lagged behind the others. "Did you ever want to hurt the girl who hurt you?"

He asked it so softly I had to bend over to hear him. "Yes. Of course."

"But you didn't?"

I couldn't, I wanted to say. I was too hurt and, by the time I was well enough, she was gone, committed to a mental institution. Then I had a new life, and I couldn't jeopardize it for something as stupid as revenge.

"No, I didn't."

He seemed so solemn as he considered that. Children, I thought. So innocent.

"I would have," he declared. "I would have killed her." He scampered away to catch up to his friends.

I watched him go. Children, I thought. So primeval.

I put my design plans in my car then took a few minutes to walk around the soon-to-be garden. The heat of the day had settled in and the air was hot and still. I hoped Dillan was taking a break. I was tempted to call and check in. The last thing I wanted was him, passed out from heat exhaustion.

I pulled out my phone but stopped when I remembered I didn't have his phone number. Good heavens, did Pop get any details from Dillan, like address, phone, social security number? I had a small payroll account in my garden business and I would need to get his information entered in order to write a check this Friday for a week's worth of work.

For that matter, what hourly rate did Pop quote him? I suppose I was so relieved to have the help that I let those details slip past me. At this point, I didn't care if Pop quoted him an arm and a leg. Dillan was proving to be worth his weight in gold when it came to yard work.

I spent twenty minutes walking the proposed site then I went back to my car. The boys were clambering into a mini-van and they waved to me when the van drove away. I was pleased with the day's work. The kids were curious, but I expected that. And they were polite. I hadn't expected that. If I served as a teachable moment, then I wasn't unhappy.

The one child's words percolated in my brain while I drove away from the facility. Why didn't I confront Tanya? For that matter, why didn't I confront Shaw? I should have faced him to find out why he abandoned me. No matter what I told him, if he loved me, he should have defied his father and helped me.

I knew the answer. Because it was easier to be a victim, a little voice in my head whispered. Because I knew he didn't love me. I was his way of spiting his father and trying to break away from his mother.

And I didn't love him. Perhaps that was the saddest part of all. Tanya ruined my life because of a man I didn't really love. I was in love with his lifestyle, so different than my middle-class upbringing. If we'd married, it would have lasted a few years, then I'd be on my own, probably with a cash settlement to keep me away. I wasn't sure our love would survive it and I didn't want to find out. I was afraid that if I asked, he wouldn't be there. So I didn't push it. It wasn't any more complicated than that.

I entered the main road, a busy two-lane county highway. Damn Shaw, anyway, for popping back up in my life. Why now? I suppose it was because of his father. His father died, and I was peripherally involved. That brought me back onto Shaw's radar screen.

I cranked up the volume on my iPod, plugged into my car's audio. I was working my way through Broadway showtunes and I had just finished *Beauty and the Beast.* I was on *Phantom of the Opera* now, a play that resonated with me. I didn't understand obsession but I certainly understood alienation.

I checked my side mirror and saw a big black pick-up behind me. It seemed like anybody who owned a big SUV or truck loved to tailgate those of us with smaller vehicles. I sped up, making a mental list of the stops I needed to make.

Grocery store for milk and a few other essentials. Stop at the local nursery for landscape fabric and a new pair of gloves to replace mine that sat out in the rain. As I drove, the county highway morphed into a busy four-lane city street with businesses on each side of the road. I slowed for the reduced speed zone ahead. The truck behind me loomed suddenly in my mirror, the reflected sun hiding whoever was driving.

My phone, synced to my car audio system, rang

shrilly. I glanced at the embedded display, but I didn't recognize the number. I debated answering, my left index finger hovering over the icon on the steering wheel.

"Oh, what the hell," I muttered. I pressed the icon for *answer*. "Hello?" I said loudly, over the sound of the car motor.

"Lilith? It's Olivia Meredith."

"Olivia?" On my side of the road was a messy roadkill, a deer that appeared partially disemboweled given the amount of nastiness spread across my driving lane. I always averted my eyes whenever I saw death on the road. I closed my eyes when I neared the corpse, breathing a silent prayer that its death was swift and not as appalling as it appeared. "Olivia, I'm in the car. Can I—"

When I opened my eyes and glanced in my rear-view mirror, I saw Tanya Sidero peering at me over the steering wheel of the black pick-up.

Chapter Seven

"Oh, my God!" I almost drove off the road.

"Lilith? Are you okay?"

"It's Tanya Sidero. She's in the car behind me." I ventured a peek at the mirror and glimpsed the Three Sisters logo, three women in a circle with their arms raised. It stood out in sharp white paint on the hood of the black truck.

"You have a restraining order against her, don't you?"

I nodded then realized how stupid that was. "Yes. I renewed it a few months ago. What do I do?" My head whipped around frantically. "She's close behind me. I can't get away from her. There's too much traffic."

"Where are you?" Olivia's voice was brisk but calm.

"Almost to the Walmart and the Sam's Club off of 19th Street in Le Prince." I gripped the steering wheel, hazarding a peek in the rear-view mirror. The damn truck was right on my bumper, filling my vision.

"I'm calling dispatch. You get to the parking lot and you run into the store. You'll be safer with people around you. Do you hear me, Lilith?"

My instinct was to park the car and cower inside, but Olivia was right. There was safety in numbers. "I hear you," I managed to croak. "I'm turning into the parking lot."

"Okay. You hold on to the phone. I'm with you, Lilith."

Hold on to the phone. Shit. I wasn't on the phone, I was talking to my car. I dumped my purse on the passenger seat while I drove randomly around the parking lot, looking for I don't know what. "I can't find a parking spot," I said. "She's still behind me."

The two stores were side-by-side. Did I have a Sam's Club card? I was so rattled I didn't know. I knew I had to have a membership card to get inside, though, so I changed direction and headed for Walmart, pawing through the purse contents on the seat next to me.

I spied a spot in the next aisle over, not far from the parking lot exit. The black pick-up was a car length away, too close for comfort. "She's still there, Olivia. I can't get away from her."

"Hang on, honey." Olivia's voice faded, like the phone was farther away. "M.J., get on the phone. Have a squad sent to the Walmart on 19th. The woman who attacked Lilith is stalking her."

I heard a vague interrogatory noise.

"Damn it, call them now. She'll be in the front of the store. Send a squad there now! Lilith, I'm back. Where are you?"

"I'm almost to a parking space." Tanya stayed so close to my bumper I was afraid to even slow down, much less stop. I didn't know how I'd shake her until I saw an elderly woman tottering out of Walmart pushing a cart. I tapped the gas and got past her, but Tanya wasn't as fast and had to wait for the woman to cross.

"I'm at the store. I'm parking now. Hold on." I sped into the parking spot, jammed my car into park, and fumbled off my seat belt. I ran for the store, car keys and cell phone clutched in my hand. As soon as I shut off the car, the call switched to my phone. "Olivia?" I gasped. "Are you there? I'm going into Walmart now."

"I'm here. You stay on the line."

"Almost to the front door." The heat of the pavement combined with my panic to make me so hot I was dizzy. A few more steps, I repeated silently to myself. I didn't dare glance back. I didn't dare slow down. Just a few more steps.

Ah…air conditioning. I didn't pause to enjoy it but pushed ahead, moving through a herd of elderly people queued up near the door. Panic had me in its grip. "Where should I go?"

"Try to stay near the front. It's usually crowded there."

I never shopped here so I had no idea what was where. Aisles stretched ahead of me, with a relatively open space to my right full of racks of clothing and purses. I headed for that, ducking behind a display of jeans. "I'm inside," I said breathlessly. "I can see the front door. I think I lost her."

"You stay right there. If you see her coming, you head for the nearest security guard. There's usually one lurking around the front of the store."

I left the safety of the display and wended my way through racks of clothing, peering at the checkout lanes. I didn't see anyone who seemed like a security guard. I dodged around a series of fitting rooms, trying to get a better vantage at the front of the store. As I rounded the corner of one of the rooms, someone grabbed my left arm, jerking me around so hard I almost crashed into the fitting room wall.

"What's the rush?" Tanya demanded.

"Let go of me!" I struggled against her, my car keys rattling in my grip when she tugged on my arm, dragging me away from the fitting rooms.

"Lilith, what's happening?" Olivia's voice came through loudly on the phone clutched in my right hand.

I didn't dare raise it to my face. I was still struggling against Tanya, who dragged me to a wall display of blouses. "There's a restraining order," I said, trying to dig in my heels on the slick flooring. "You're not supposed to be within fifty yards of me." I tugged at my arm, but she had my left wrist in a vise-like grip.

I hadn't seen her in years. She was still slender and tall with large breasts and an olive-skinned complexion. Her pale blue polo shirt with the Three Sisters logo was partially unbuttoned and strained across her chest. Her skin-tight jeans were so snug I clearly saw the outline of a phone in her front pocket. Fitted clothing was impossible for me because of the scars and it pissed me off to see her flaunting her body, something I couldn't do anymore.

I also felt a flash of jealousy at the sight of her hair. I had to keep my hair short because I no longer had the flexibility to maintain any kind of hairstyle. My once long, dark blonde hair was now liberally streaked with gray, unlike hers which was mahogany brown, shoulder-length, and untouched by any sign of age.

"What will you do? Call the police? They won't bother with a restraining order from something that happened twenty-five-years ago."

I raised my phone. "Did you hear that, Olivia? She said the police won't come."

"That's bullshit." We both heard Olivia's voice clearly. "They're on the way. They sure as hell act when an ex-cop calls them."

I lowered the phone. "What do you want?"

"Well, that's rude." Tanya pouted at me then released my wrist. "I guess I'll have to talk fast. I wanted you to know that I don't hold any grudges about what happened."

I almost dropped the phone. "What?"

"You heard me. I needed help and, if it weren't for you, I wouldn't have been sent away." She smiled prettily. "It gave me a chance to spend some time with someone I love, quality time."

"You're crazy," I spat. "I haven't forgiven you."

"Really? Well, my therapist said I need to tell you, so I did." She shrugged. "Whatever." Her gaze raked over my neck then to my hand. "It doesn't seem that bad."

I wanted to howl with rage. Instead I said, "I was lucky I fell in the pool."

"I suppose." She sounded bored, like this was a waste of her time. "I do want to warn you, though."

I took a step back. "What do you mean?"

"Lilith, get the hell away from her!" Olivia sounded as scared as I felt.

I stumbled back another step, but Tanya followed me. "Get away!"

"Oh, grow up. I won't do something to you here, where everybody can see." She leaned close to me and I cringed. "But if you think you can have Shaw, you're insane. You thought you took him from me once but not again, do you hear me? Anything between you is temporary. I won't have it any other way."

"You're the insane one," I whispered, so terrified I could barely speak. "Today was the first time I've seen him in years. Why do you think I want to be with him?"

"Because you love him. He told me you do." She straightened, glaring at me from the height of her stylish sandals. "You might get him because he needs you now, but it won't last. And I'll be there to pick up the pieces."

Good Lord, what was she talking about? "He's insane if he thinks I'd have anything to do with him." Anger was starting to replace fear.

Her eyebrows drew together in confusion. "He told me he talked to you about it. Didn't he discuss it with you? Aren't you going to the funeral with him?"

"I don't know what you're talking about. I saw him today and we talked briefly. I won't go to the funeral with him."

Tanya stared at me, her brown eyes lit with manic intensity. "But he said you and he would have to—" Her eyes narrowed. "Wait a minute. Was he lying about that?"

I gave up on trying to decipher her crazy ramblings. "You leave me alone. Do you hear me? I'll take action if you don't leave me alone."

"Take action?" Tanya crossed her arms and regarded me with haughty disdain. "What do you think you can do?"

I leaned toward her, my phone raised. "You won't fool me again, Tanya. I know what a bitch you are. I'll defend myself. Watch out for your own safety."

A male clerk approached, probably summoned by a checkout person who had seen our argument. "Ladies, if you have a disagreement, please go outside."

I turned on him. "This woman threatened me."

"Me? Threaten her?" Tanya straightened, thrusting out her ample bosom. "She threatened me. If she doesn't quit harassing me, I'll call the police." She leaned around the intervening clerk, giving him a good look at her nipples, which were clearly outlined by the polo shirt.

"I won't be intimidated by you." I pushed past the flustered man. "You leave me alone or you'll face the consequences." I strode away, glancing back once. Tanya glared at me over the man's head then she shifted her attention to him, smiling as if agreeing.

"I'm leaving the store, Olivia," I said into the phone, still clutched in my sweaty hand. "We can cancel the police."

"No way. You wait right there until they get there. They'll escort you home."

Good heavens, if I showed up with a police car escorting me, Pop would have a heart attack. "No, I think it's okay now. I'm at my car and I'm leaving now." I swung open the door and dropped into the driver's seat. "Hold on."

I turned the car on and within seconds my call switched back to the car's audio system. "It's okay. She hasn't left the store."

"Are you sure?"

"I can see the doorway. My car is facing it." I shot out of the parking space. Thank God the aisle was empty behind me, otherwise I would have rammed into someone. "I'm leaving the parking lot now." I glimpsed a squad car at the traffic light in the distance. "I think I see the police. They don't have lights or sirens on."

"They're coming in quiet," a man's voice said from

the phone. "They'll stop her from leaving the store if she's still there. What kind of car was she driving?"

"A black pick-up with the Three Sisters Landscaping logo on it." I made a right turn at the street as the squad car entered the parking lot behind me.

"They'll stop her from following. Do you want to meet to talk about it?" As always, Olivia's calm voice soothed my jangled nerves.

"Not today," I said. "I need to get home. I have a new person helping at the house and I need to do some close supervision until I'm sure he knows a weed from a flower." I managed a credible chuckle. "I'm not sure he does."

Olivia said, "Oh, you never know about people. Anyway, I'm happy to meet with you any time. And if you want me to talk to the police about what I heard, I will."

"Thanks. I'll talk it over with Pop and I'll get back to you."

"I'm glad to help. I'll call you later about the conference."

The conference? Oh, that's right. She thought she'd attend my talk. "Thanks again." I managed to disconnect the call, sweat beading on my face. I couldn't believe it. Tanya, following me like that. I drove away, my mind in a fog.

Thank God Olivia called. At least I had a witness to Tanya's insanity. I took a circuitous route to the grocery store, reasoning that if Tanya were somehow following me then I'd spot her. I didn't spy the black pick-up truck anywhere around me, so I raced into the store, bought my groceries, and ran back out in record time.

The hardware store was on the way home and it only took a few minutes for me to find what I needed and get out. I pulled into my driveway at around three-thirty, exhausted from the stress of my meeting and the confrontation.

I went into the house, expecting to find Pop either in the living room or the porch, but he was nowhere in sight. I paused, debating whether to find him and tell him what happened, or wait.

I chose waiting. I needed to think about it and decide how to proceed. I didn't want him getting in an uproar until I had a chance to process what happened. Satisfied with that logic, I went upstairs and peeked out into the backyard, ready to chastise him if he was working. He and Dillan were sitting in the shade talking, the cooler on the ground between them. The yard looked great. Most of the thyme was replaced, the tree area was raked, and mounds of mulch sat at convenient spots, ready to be spread. Obviously, Dillan had been hard at work, so I didn't begrudge him and Pop shooting the breeze on a break.

I stripped off my "professional clothes" and washed my face then lay down, naked, on my bed, my left arm over my face. I focused on an old meditation exercise that Olivia taught me. Whenever bad thoughts intruded, I gently nudged them to one side and substituted a pleasant thought.

I pushed my memory of Tanya's face off to one corner of my imaginary room and instead visualized the eager Boy Scouts, so young and optimistic. Now that the meeting was over, I could acknowledge I'd been worried how they would react to me. Their acceptance and frank curiosity was a relief. I played the meeting over in my mind, making little notes on my mental whiteboard about what to work on next.

"Lily! Lily, are you okay?" Pop's voice boomed up the staircase to me.

I opened my eyes. I must have dozed. The bedside clock said four-thirty. I yawned and stretched cautiously. "I'm upstairs, Pop. I'm fine." I sat up, dragging the coverlet over my legs when I heard footsteps in the hallway. Pop had helped dress my wounds and participated in my physical therapy, so I wasn't shy about him seeing my scars, but it was chilly upstairs with the air conditioning going full tilt.

My bedroom door burst open, and Dillan lunged into the room. I was so stunned, I stared at him. Then I remembered I was naked, and I tugged the coverlet higher, which barely covered me because I was sitting on it. "What are you doing? Get out of here!"

"Are you okay?" He prowled around the room, even pulling open my bathroom door and going inside.

"What do you think you're doing?" I demanded, scooting to the edge of the bed to gather more bedspread around me. "Leave my room."

"Lily, are you okay?" Pop came into my room, his face red. He staggered, grabbing for the doorway.

"Pop!" I forgot decency and dropped the bedspread to run to him, sliding my arm around him under his shoulders.

He sagged against me, panting. "I—just—can't—get—my—breath—" he stuttered.

I gritted my teeth and supported him, his body pressed against my right side. "Come on," I whispered, longing to scream with pain. "Come on, let's get to the bed." I took a step, then another one, feeling as if my skin was flailing off my side.

"I'm hurting you," he murmured, his voice faint. "Let me go, I'll be okay. Let—"

"Shit." Dillan scooped up Pop, pulling him away from me and depositing him on the bed. I stumbled forward, landing next to Pop, who sprawled on the disarrayed bedspread, gasping for breath.

"Call an ambulance," I said to Dillan, who leaned over Pop on the other side.

"I'm okay," Pop wheezed. "I'm just winded. And scared." He gazed up at me. "Are you okay? Did that bitch hurt you?"

I shivered when the air conditioning drenched me with frigid air. Damn. I was still naked. I snatched up the blouse I wore that morning from the chair next to the bed and dragged it on. "What's going on? Pop, we need to get you to a doctor." I glared at Dillan. "Get out of my bedroom."

"Like hell I will." He held up something. "What happened today?"

"What's that?"

He shook his cell phone at me. "Were you going to tell us about it or not?"

"I don't have to tell you a damn thing." I stood up, my hands on my hips.

My bare hips.

His eyes went to my stomach, went lower, then he snapped his head up. I kept my gaze fixed on him. "Well?" I demanded. "Why should I tell you anything?"

He threw up his hands, jammed the phone in his shorts pocket, and stormed out. "You tell her!" he shouted over his shoulder.

"Tell me what?" I shouted back, striding to the door.

"Damn it, Lily." Pop pushed himself upright. "Dillan, get back in here! Lily, you get some clothes on before you give Dillan a heart attack."

"You're the one with the heart I'm worried about." I grabbed my pants from the chair and yanked them on. "Pop, are you okay?" I leaned over him, touching his face. His color was almost his normal ruddy pink. "What's going on?"

Dillan appeared in my bedroom doorway. "Will you tell her?" he demanded. His gaze went anywhere but at me, his arms crossed on his sweaty green T-shirt.

"It's just that I was worried." Pop sat up and swung his legs off the bed. "Mark and I talked about it and we thought it might be good to have somebody around who could help."

I looked from him to Dillan, who still refused to make eye contact with me. Icy air drenched me again. Damn it, my blouse was unbuttoned. I haphazardly buttoned a couple of buttons, then faced him. "Better?" I demanded.

Dillan's face changed to beet red.

"That's why your friend recommended this guy?" I jerked at thumb at Dillan. "Because I needed somebody for yardwork?"

"Well, yeah, but it's more than landscaping." Pop peered around me. "You tell her."

"I'm not telling her. You tell her."

I threw up my hands. "What?"

"I'm supposed to be your bodyguard," Dillan muttered behind me.

I turned slowly to stare at Dillan. "My what?"

He met my eyes, his face still flushed. "Bodyguard," he enunciated.

I counted to five, then I wheeled around to face Pop. "You hired a bodyguard?"

"I hired a guy to work in the garden, and he can also be a bodyguard." Pop put his hands on the edge of the bed and stood.

I took his arm, holding him steady. "I still say you need to go to the doctor."

"I will. Or I'll call," he amended.

"I'll call and you'll see him." I got on Pop's right side and helped him walk to the door. "Let's go sit and try to talk about this like rational people."

"I can help," Dillan said, moving forward.

"You can get the hell away from me," I snapped. "I've had a shitty day starting with you scaring the crap out of me at the crack of dawn and ending with a psychotic bitch scaring the crap out of me an hour ago. I'm going to make a drink, sit down, and try to make sense out of my life. You can join me or not, but you will move, do you hear me?" I shot him a glare that would have eviscerated him if my eyes were lasers.

Dillan's mouth twitched. I think he wanted to smile. Lucky for him, he restrained himself. He pressed hard against my doorway, giving Pop and me a wide berth. I steered my elderly father from the room, and we shuffled to the steps. I held his arm while descended, then I guided Pop to the porch.

"You sit. I'll mix us a cocktail," I ordered.

"Let me do it," he muttered. "I'm not infirm."

"No, you're old. And I may be beat up, but I'm younger. So sit down, shut up, and tell me if you want a martini or a gin and tonic."

Pop sighed. "A martini would hit the spot."

"Two martinis coming up." I eyed Dillan, who had followed us, pausing in the porch doorway. "You. Come with me. You can carry the chips."

"Yes, Boss." He said it so fast it was like one word.

I stalked into the kitchen. "I can't believe my father hired a damn bodyguard," I fumed while I snatched open the fridge door and rummaged inside. "I don't need a bodyguard. I need a strong back to—" I slammed the door. "Get that tray for me." I pointed to the decorative bamboo serving tray hanging on the wall.

"Yes, Boss." Dillan got the tray and held it out.

I put dip and chips on the tray then added a can of beer nuts. "Take that out to the porch. I'll make the drinks and bring them out."

"Uh, drinks?" He eyed the gin bottle I pulled from the freezer.

I sighed. "You don't drink?"

"Beer?" he asked hopefully.

"Doable. Now go."

"Yes, Boss." He bobbed his head then scurried away.

I fixed two martinis and got a beer from the mini fridge in the mudroom. I put everything on another tray and went out to the porch, where I found the two men deep in conversation, Dillan on the couch and Pop in his chair opposite mine.

"Before you get all hot and bothered, hear me out," Pop said as soon as I sat after dispensing the beverages. "We needed help in the garden and he was available. It was an added bonus that he has some law enforcement experience. It might come in handy. I mean, you did find a dead body, Lily."

Damn it, that made sense. I wasn't in the mood for sensible, though. "You should have told me."

"You would have told me to leave." Dillan ignored my icy glare. He rubbed his head, his gray hair standing up in little spikes. "You know, I had a bad day, too. First of all, you hit me."

"I didn't hit you that hard."

"You hit him?" Pop asked.

"It was an accident," I assured him.

"It was an attack. And look at my arm. Your damn roses got me." He held out his forearm for my inspection.

Sure enough, he had long thin scratches on his right arm. "I should have warned you," I admitted. "It's as bad as the Gertrude Jekyll."

"The what?"

"I think Harrison's Yellow is worse," Pop commented.

"You might be right," I conceded.

"Are you guys talking in code or something?" Dillan's gaze went from Pop to me.

"Gertrude Jekyll and Harrison's Yellow are rose varieties," I explained. "Some people have been known to plant those as security measures. Grow one of those vines on a fence, and no one, man nor beast, will get through." I put down my drink. "I'll get you some antiseptic salve. You need to treat those before they get infected."

"Sit down." Dillan put his hand over mine on the chair. "I'll live for another few minutes. Tell us what happened. Did she really attack you?"

I relaxed back in my chair and he released my

hand. "She didn't attack me. She—" I searched for the right word while I sipped my martini. "She accosted me. In the middle of a flippin' Walmart." I described how Tanya followed me and the confrontation. "How did you find out, though?"

Dillan fished his phone from his shorts pocket. "My mother called me."

"Your mother?" I stared at the phone in disbelief. "Olivia?"

He nodded.

"But—but—" I struggled to put one word after the other. "Your name is different."

"She kept her maiden name because she worked with cops and she didn't want people to know she worked with a cop. Mark's name is kind of unusual."

I turned to Pop. "Your friend?"

"Yep. Mark Eames."

"You kept your father's name," I stated. "Her first husband."

"Yep." Dillan took a long swallow of beer.

I sipped some more gin. It certainly helped make things clearer. "You devious old man," I murmured.

Pop raised his glass. "Takes one to know one."

Dillan's phone chimed. "Speak of the devil." He put the phone to his ear. "Hey." He watched me as he spoke. "Yeah, she knows." Pause. "You might say that." Pause. "Well, I'm not fired."

"Yet." I extended my hand.

"She wants to talk to you. Hold on." He put the phone in my palm. "It's Mom."

"Yeah. I guessed that. I'm getting a refill." I got up, phone to my ear, and picked up my martini glass.

"I can't tell you what it means to me that you gave

Dillan this job," Olivia said before I say a word. "He's been at loose ends. He has his teaching job, but he only had one semester of that and now he has the summer off. I was so worried about him. Teaching is such a huge change for him from police work."

"Olivia, why did—"

"He was put on disability because of that last injury. Thank God, too, because I was afraid he'd be killed if he kept on with that department in L.A. I think he likes teaching but he's afraid to admit it." She made an exasperated noise. "I suppose I can understand. Going from being a cop to a teacher is a bit of a leap. I think he's been adrift and he needs a solid purpose."

"And I'm it?" I managed to wedge in.

"Maybe. I mean, let's face it. If he'd been with you today, Tanya would never had approached you. Keep him around until they get the Kelleher thing solved. It'll be good for both of you."

She had a point about Tanya. I glanced to my left. Dillan watched me from the porch couch. "Okay," I said. "He can stay."

He raised his beer can in salute. "Thanks, Boss."

Chapter Eight

"You can't sleep out here." Dillan pointed to the porch couch.

"Wait a minute. I said I wouldn't fire you. I didn't say you can tell me what to do." I peered at Dillan through the darkness on the porch. It was two martinis for me and Pop, two beers for Dillan, and a frozen pizza later. Night had settled in around us.

"I'm the bodyguard. That means I get to tell you what to do when it comes to your safety. I know about shit like this."

"But—"

"I'm going home, I'll clean up, change clothes, and come back here. I'll sleep on the porch." He stood staring at me, his face ghostly in the reflected light from the kitchen behind him.

"Lily." Pop's voice was soft. "We'll talk while he goes home. Dillan, I'll give you a call in a half-hour and let you know if you need to come back."

Dillan faced Pop. "Now wait a minute. We talked about this. You—"

Pop stood and put a hand on Dillan's arm. "She and I have been taking care of each other for a long time. We need to talk over if we want anybody else taking care of us now."

It was laughable. There was Pop, half-a-foot

shorter than Dillan and outweighed by at least fifty pounds. Dillan just stared at him then inclined his head in grudging assent. "I get it. Whatever you decide." He peered over his shoulder at me. "Don't let your pride get in the way of your common sense."

He left before I came up with a scathing reply, going out the front door. A few minutes later I heard his motorcycle throttle into life, chugging up the hill.

Pop sat down, the left side of his face illuminated by the light from the kitchen. "This whole Kelleher thing—this thing with Tanya—it's brought it back, hasn't it?"

I leaned back in my chair, startled by the sadness I heard in his voice. "I suppose it has," I admitted. "Seeing Shaw again was a shock."

"I never told you this. I guess I decided it would only add more hurt to what had happened." His hands flexed on the arms of his chair, a faint glow showing on his wedding ring. "Blake Kelleher came to me after you and Shaw began dating and offered me twenty-thousand dollars if I would encourage you to go away, to separate you two."

I was so stunned I didn't speak for a minute. "I don't understand."

"Kelleher saw that Shaw was getting serious about you." Pop's hand clenched into a fist then relaxed. "Or as serious as that asshole could be. His father wanted to separate you two. He wanted Shaw to marry Tanya. He said it had been planned for years. The two families were close and everybody expected it." Pop shifted in his chair, the light fading away from him. "Nobody expected you."

Good Lord. Twenty-grand? Back then, it was a

fortune.

"He wanted you gone," Pop said flatly. "I always wondered if he put Tanya up to it. I always wondered about that job in Chicago."

"You mean that audition? Do you think he arranged it?"

"You were planning to leave town. Do you think if you went to Chicago for an acting career that you and Shaw would still have gotten married?"

I closed my eyes against the tears that threatened. I knew the answer to that. Our relationship was based on sex and fun. Take that away and nothing would have remained. "No," I whispered. "I don't think we would."

Pop leaned forward, clasping his hands between his knees. "I turned him down. I told him it was your life, and I wouldn't interfere. I should have interfered, though. If I had, none of it would have happened."

"Oh, Pop." I heard the guilt and the anguish that he had kept hidden all these years. "It was Tanya's fault, not yours."

"Honey, I didn't protect you then. And I don't know how to protect you now. I'm not sure that you're in danger, but Mark thinks there's a reason to be worried, and that's good enough for me. I couldn't bear it if you were hurt because I didn't do something to keep you safe. You've been hurt too much as it is. Please."

"Pop, it's just that there's no reason to—"

He raised one hand. "A dead body in the labyrinth. A broken lock on the gate. Another gate we thought was locked but was open. Tanya confronting you." He ticked the items off his fingers. "Something's brewing. I don't know what it is, but you're right in the middle of it."

I peered at him. He was so haggard and frail, like a man carrying a burden that was too much to bear. I was that burden. For years he cared for me and watched out for me. He might have had a new life after Mom died but, instead, he was saddled with a child who required post-surgical care, occupational therapy, and emotional support. I was a continual reminder of guilt, however misplaced.

"I'm sorry, Pop." I went to him, kneeling to wrap my arms around him. "Of course. If it'll help you, we'll do it."

"Thank you." His face pressed against mine, and I felt his tears.

****

Two hours later Dillan entered the side yard, closing the gate behind him. I was forewarned by Pop, who had called him. I sat on the porch, reading a book on my Android tablet. I twisted in my chair when I heard him.

"I didn't hear the cycle," I commented.

"I brought my car. I have to pick up the cat in the morning. The vet called and said he came through it with flying colors." His voice was muffled, and he still stood at the gate, his back to me where I sat on the porch.

"What are you doing?"

"Putting on a new lock. That old one is too easy to manipulate." I heard rustling, clicking sounds. "You can still get around the gate if there's an emergency. There's enough space between the gate and the trees."

"Just barely," I muttered. "I'd better not gain any weight."

A few minutes later he entered the porch via the screen door, dropping a bulky bag in the corner. He'd changed into jeans and a polo shirt with some kind of logo on the breast. "The vet said the cat is doing good."

"You mentioned that. It's still not negotiable. I won't keep him." I stood, closing the cover on my tablet. The porch faded into darkness, the only illumination a faint glow from the light over the stove to the left of the French doors. I switched on the low-wattage lamp near Pop's chair at the door.

"Well, he's fixed up now so maybe he'll get adopted."

I doubted it but didn't bother to argue. "Good night." I went into the house.

"Your father loves you a lot."

"The feeling's mutual." I evaluated his silhouette then the couch. "The couch isn't very comfortable."

"Yeah. I figured." He tilted his head toward the bundle he dropped. "That's why I brought my sleeping bag."

I hesitated. "Thank you."

He smiled, the first real smile I'd seen. He had dimples. "Don't worry. I'll guard those roses. Good night, Boss."

"Good night." I stepped into the kitchen and poured myself a glass of wine then clicked off the air conditioning and switched on the overhead fan. I went to the living room where Pop sat in his recliner, TV remote in hand. "I'm going up, Pop."

"I'll check in on Dillan before I go up," he said with a wink. "Show him where to brush his teeth and all that."

"Good thinking. 'Night."

He waved a hand and went back to watching his favorite renovate-a-junker-into-a-treasure car show. I switched on the living room fan and went upstairs.

I decided tonight required some sleep assistance, so I took three over-the-counter sleep aids, washed down with the rest of my wine. I went to the window to stare at Labbie. All was quiet. I hated to admit it, but I felt much better knowing Dillan was sleeping downstairs. Maybe things would stay quiet now that he was here.

I fell asleep and had the best night's sleep that I'd had in years.

****

I woke at dawn, showered, and dressed for a day of work in the garden. I was pulling on my blouse when I remembered Dillan's expression yesterday, seeing my naked body. He hadn't been repulsed. Startled, yes, and embarrassed, but I saw no disgust.

That reminded me he was sleeping downstairs. I went by Pop's room, hearing his snores, then went to the dining room, tiptoeing through it to the kitchen where the French doors were open. I peeked out to the porch, but the couch was empty. Hmm. I made coffee then went to the back door, peering out into the yard.

Dillan stood to the right on the permeable pavers. He was facing away from me, his arms upraised. Today he wore pale brown cargo shorts and he was shirtless. The scar on his back rippled when he moved, stepping forward in some stylized dance.

Tai-chi. I recognized it. I used to practice it after the attack, but it was years since I had tried it. I somehow lost the concentration needed to go through the forms correctly. I watched him, memory filling in the names of the movements. Work at shuttles. Needle at sea bottom. Flash the arm. Turn, parry, punch. Close up. Cross hands. Closing.

Dillan moved with controlled power and grace. He'd obviously been doing this for years because the transition between the forms was seamless. I had never understood how it was used for martial arts training but seeing him practice the moves made me visualize it, vividly. I could almost see a sword in each of his hands, moving flawlessly to attack an enemy or parry a blow.

He ended up facing east, head bowed. I waited a few seconds then stepped outside. His head whipped up and he pivoted when he heard the door open. When he saw it was me, he went to his T-shirt, lying on the ground. He picked up something lying on top of it and to my shock, he stuffed it down the front of his pants.

A gun. Good Lord, he had a gun.

"What are you doing?" I demanded, staring at his shorts. "Are you armed?"

He pulled on his T-shirt. It was dark blue with a logo on the front. I didn't pay attention to that. I was more fixed on the inconspicuous bulge in his pants soon covered by his shirt. "Yep, I'm armed."

"But—but—it's a gun," I stammered. "Aren't you afraid it'll go off?"

He grinned while he tucked in the shirt. "It only goes off if it's touched." He wiggled his eyebrows.

"Oh, for heaven's sake, you know what I mean." My face got hot with color. "You can't go around carrying a gun in your pants."

"Of course, I can. Cops do it all the time." He patted his belly, which now was like a regular tummy, albeit perhaps a tad bulgy. "Concealed carry. There are a few brands. Thunderwear, Safe Carry—all designed to carry a weapon where nobody sees it." He winked. "Except my close friends. I won't carry it when I'm working in the yard. It gets too hot and it can be restrictive. But the rest of the time, yeah, I carry." He brushed by me to go to the house. "What's for breakfast?"

I hinged up my gaping mouth. "Breakfast? I usually have toast."

Dillan shot me a disbelieving glare over his shoulder. "I'm moving a tree today. I need more than toast."

I hurried after him. "What do you mean you're moving a tree?" He went into the mudroom and padded through there to the kitchen. "You're barefoot."

"Makes it easier to do Tai Chi. I asked a few friends to come over today. I figured we'd get through some of the big stuff on your list." He went to the fridge. "How about eggs? You're not a vegetarian, are you? Oh, yeah, that's right. We had sausage pizza last night. Whew. That's a relief." He pulled out a carton of eggs. "Any bacon?"

"Wait a minute. What do you mean, you asked a few friends to come over?"

"I'll make the food since you're providing it. Where's a skillet? Do you have bacon?" Dillan opened the freezer and peered inside.

I came around the island and pushed him away. "Don't go rummaging around in there. I have things organized."

"I'm sure you do." He grabbed the foil-wrapped packet as soon as I touched it. "Sit down. I'll cook. Where's the bread? You can make the toast."

"You're bullying me." I sidestepped, blocking

access to the stove. He dodged me by going around the other side of the island.

"I'm being efficient. We have a bunch of work to get done. I've only got the guys for a couple of days. Where's the pots and—" He bent over, poking through cupboards. "Are you making toast or not?"

"I thought I was the boss." I glared at him, hands on my hips.

"When it comes to the garden, you're the boss. Otherwise, it's negotiable."

"It is not."

"Is, too. Make the toast." He put my skillet on the stovetop and unwrapped the package of bacon. "We need more than this."

"That's a single serving."

He made a noise. "A single serving for a mouse. Get me three more."

"What's the fuss?" Pop came into the kitchen, yawning. His T-shirt was on inside out, but he did get it tucked into his baggy jeans.

"Dillan demands to be fed." I went to the fridge and got two more packets of bacon. "I don't need any. Catch."

Dillan turned and I tossed the frozen food at him, one at a time. He caught them easily. "You need to eat some protein in the morning. It's good for you."

Pop meandered to the coffeepot. "I keep telling her that, but she never listens. She's worried about her slim, girlish figure."

Dillan eyed me. "Your figure is fine. I saw it, remember?"

"Fix your own toast." I slammed a loaf of bread on the island then stomped to the coffeepot and filled a mug. I went to the porch to hide my smile. What a pair.

I slipped out the screen door and walked to Labbie, sipping my coffee. The heady aroma of thyme underfoot mingled with the woody smell of mulch and the sharp tang of salvia in the side flower beds.

I examined the serviceberry bush that needed to be moved. It was a monster, easily eight feet tall and with roots that probably went as deep, if not deeper. That would take most of the day to transplant because the viburnum to swap with it was as big. I wanted to have them transplanted two years ago, but somehow that never happened. I hoped Dillan had big friends.

I went into Labbie and checked my grow lights. The buds were much bigger, taking on that bottom fatness that signified they were getting ready to bloom. If the weather held, I might have blossoms by Saturday. Of course, if the weather held that meant I needed to water. I retraced my steps, working out a watering schedule in my mind.

"Chow time!" someone bellowed from the house.

I hurried to the porch and went inside to find Pop and Dillan seated at the island, an empty seat between them with a plate waiting for me. I slipped onto the stool and dug into the fluffy scrambled eggs. I had one slice of bacon compared to Dillan's four and Pop's three, but it was more than enough.

We ate in companionable silence for a time then Pop asked, "What's on the calendar for today?" He grimaced. "I screwed up yesterday, and I don't want to screw up again."

I leveled my fork at him. "You didn't screw up. Swanny is coming at ten and the Showcase organizers are coming for a walkthrough at noon." I looked at

Dillan. "I'll show you what needs to be done, but I probably won't be able to help much."

"Who's this Swanny guy?"

"My physical therapist. It can be painful. He usually comes three times a week, but with the Fourth tomorrow, he couldn't, so we're doing Tuesday and Friday this week. That reminds me. I suppose you'll want tomorrow off."

"Actually…" Dillan pushed his plate to one side. "Mom and Mark are having a party and wondered if you guys would come."

I started to murmur a polite refusal, but Pop said, "That sounds great. Can we bring something?" He ignored my quelling stare. "With the help we've had we can take a day off, can't we?"

He sounded so anxious I hesitated.

"Mom was hoping you'd join us," Dillan said.

"Us?"

"I'll probably drop in. I've got nothing else planned." He checked the clock over the sink. "I'd better go get Beast now, so I can get back by the time the guys get here."

"Beast?" I peered up at him when he stood, forcing my gaze to avoid his shorts where I knew a gun was hidden. I still couldn't wrap my head around that.

"Beast Griffen. That's his name." Dillan dug a hand in his pocket and pulled out a set of car keys.

"I told you, we're not adopting a cat."

"Maybe we should have one," Pop said. "You know, to handle the mouse problem."

I rounded on him. "We don't have a mouse problem."

"This is where I came in. I'll be back soon." Dillan

took a swig of coffee from his mug then scurried away, heading for the front door.

I picked up the plates. "We don't need a cat, Pop."

"It might be nice. You know, company on those winter nights when you're out and about and I'm here alone."

I scraped plates and loaded the dishwasher. "I'm seldom out and about."

"But you are sometimes. It might be pleasant to have a cat on my lap." He smiled wistfully.

I seriously doubted the monster I saw would be a lap cat, but I didn't point that out. "We'll see," I said. "The cat may not like it here. Maybe another home would be better. I'm going to do some watering. Can you move the porch furniture back into place before it gets too hot?"

"The weather's supposed to break tomorrow night." Pop slipped off the stool. "Storms coming through."

"That and a buck will buy me coffee. I doubt they can forecast anything that far in advance. I'll water anyway." I left before he could argue any more.

I got out the hose and did some spot watering, mainly focusing on the flowering plants and the roses in Labbie. By the time I was done, Dillan had returned, cage in hand.

"Here he is, ready to rule the roost." He lifted the live trap and the cat glowered at me. His face wasn't as puffy and the broken tail was now gone, replaced by a bandaged three-inch stump.

"He'll chew that bandage off," I said, winding up the hose to stow away.

"The vet said we need to put this stuff on the

bandage while the tail heals." He gestured with a bottle. "It tastes like crap, so Beast won't bother the bandage. Should I put him on the porch?"

"How about the basement? It's cool there and you can set up his litter box and food dishes there."

"Litter box?"

I prayed for patience. "Take him downstairs. There's an unfinished room where you can stow him. I'll run to the store and get a box and some food."

"Soft food," Dillan cautioned. "He had a tooth pulled. And have your dad go. I'd rather you didn't leave unless I can go with you and the guys will get here soon." He hurried away, cage swinging. "Come on, Beast. We'll get you set up. Trust me, you'll like it here."

The cat hissed and made an ineffectual grab at the cage bars. I went to the front porch where Pop was arranging the furniture. "Did you meet your cat?" I asked.

"Yeah. He's a big one. I'm sure once he gets used to the place, he'll settle down." Pop went to the top step when we heard a car door slam below. "Look at that. Dillan did call in a few friends."

I joined him on the step. Four young men, probably in their twenties, were walking toward us, two black and two white. Three of them had the same kind of build as Dillan: deceptively tall and lean but muscular. The fourth, one of the white guys, was enormous with bulging biceps and thighs that strained his gym shorts.

"Hey," one of the black guys said when he saw us. "We heard you folks need some help jamming up the Three Bitches Landscaping company. We are here to lend whatever aid we can."

One of the slender white guys slapped him on the shoulder. "Language, man, language. She's a lady."

I laughed. "I've heard worse, believe me." I regarded the black guy who spoke. "You have a beef with the Three Sisters?"

"I applied to work there. They declined to hire me because they were worried what some of their lily-white clients would think when they saw a black guy working in the yard." He and the other paused on the top step. "Hey, Dillan."

Dillan came out of the house. "Hey. I see you met Lilith and Grif. This is Alec, Mel, Mason, and Amil. Students of mine."

The various men nodded their greetings. I gestured them to the path leading around the side of the house, falling into step with Mason, the black guy who spoke. "They didn't hire you because you were black? They said that?"

"Not in so many words. But you tell me—how many black guys they got working for them?"

Well, he was right. The Three Sisters landscaping service was known for handling upscale clients, working on the million-dollar homes that had sprung up in some of the elite suburbs. They were probably worried about their 'reputation' when it came to hiring workers.

I led the way through the gate into the backyard. "I know some people in the business I can contact if you want some work. A strong back is a strong back."

"I wanted to get some experience in landscaping because I wanted to put together a program for prisoners. I figured that might be a smart job opportunity for some guys when they get out." He surveyed my yard. "Now, this is a garden. I'm telling you, if some of those boys at prison could work in the outdoors and see stuff growing like this, they might get a new lease on life."

"Is that a maze?" Amil asked, going to Labbie.

"It's a labyrinth," Pop said. "A maze has several ways in and out. A labyrinth has one. It's used for meditation."

"Cool. That must have taken a long time to build, man."

Pop launched into the history of the labyrinth, taking two of the workers with him while he talked. I heard 'deadly injury' and 'rehabilitation' and knew that he would allude to my burns. Hopefully, nobody would be shocked when they saw my wounds. I silently blessed him for his tact.

I regarded Mason, who stood with Dillan, turning to view my yard with an expression of stunned enlightenment. "I never seen a garden like this," he said. "I thought, you know, a garden—vegetables and a few flowers. This is like—it's like planned and the right colors are in the right place and—"

"A garden is more than color. It's texture and sound and smell. Close your eyes." I smiled at his disbelieving expression. "Go ahead. Try it." He squeezed his eyes shut. "What do you hear?"

"Birds," he said immediately.

"How many? What kinds?"

He shrugged. "I don't know."

"I've counted a dozen varieties and I'm sure there are more I haven't identified. What about that chirping sound?"

"That's a bird, right?"

"Nope. Chipmunks. What about the silver birch leaves? They make a papery sound. The daylilies rustle when they move, and on a humid day, you can hear them opening. Now take in a deep breath."

He did, expanding his chest and straining his T-shirt. "Man," he murmured. "What is that?"

"Peonies. Daisies. Ornamental chives. Thyme. Salvia. Earth. Mulch." I squeezed his arm, which was as solidly muscled as it appeared. "Open your eyes. Now what do you see?"

He peered about then shifted his gaze to me, smiling. "I see a garden. If I could reach out to some folks at the prison and show them this—" He shook his head.

"You might be able to work with the Master Gardeners on a prison program. I can put you in touch with some people. I've been designing therapeutic gardens for a few local nursing homes and hospitals. I'd love to take a stab at some kind of productive therapeutic gardening program for the prison population." I turned to Dillan, who stood behind me, watching. "Maybe you can work this into some of your coursework. Or perhaps he can get course credit for some of the work."

"Maybe," Dillan said with a smile. "But now we have other work to do. Show us what's needed, Boss."

I smiled, too. "Right this way."

Chapter Nine

"Wow. Look at those guns." Pop stared out the kitchen window at the workers in the backyard.

"Guns?" I dropped the ice cube tray in the sink and raced to his side. Swanny had come and gone, and I was preparing for the five members of the Showcase committee to evaluate my preparations for Saturday's judging. Holy God, I couldn't have guns sitting around when the committee walked through. "Guns? Where?"

"Those guys. Dillan said they played football and you can tell. Man, those biceps. That guy must bench press three hundred."

I sagged against him in relief. "I thought you meant guns. You know, guns. Dillan carries a gun."

"Yeah, I figured he did."

"But—Pop, he carries a gun!"

"He knows how to use it, so what's the problem?" Pop glanced at the clock. "Your committee's due to arrive. You'd better get out front."

I hastily put the finishing touches on the cooler of lemonade I was making, adding lemon slices and more ice. "Tell the guys to break for lunch," I said over my shoulder. "They need to get out of the sun. They've been working hard."

"Will do. I'll have 'em store the serviceberry in the garage so it doesn't take the heat of the day." Pop headed to the back yard, where the 'crew' had worked all morning, digging out the serviceberry for transplanting.

I lugged the cooler to the front porch in time to see three ladies and two men trudge up my steps. As I expected, they were dressed in what I thought of as "summer togs," a description I remembered from my Nancy Drew reading days. The women were in designer capris with matching tops, the men in lightweight trousers and crisp short-sleeved shirts. All were carrying clipboards and wearing fancy sunglasses.

"Miss Griffen?" A tall, imposing woman with blunt-cut gray hair extended her hand. "I believe this is the first time you've been entered in the competition. It's a pleasure to meet you."

I shook hands with her, something I normally didn't do because it was painful, especially with someone like her, who had a firm grip. I forestalled the others by offering a glass of lemonade and we stood on the porch for a few minutes while they sipped and evaluated the front garden.

"The steps are a challenge," one of the men said.

"We'll have accessibility via the driveway." I gestured to my left. "We'll move our cars for the day, so people can park in the garage if needed."

"Good." The man ticked off something on his clipboard.

"Why don't you show us the tour?" the woman suggested. "We'll make notes as we go. If you'd like a member of your grounds crew to join us, that would be fine."

My grounds crew? "They're busy at the moment. We're doing some last-minute transplanting." As I spoke, Mason rounded the corner of the garage, tucking in one of Pop's T-shirts—a clean blue one, which strained across his chest.

"Sorry, Boss. I lost track of time." Mason hurried to my side, smiling at the committee members. "Sorry, folks. Mr. Griffin mentioned that you'd like the head of the crew to be here while you're evaluating the site. He said he read it in the rulebook." He snatched up the clipboard I had set on the porch chair. "Ready when you are."

Bless you, Pop, for remembering that. He and I had discussed it and how to handle it (or not handle it), but it totally slipped my mind. "I thought we'd have people come through starting here." I led the way to gate near the garage.

"This is a much smaller site than we usually have on the tour. How many acres?"

"Two," Mason said before I could answer. "But jam-packed full of goodies."

"There's a rather sharp edge there," one of the men said, pointing to the gate. "A screw might be loose and sticking out. You'll want to fix that."

Mason made a note on his clipboard. "Will do." He led the way into the backyard where Pop met us. "The crew is taking a lunch break," he said after introductions were made. "I told 'em to be back at one."

"Good." I turned to the committee. "We're still doing some last-minute touch-ups that I didn't get to earlier." I escorted the group around the garden, noting items of interest and showing what still needed to be done. They took their time, examining the area for hidden hazards and for the more unique plants that I had growing. They occasionally made comments ("that paver needs to be leveled"; "make sure there's signage here about the thorns"; "put some caution tape here to show the drop-off"). Mason dutifully scrawled on his clipboard, smiling the whole time.

We made a circuit of the perimeter then came to Labbie. I led the way inside and belatedly remembered I still had grow lights in the interior. I was prepared to make excuses but when we entered the center, the lights were gone. I breathed a sigh of relief.

"Such a unique feature," one of the women said. "But rather tight quarters. You'll need to have someone at the entrance to monitor who can come in. And netting to keep the roses back. Those thorns are a problem."

"We'll post signs about the roses. Don't touch. And my niece will be here to help," Mason said promptly.

"Good." The woman made a note on her clipboard.

"She is?" I murmured to Mason.

"She is now," he said out the side of his mouth.

We ended the tour at the porch. As we passed by, I heard the phone ring inside. "I'll get that," Pop said and he dashed into the house.

I led the committee to the side gate. "It's a beautiful property," one of the men said. "Truly a small jewel compared to some of the other properties we're highlighting." He exchanged a glance with the other committee members. "I'm pleased it's on the tour. It will give homeowners a chance to see what a home garden can be."

"What it can aspire to be," Mason said. "It takes the right designer to put it into place." He nodded wisely, and the man nodded, too.

"Absolutely. Thank you for your time. We'll look forward to Saturday." They left, pausing on the steps to talk and point to various shrubs while they descended.

"What is this Showcase thing?" Mason asked. "I mean, I know it's important. Dillan said it was, but what's it for?"

"People pay to go on a tour of a dozen gardens in Le Prince and Beaumont. The money goes to charity and the people who design the gardens get a chance to showcase their talents—and maybe get a few new customers."

"Well, that's good, but most people can't afford somebody like you to design their gardens." Mason frowned at the committee members, barely seen above my shrubbery at curbside as they got into their large sedan.

"I set my fees according to what a person can pay. Not everybody does that, but many designers do. It's more affordable than you think."

"Huh. That's cool." Mason studied the clipboard. "I'd better get working on this stuff."

I took it from him. "You need to get lunch. Thanks for your help."

"Lilith?" Pop leaned out from the front door. "Phone is for you. I told him you were busy, but he said he needs to talk to you."

"Who is it?"

"Some lawyer. Said he has to talk to you as soon as possible."

"That's trouble," Mason muttered.

Movement on the street below caught my attention. The sedan with the organizers was pulling away but in its place was a new sedan. "Can't talk," I called out.

138

"More company is coming."

"That isn't company," Mason declared. "That's a cop if I've ever seen one." He pulled out his phone and headed for the house. "I'm calling Dillan. He needs to be here."

Mason was right. Detective Hunter was climbing the steps to my house accompanied by another man similarly dressed in dark pants, a lightweight sports coat, and a pale blue dress shirt. Hunter glanced around curiously while he climbed toward me, obviously surprised by my abundant front yard. He hadn't been there the day Blake Kelleher was found, so this was the first time he experienced my garden first-hand.

I waved. "Detective, what are you doing here?"

"Lilith, you wait for me." Pop dashed from the house to join me.

Hunter and his companion paused on the step below me. "Miss Griffin, we need to talk. This is Detective Chase. Can we go inside, please?" He smiled so briefly I wasn't sure if I really saw it.

"Of course. Can I get you a glass of water or—" I whirled when I saw another car zooming down the street, screeching to slow down, then making a sharp turn into our drive. "Who is—"

Dillan leapt from the car before it even stopped, phone in hand. "What the hell is going on?" he demanded, striding toward us. The rest of the crew piled out and followed him. It was an intimidating sight—four angry men, sweat-stained and dirty, advancing on us.

"Dillan, this is Detective Hunter and—" I turned to the other man. "I'm sorry, I didn't get your name, I think it was—"

"I know who he is. What are you doing here?" Dillan demanded.

Hunter didn't blink an eye. I guess facing angry citizens was a normal part of his day. "Lieutenant Lyall, is it?"

"Lieutenant?" Pop said.

"Mr. Lyall," Dillan snapped. "I'm a civilian."

"In that case, stay out of police business." Hunter put a hand on my arm and gently tugged me toward the house. "Let's go talk, shall we?"

"Oh." I didn't say it loudly, but his grip was too tight on my burned right arm. I instinctively pulled back, but that only made it worse. Dillan lunged forward.

I twisted, putting myself between him and Hunter. "No! Don't! He didn't know." I leaned into Dillan, who struggled to get past me. "Dillan, it's okay. He didn't know."

Hunter released my arm and stepped back. "What's wrong?"

I rolled up my sleeve and pushed the fabric along my arm. "It hurts." Dillan put his hands on my shoulders, holding me when I swayed.

"Shit," the man with Hunter whispered when he saw the burned flesh.

"Holy crap, what happened?" one of the crew muttered.

"I'm sorry," Hunter said. "I forgot."

"It's okay." I pushed back again. This time Dillan stepped away, releasing his light hold on my shoulders. "Come inside and we can talk." I smiled at the work crew, standing in a semi-circle behind Dillan. "We'll be back in a minute. Nothing to worry about." I moved toward the house and the crowd parted, letting me pass.

"Hey, Boss," Mason murmured when I passed. "You need anything, you holler."

"Will do," I assured him. I went to the house, walking a bit unsteadily amidst the testosterone surrounding me.

"We need to talk to you," Hunter said behind me. "In private."

"You'll talk to me, my father, and my bodyguard," I said without missing a step. "Or you'll take me into custody and charge me with something. This is an informational visit, correct? Or do I need to call a lawyer?" I turned to see Hunter glaring at Dillan, who was a foot or so behind me.

Hunter blew out an exasperated breath. "Okay. Bodyguard?" he muttered when he brushed past Dillan to follow me into the house.

"You go, girl," Mason called out.

I entered the house, going to the right to the living room. When I came into the room, the cat was on Pop's chair. He got one peek at the people coming toward him and took off at a run toward the open basement door at the back of the room. The last I saw of him was his pink, fur-less flank, furry backside and the white bandage on his tail stump.

"It was lonely downstairs," Pop said when I whirled to face him. "Him and me split some tuna for lunch. He has a good appetite." He gestured to the couch. "Have a seat, gents. What's going on?"

Hunter and his companion sat down. Dillan leaned in the entryway, arms crossed. I pointed to a chair, but Dillan gestured to his dirty clothes. "Nope."

I sat in the armchair next to Pop's recliner. "What

can I help you with?"

Hunter sat on the edge of the sofa like a man ready to sprint away. His partner pulled out a small spiral notebook and balanced it on his knee, a pen raised. "Where were you last night between nine o'clock and midnight?" Hunter asked.

Dillan straightened and opened his mouth, but I got in first. "I was here with my father and with Mr. Lyall."

"Mr. Lyall?"

"I was here all night." Dillan met and held Hunter's stare. "All night."

Hunter pursed his lips. "And you can verify that Miss Griffin and her father were here as well?"

"Yep."

"What about you, Miss Griffin? Can you verify that Mr. Lyall was here all night?"

I met Dillan's gaze. "Yes, I can." I glimpsed the surprised expression on Pop's face quickly hidden. "Why do you want to know?" I tore my gaze away from Dillan.

"Tanya Sidero was killed last night," Hunter said. "She was murdered."

It took a second for me to process what he said. "Oh. Wow."

"You don't seem surprised."

"Surprised? Yes, I am. I'm surprised anyone managed to catch her unawares. She was always a careful person. Was it a robbery or something?"

"Murder," Dillan muttered. "Not manslaughter."

"I don't understand."

"Murder is planned. Manslaughter happens in the course of another crime. Right?" Dillan asked Hunter.

"Generally speaking." Hunter kept his gaze fixed

on me. "You don't seem particularly upset that someone you know, someone you recently spoke to, was murdered. That's the second person who's died near you in the past few days."

"Upset? My main feeling is one of relief. I've had nightmares about that woman for twenty-five years, so excuse me if I don't feel any sadness that karma finally bit her on the butt. This means I can quit looking over my shoulder." I raised my arm. "My injured shoulder. Neither she nor Blake Kelleher were 'near' me, except in physical proximity recently. They weren't close to me in any way that matters."

"I meant proximity, but I see what you mean."

"Why are you asking Lilith?" Pop asked. "You can't think she killed that bitch."

Hunter shifted his attention to Pop. "No, but someone who loves her might do it. Someone close to her." His eyes flickered to Dillan.

"Why wait twenty-five years?" I demanded. "She was released from that psychiatric hospital years ago. Why wait until now?"

"Maybe it's someone who recently met you." Hunter stared openly at Dillan.

"Now just a darn minute," I snapped. "You have no right to come in here and—"

"There's something else," Dillan said. "What is it?" He appeared curious, not concerned that he might be considered a murder suspect.

"Miss Griffin argued with both victims," the partner said. "We have witnesses."

I waved a hand. "Blake Kelleher was an obnoxious old man and Tanya Sidero was a class A, number one bitch. I'm sure they argued with dozens of people." I leaned forward expectantly.

He pulled something from his inner suit coat pocket and tossed it on the coffee table in front of the couch.

I got up to peer at it.

It was a blue rose.

"Why that little bitch! It was her—she cut my roses!" I pointed at the poor battered rose in the plastic baggy. "That's from the center of my labyrinth. We found the roses gone. I thought your men did it but when we found the footprint I realized—wait a minute. We found a footprint. Whose was it?" I lifted the plastic baggy, touching the forlorn flower. "That evil bitch. Oh. That reminds me." I turned to Dillan. "We need to set up the grow lights again."

Hunter's partner stared at me, his jaw sagging. "What lights?"

I waved a hand. "You wouldn't understand. We had to remove them for the organizing committee." I smiled at Dillan. "Thank you for that."

He inclined his head. "Glad I thought of it, Boss."

"This is proof that she cut my roses." I shook the bag at Hunter. "You need to arrest her or—" I stopped. "She's dead. Damn. You can't arrest her. That bitch. Now I'll never get an answer."

"Answer to what?" Dillan asked

"Why she did it." I touched my neck. "She said she wanted to hurt me, but it had to be more than that, didn't it?" I sat back and spread out the baggy on my leg. "My poor flowers."

"Sweet Buddha in a bikini," Pop muttered. "What was she doing with that?"

"That's a mental image I'll carry for a long time."

Dillan glanced at Hunter and his partner, who appeared somewhat stunned. "The roses. She's been breeding them for years," Dillan said into the dense silence that settled over the room. "They're very rare. Very valuable."

"Ah." The two policemen breathed a sigh of relief, probably glad that something made sense in my incoherent ramblings.

"What about that footprint? Was it hers?"

"You saw that?" Hunter asked.

"Dillan saw it. He said you did a plastic mold thingy, so you could find out who it belonged to. Was it Tanya's?"

"There were two," Hunter said after a pause. "One in the maze and one near the gate."

"Damn. I didn't see that one," Dillan muttered.

"It was off to the side, near the fencing," Hunter's partner said. "Easy to miss." He closed his notebook. "You're Captain Eames' kid, right?"

"Stepson. Did you get any positives from the footprint?"

"We're working on it."

"I know what that means." Dillan said it with a grudging smile. "I've said it myself enough times during the course of an investigation."

Hunter stood, followed by his partner. "We wanted to verify that you can identify that rose. It was found in the pocket of the victim."

"That little bitch. The whole time she was intimidating me, she had one of my roses in her pocket." I stood, too, joining the two policemen when they walked toward the door.

"I guess this proves that karma works," Pop said

cheerfully. "She got what she deserved."

"It took a damn long time," I grumbled. "I suppose this means I don't need a bodyguard anymore." I smiled tentatively at Dillan, who fell into step with us to go out the front door. "I can still use the garden help, though."

"On the contrary, Miss Griffin." Hunter went to my stone steps. "You do still need a bodyguard. The two victims are both related to you in some way. I'd feel better knowing you had someone watching you until we get this killer put away."

"Is it the same person?"

"Probably," Dillan said. "That's a big coincidence."

"We're working on that." Hunter said it with a smile. "We'll be in touch." He and his partner went down the steps, pausing midway to look around at my garden.

"I didn't ask." I watched Hunter bend over to examine a coneflower. "How was she killed? How was Blake Kelleher killed?"

"I'll find out." Before I could stop him, Dillan dashed away to catch up to the two detectives.

"They're probably talking about cop things," I commented to Pop.

"You can bet on it," he agreed.

"Everything okay, Boss?" Mason peeked around the side of the garage. "You need us to bash any cops or anything?"

"No, we're good." I checked my watch. "Let's get going on that transplanting. Maybe you guys can finish at a reasonable hour."

"You need to get some lunch," Pop said firmly. "And some rest. You had P.T., then you had those organizers. I know how your sessions hurt you. Get something to eat then lie down. I'll manage the tree moving."

"Don't you dare lift anything heavy," I warned. "You can watch, but that's all."

"I'll give orders. I'm good at that." He waved me off. "Go inside and catch up on your beauty sleep. I'll whip these kids into shape."

I reluctantly went inside. I trusted Pop's judgement on the transplanting, but I didn't trust that he wouldn't overdo it. Well, Dillan would make sure Pop took it easy. I could count on Dillan.

I paused in the foyer. I could count on Dillan. What an odd thought. For decades, I hadn't counted on anyone but myself and Pop. I went to the living room, but I spied the cat, dozing on Pop's recliner. He sensed my presence and eyed me, muscles bunched to spring.

"Relax, Beast," I murmured. "I'm going up for a nap." I'd grab a bite to eat later, after I rested. For now, all I wanted was a chance to stretch out and doze.

I changed into denim shorts and a shapeless, short-sleeved T-shirt, then smeared on the icy gel that would soon transform to healing warmth. I lay down, staring at the ceiling.

Tanya, dead. Thank you, God. Would the nightmares stop now? Probably not. Who would want to kill her? Murder was a huge step. I understood accidental death or even killing somebody during a crime, but murder? People planned murders. People had a chance to think about it ahead of time and they still went through with it.

With those happy thoughts dancing in my head, I napped, crazy dreams keeping me twitching and tossing on the bed. Dillan, Shaw, Pop—they intertwined with the garden site at the nursing home, arguing with me about a tree I wanted to remove. Then the scene shifted, and I was in Labbie, but it was changed, dark and dismal. I struggled to get out, but the path kept shifting and the walls moved, closing me in.

I woke, gasping and disoriented. I doubt if the nap did much good. My poor muscles were as tense now as when Swanny worked on me. Oh, well. I looked out the window. The guys had the trees swapped, dirt piled around the base of the viburnum now in the backyard. Wow. That would have taken me and Pop two days to do, if not more. It was sure nice to have a crew.

I went downstairs and brought in the cooler from the front porch, refilling it with lemonade and lemon slices. I went out to the back stoop in the shade of the overhanging awning, intending to set it out for the guys when they took a break.

Which they were doing—all of them sitting in the shade of the garage, talking. "Hey," I said, leaning out the door. "Here's something to drink." I brandished the cooler in my left hand, letting it dangle by its handle.

Dillan swiveled in his seat on the step. "Hey, Boss. Come on out and join us." He tapped the step next to him.

I shook my head, mindful of my shorts and top. "Nah, that's okay."

He grabbed the handle of the cooler and tugged gently. Pop was sitting opposite Dillan in one of our old lawn chairs. He smiled. I switched my gaze to Dillan, who smiled, too. "Come on, Boss. Join us."

I could count on Dillan. I released the cooler and stepped outside, sinking down to sit next to Dillan on his right, my right side exposed to the crew. "Hey, guys."

"Hey, Boss," they murmured.

"You guys did an awesome job."

"Yeah, we're sure to get that trophy," Pop said, jiggling his crossed leg.

"What trophy?" Mason asked.

"It's nothing," I said.

"It's something," Pop insisted. "The winner of the popular vote gets a nice trophy that would look real fine on our mantel."

"We don't have a mantel," I pointed out.

"I'll build one."

"Well, first we have to win it. And thanks to you guys, we might. What do I owe you?" Their gazes flickered over my bare legs and arms, eyes darting to me then away.

"We still got some stuff to finish up," Amil said. He'd been mostly silent while they worked, not laughing and joking around like the other guys. "We'll be back." He swiveled his head to regard his friends and they nodded.

"You know, I gotta say it." Mason came forward and filled a paper cup from the cooler. "That chick got what's coming to her, Boss."

"Amen, brother," Amil murmured.

"No shit," someone else said.

Dillan nudged me. He was a warm presence next to me on the step—sweaty, smelly, and solid. "Karma's a bitch, huh?"

"It's only a bitch if you are," someone murmured.

I bobbed my head, unable to speak. I was accustomed to pity. I wasn't accustomed to sympathy, especially not from strangers like this. I think Pop saw my emotion because he asked, "How did she die, Dillan? You talked to the cops about that."

"She was suffocated." He saw my shocked expression. "Not strangled. Suffocated."

"How does that happen?" Mason asked. "Hey, this is part of our education," he said when Pop frowned at him with an arched eyebrow. "Criminal Justice, remember?"

"She was drugged then killed while she slept." Dillan sounded briskly professional. "Probably a roofie in a drink. They found fibers in her mouth and nose."

Pop murmured, "Roofie?"

"Rohypnol," Dillan said. "A date-rape drug."

The others perked up. I could almost see little wheels spinning in their heads. "Roofies are easy to find," Mason agreed. "You can buy those on a street corner. Hard to trace, too. What about the old man? Is it connected?"

"It's got to be," Mel stated. He was the big kid with the big guns. "Two people connected to the same person."

"Me," I said.

"And Shaw Kelleher." Mel shrugged. "Kelleher knew both the victims, too."

Dillan smiled. "I like the way your mind works. Good. You're not seeing only the obvious suspect. Study everybody around the victims. Find the commonality in circumstance. Blake Kelleher's death was apparently a heart attack. He was an old man and you know—"

All four of the crew members laughed. "Yeah, right. And I got a bridge for you in New York," Mel scoffed. "What'd they find?"

"Tox screen is still being processed."

"We know what that means," Amil said. "Definitely not natural causes."

The phone rang inside the house. "I'll get that." I stood, putting my hand on Dillan's shoulder to steady myself.

I heard him say behind me, "Time to get back to work, guys. Let's get those trees put to bed."

Thank God for a crew, I thought. I picked up the phone in the kitchen. "Griffin residence."

"Lilith? It's Shaw Kelleher."

"Shaw." I peeked over my shoulder guiltily, as though he might have heard people speculating about his murderous intent. "How are you doing?"

"That's why I'm calling." He sighed. "Lilith, I need to see you. I feel like my past is being stripped away from me." I heard the tears in his voice. "Mother, Father, Tanya—they're part of my past. You're part of it, too, Lilith."

I understood his bewilderment. After the attack, everything changed for me. People who used to be friends suddenly vanished. My world was topsy-turvy. "I know, Shaw. It must be shocking."

"I was wondering—can we get together? I'd like to see you. I'd like to talk to someone who, well, someone who knows me. Someone who knows me from the past, not from now." He gave an unsteady laugh. "Does that make sense?"

It did. "Do you want to come over?"

"No, I can't. Not now. I was hoping we might have dinner tonight. I know it's late notice and all, but I was tied up with funeral planning and Tanya's family and—

God, it's been horrible. Please. I need some connection to who I was so I can go forward. I feel like I'm floundering."

I heard the back door open. "Boss, do you—" Dillan stopped. "Sorry."

"I'd be glad to, Shaw. Where?"

"How about La Restaurante 1740? I'll make a reservation for seven o'clock. Is that okay for you?"

Dillan started to speak, so I raised a hand to stop him. "That's fine. You don't have to pick me up. I'll meet you there."

"Thank you, Lilith. This means the world to me. I'll see you tonight."

I hung up the phone to find Dillan glowering at me. "What's wrong?"

"You're meeting Kelleher? Where and when?"

"It's a date, Dillan. I don't think you were invited." I tried to move past him, but he shifted so I couldn't get by. "It's only dinner."

"I'm going with you."

"No way. How would I explain a babysitter with me?" I tried, once again, to evade him.

"Tough shit. I'm going with you."

"But—"

He glared at me. "I'm going."

Damn. I guess I had a babysitter for the night.

Chapter Ten

"Well, this is awkward." I smiled apologetically at Shaw over the top of the engraved menu. We were seated in the restaurant, an elegant space at the atop the tallest building in Beaumont, Hotel 1740. The restaurant was a subdued, discreet place with tables against a wall of glass above the city below. The room was tiered, so people seated in the interior of the space still had a view of the outdoors, as well as a view of those of us who sat closest to the windows.

"It doesn't bother me in the least." He glanced to his left. Dillan sat at a table far across the room, facing us. "I hope he can afford it."

I didn't tell Shaw that Dillan's meal would be on my tab. I insisted on that when Dillan insisted on driving me and escorting me to my dinner. "The least I can do is pay for yours," I'd said.

"I can buy my own damn food."

"What has your Jockeys in a jam?" I snapped back. "I'm meeting an old friend for dinner, that's all."

"An old friend who was indirectly responsible for your initial injury and who is directly related to two people murdered in the past forty-eight hours. He's a suspect, Lilith. A damn good one."

I laughed at him then and I smiled at the thought now. Shaw Kelleher, a murderer? Spoiled, pampered, indulged Shaw? He wouldn't have the first notion about how to murder someone, much less have the guts to do it. I could imagine Dillan doing it, but Shaw?

"A penny for your thoughts," Shaw said, laying aside his menu.

I set mine aside as well. Mine had no prices in it, which told me everything was expensive. I wondered what my tab for Dillan's meal would be. "Only a penny?"

He smiled. "Okay. A dollar."

He really was the handsomest man I'd ever known. Even now, with his face haggard from tiredness and grief, he radiated sex appeal, charm, and confidence. I saw no arrogance, though. Shaw somehow acknowledged his beauty, pushed it aside, and was simply himself.

His suit was perfectly cut to emphasize his shoulders. The dark gray fabric of the coat and trousers shone faintly in the subdued lighting and his silk tie was knotted precisely, the muted burgundy and gray colors a subtle contrast to his dark shirt.

I wore my summer weight "nice night out in public" outfit, a loose chiffon ankle-length dress, beige with darker beige accents. The dress was high-collared, covering most of my neck wound, with the shear jacket covering my arm scars. I had a similar 'winter night out' dress in a darker color and heavier fabric.

"I'm amazed at how I've changed and how little you have." I took a sip of the fine French wine, far finer than any I stocked in my pantry at home. "I guess it's true. Women get old and men get handsomer with age."

"You're still beautiful. No, you are." He propped his elbows on the table and rested his chin on his clasped hands. "You're beautiful in an unusual way now. Back then, you were fresh and sort of unspoiled and reckless. You had a devil-may-care attitude and it came through in everything you did. Now you're quieter, calmer. You radiate beauty now. Back then, you flaunted it."

I didn't know what to say. It was years since anyone had complimented me so lavishly. "Thank you, Shaw. I guess that devil-may-care part of me faded with time." I fiddled with my napkin, embarrassed by his unblinking, intense gaze.

"What happened to you was a travesty," he whispered. "I've regretted it since it happened. I'm relieved to see that you recovered so well. Your scarring is barely noticeable, although I'm sure it's still painful."

Something in his voice didn't quite ring true. Maybe it was the way he stole glances at my neck or my hand, resting on the table. His face stilled then his lips thinned as though he was repressing an expression. Was it disgust? Revulsion? Pity? I couldn't tell.

"Yes, it is painful sometimes. I have limited range of motion."

"And yet you've made such a good life for yourself." He leaned back when the waiter came to the table.

"Would the gentleman care to order?"

"The lady can order her own meal." Shaw's eyes twinkled with laughter. "I wouldn't dream of deciding for you."

The waiter shifted his attention to me. "Grilled filet mignon," I said. "Medium rare. Plain mashed potatoes, please."

"Excellent choice. And for the gentleman?" The waiter turned to Shaw.

"The bone-in rib-eye, medium. We'll have a bottle of Cabernet Sauvignon with the meal. I leave it to your discretion to choose the right wine."

The man left, probably evaluating wines in his head and wondering how expensive a bottle he could get away with. "It appears we're going for the carnivorous meal tonight."

"I've been living at home for the past few years. Mother was ill and I think she enjoyed my company. Father never cared for steak, so I always enjoy it whenever I get the chance." Shaw's hand paused over his wine glass. "I suppose I inherit the house. I never thought much about it."

'The house' was an estate north of town, an enormous McMansion set on fourteen acres of rolling hillside, trees, and an expanse of lawn that probably needed three people to keep it trimmed at least twice a week. The swimming pool was in the back of the house near a putting green and driving range.

"Will you keep it or put it up for sale? It's a big house for one person."

He toyed with his wine, swirling it around in the glass. "I'm not sure," he said. "There are so many things about the house I love. I guess I haven't thought much about it. So much has happened so fast." He took a swallow of wine, then his gaze went to Dillan. "You didn't actually explain him."

I managed a credible chuckle. "The police think it might be useful for me to have a bodyguard. Plus, he's helping us get the garden into shape."

"For how long? Isn't it a bit intrusive to have him

around all the time?"

"Just for a few days. The police seemed confident that they'd solve—they'd figure out—" I stammered to a halt. I was talking about the murder of his father and a family friend. "You know."

"You have more confidence in our police department than I do." Shaw gave a little shrug, as if to say *irrelevant*. "I'm sorry about Tanya. She was a troubled person. I always knew she had problems. We grew up together, we were in and out of each other's houses, we went to school together." He swirled the wine in his glass.

"I had no idea. I didn't know her well, of course. I didn't meet her or any of your other friends until after you and I began dating."

"That time with you was the best time of my life." He regarded me through his eyelashes, almost bashfully. "I never felt about anyone the way I felt about you. It was as if my life was being remade. As if I was being remade."

I didn't remember it that way. We had fun together, usually doing something I had never experienced before. Shaw was rich and loved to party. We met when Pop worked on one of his cars. A total accident but the chemistry between us was there from the start. I was shocked when he proposed. I think I knew even then that I didn't love him the same way he loved me, but I didn't care. He was the catch of a lifetime.

"I didn't think she cared about me. I was so stunned when she did what she did. I don't think she cared that you and I were together. She thought people were laughing at her. They weren't, of course. She wanted to prove that she had the guts to do something drastic. Nobody cared who was with who." He smiled sadly. "That's how it was back then. We were so careless, so unmindful of who we hurt."

Some of us were, I thought. It was hard for me to remember who I was back then. Too much had happened between then and now. "It was an odd time," I murmured. "Another lifetime."

"Sometimes it feels like yesterday." He sipped his wine then said, "How much do you know about him?"

"Him?"

He inclined his head toward Dillan.

"Oh. His stepfather is a friend of my father. He's an ex-cop." And he carries a gun, I thought but didn't say. "I think he used to live in California."

"I did a bit of research. We have people on the payroll who do background checks for us and I asked them to check into Mr. Lyall's background."

"You know his name?"

"Our people are good at what they do." Shaw said it without a hint of condescension, as though spying on another person and gathering information about them was a normal part of business. Well, it probably was for him, I reasoned.

"I don't know if you know all there is to know about your so-called bodyguard. He was in a motorcycle gang in California and killed a man in a fight over a woman."

"What?" I almost dropped my wine glass.

"It's true. Ask him about it." Shaw smiled briefly. "After we eat, please. I'd rather not have any unpleasantness mar our meal. Yes, his stepfather had to intercede to make sure his stepson didn't go to jail. As it was, Lyall was forced to do community service."

"But he's a cop. I mean, he was a cop. Why would they allow him into the police school or whatever it is? Aren't there rules about that?"

Shaw raised one elegant shoulder. "Maybe someone paid someone to make sure his stepson was admitted."

That didn't sound like the man who was Pop's friend and Olivia's husband. Mark Eames sounded like a rigid, moralistic man who would be horrified to break a rule, either willingly or inadvertently. Pay someone to let his stepson into cop school? I doubted it.

I didn't voice my doubt. "I'm sure Dillan has an explanation for his past."

"I'm sure he does. And I'm sure it's a good one. But let's not talk about him. Tell me about your garden and the showcase coming up."

I was relieved to be off the subject of my temporary bodyguard. I launched into conversation about the Showcase, the rules, the judges, and my competition. "So Tanya's company is your main competitor," Shaw murmured. "How apt that you and she were in competition."

"Apt?" I leaned back to let the waiter set our food on the table.

"Perhaps not apt, but an interesting convergence of your past and your present." Shaw tasted the wine the man poured and nodded his approval.

We tucked into the food, some of the best eating I had in a long, long time. I savored every bite, knowing I probably wouldn't taste the like of it again for a long, long time. This is the life, I thought. Dining in a beautiful restaurant, a handsome man paying attention to me, fine wine, candlelight…a normal life for normal people, albeit normal *rich* people. I let the wine mellow me and I enjoyed every minute.

We talked over coffee and cognac, Shaw telling me about the family business and me telling him about my therapeutic garden clients. When we finally pushed away from the table, I was relaxed, happy, and almost forgot that a petulant man waited for me near the elevator.

Shaw walked with me through the restaurant, his hand resting lightly on my back. We paused a few feet away from Dillan, who stood at the elevator, hands clasped in front of him like some kind of military guy.

"Thank you so much for joining me tonight," Shaw said. We stood near a step below a container of plants, which hid us from the tier above, where Dillan waited for me. "It's been a long time since I was able to relax with anyone. It seems like most people I interact with are more interested in my business connections or my money than simply talking about, well, about whatever comes up." He lifted my left hand and kissed the back of it, his lips soft on the skin. "Thank you."

"Thank you," I said. "I haven't had such an enjoyable evening in years. It was nice to connect again with you."

"Let's make sure to do it again. Let's do it again soon. I don't want to let you slip away now that I've found you again. Can we get together tomorrow? Perhaps tomorrow evening?"

"I'm supposed to go to party in the afternoon." I thought about Dillan and the way he was acting. "It's up in the air if I'll go or not."

"If you go, maybe you can slip away?" He held my hand. "I have the funeral on Thursday to endure, and

I'll have to attend Tanya's funeral, too. I don't know when that will be. The police are apparently examining the body."

"I'm sure they are," I said. "Those things can take time."

"Those things?"

"Investigations." I smiled ruefully. "What do I know about it? I sound like I know what I'm talking about. Just because Detective Hunter talked to me, I don't have the inside scoop on anything."

"You've been talking with the police?"

"They were talking with me. They came over today to question me about Tanya's death."

Shaw frowned. "Why?"

"They found something on her body that tied her to me."

"What?"

"I'm not sure if I'm supposed to talk about it. It might be a secret."

"I'm pretty damn sure it is." Dillan stepped behind Shaw. "Are you ready to go or do you want to blabber some more police business to a murder suspect?"

"I beg your pardon?" Shaw turned.

"You heard me," Dillan snapped.

Shaw considered him, his head tilted to one side as though examining a new form of wine offered for appraisal. "You weren't invited to join this conversation."

"Too bad. I invited myself." Dillan jerked his head. "Let's go."

For one frozen instant, I was sure they'd come to blows. Good Lord, two men fighting over me. I would have loved it if it weren't so mortifying to have it happen in such an upscale, public place.

"I'm sorry, Shaw." I didn't know what to say. "It's just that the police told—"

"Never mind." Shaw raised my hand to his lips and kissed it again, a slow, lingering caress. "I'm sorry our evening was so rudely interrupted. I'll be in touch, Lilith. I loved seeing you again. You're as lovely and loving as ever."

He released my hand and pushed past Dillan, going up the step to the right, to the bar at the end of the restaurant.

"Ready?" Dillan snapped.

"Do I have a choice?" I stomped up the steps to the elevator, the door open and waiting. I got in and Dillan followed, stabbing at the button for the street level. We didn't speak while the elevator descended. When the doors opened at the bottom, he left first, studying the hotel lobby with one hand tucked into his coat.

"You aren't carrying a gun, are you?" I demanded, following him into the hushed, tastefully decorated space.

"Of course, I am. Come on." He strode toward exit doors and the valet stationed there.

I followed at a more leisurely pace, enjoying the lovely paintings and lush area rugs on the polished marble floors. My usual travel lodge was a Holiday Inn, so this refined venue was a treat.

Dillan waited impatiently for me outside. "Let's go. We've wasted enough time here."

"Did you have a pleasant meal?" I asked, determined to be at least minimally polite.

"Not really. I didn't enjoy the atmosphere." He jammed his hands in his pants pockets. He wore a sports coat, dark trousers, and a white shirt and tie. He seemed uncomfortable, like his clothes weren't quite the right size.

"I had a marvelous time. Except for the times when I saw you sitting there, glaring at me. I don't get many chances at a romantic dinner and having a third wheel around added a nice touch." I shot him an insincere smile.

He peered at the street where the valet had disappeared into a parking garage. I didn't think he'd answer at first. "You know, for somebody who claims her scars won't define her life, you sure have let them define yours. You maybe don't get chances at romantic dinners because you have this barrier up, this poor me, my scars have ruined my life. You don't even want to talk to people, much less maybe see if there's a chance for romance."

I faced him with clenched hands, so angry I was trembling. "How dare you. You have no idea what my life was like before this."

"It was twenty-five years ago." He leaned closer. "You've lived as long with the scars as you have without them. Don't you think it's time to forget about them and move on?"

That was a low blow. A very low blow. Even as I thought that, I recognized a tiny grain of truth in what he said. That made me even angrier. "Look who's talking. How long did you live with your stepfather? How's that relationship going?"

He stared into my eyes and several emotions passed through his—mainly anger, but also sadness and bitterness, maybe. It was hard to tell. I was so angry I could barely see straight.

I should have left it there. Instead, I said, "You know nothing about me. You—"

"And I guess I won't get the chance to know you, will I? You're too afraid of what I might think to even give me a try."

"Afraid? Afraid of what?"

He was silent for a long few seconds. "Love."

I laughed. "Love? You? What do you know about that? You broke your mother's heart. She used to sit by my bed and cry about you." I suddenly remembered what Shaw said. "Did you kill a man because of a woman? Is that your idea of love?"

Dillan was so still it was like he'd gone to stone. "I see you did your homework."

"Shaw did it for me."

"Yeah. I guess that makes sense. He would." Dillan pushed past me, bumping me to one side.

"Wait a minute. Aren't you on guard duty tonight?"

He stopped then came back to me so fast I almost tipped over. "I called in a favor and got you a substitute. I know you don't believe this, but I have a life. I have things to do other than sit around here and guard you."

"Sorry." I held up my hands. "Excuse me. I thought this was a job."

"It is. A job I've handed off to somebody else." He waved a hand. A sleek sports car came to life, headlights flashing on and the motor revving. It crossed the street and came to the curb. A woman stepped out— tall, svelte, and blonde with killer legs in skintight jeans.

"Long time, no see, Dil," she purred, rounding the

car to stand in front of Dillan. Her knit top strained across her large breasts. "Is this the job?" She raked me over from head to toe with a disdainful sweep of her heavily-mascaraed eyes.

"Yeah, only for the night, Sarah. I'll take over tomorrow. Take her to Eames' house at noon."

"Wait a minute. I'm not a package to be picked up and dropped off." I crossed my arms. It was that or I'd strangle him.

"Yes, you are." Dillan started toward the parking garage.

"You wait." I darted after him, but Blondie grabbed my arm—my right arm. She pulled it, hard, and I almost dropped to the pavement. As it was, I staggered and bent over, suddenly nauseous from the pain and the anger.

"What the hell?" She pulled me to my feet.

"Leave me alone, bitch." I tore my arm away from her grip, shaking. I saw Dillan a few steps away, watching. "Leave me alone," I snarled. I stumbled in a circle and headed in the general direction of home.

The woman threw up her hands. "Dil, what's going on?"

I kept walking. I was done with this night. I didn't give a shit what happened to him or her or Shaw or me. I wanted to get home, take a Good Pill, drink too much wine, and sleep. Thank God I wore low-heeled shoes. It was a long freaking walk home and I expected a few blisters before I was done.

I'd gone two blocks when the sports car pulled up next to me at the curb. "I'm sorry," the woman said through the open window while the car idled next to me where I paused. "I didn't know."

I stopped. Adrenaline drained away and exhaustion took its place. I fumbled open the passenger door and dropped into the seat. "Do you know where I live?"

"Yeah, he gave me directions."

"Drive." I flopped back on the leather seat and closed my eyes.

"I didn't know about your injury."

"Drive."

Ten minutes later she said, "We're here."

I opened my eyes. "Park in the drive."

She did as I said. I threw open the door and fell out. Pop met me at the front door. "Where's Dillan?"

"I don't know, and I don't care." I pushed him away and headed for the kitchen. The damn cat was sitting in the porch doorway. He got one look at my face and ran to hide under the couch.

I poured the biggest wine glass we had full of white wine and went back to the front of the house. "I'm going to bed."

The woman stood in the doorway to the front porch. She and Pop were huddled together like conspirators. I ignored them and dragged myself up the stairs.

I fumbled a Good Pill from its container and swallowed it with a big swig of wine before putting the glass on my nightstand. I peeled off my clothes, let them drop, then I fell onto the bed.

Damn him to hell and back. How dare he talk about me like that? He didn't know a damn thing about me. He didn't know how I felt. Damn him and Shaw. Damn them both for making me feel like a woman again. I had relegated that to a subterranean part of my psyche. I wasn't a woman anymore because of the scars. I was only a person.

But Shaw—Dillan—His gaze. The way he moved.

I took another big swallow of wine. Who?

I knew the answer.

Dillan.

Damn him. I had built a wall between me and the world, between me and sex. Damn him for breaking it.

I swallowed the last of my wine. To hell with him and all of them. The pill began to work its magic.

I woke later than usual, unsure where I was. Gradually it came back. Wednesday. The Fourth. The damn party. I covered my eyes with my arm. Shit. I was supposed to go to Olivia's house. Well, I'd call in sick. No way was I going there.

Pop had other ideas. He and Blondie were apparently good buddies. They were in the kitchen when I made my way downstairs an hour later. The stupid cat sat on the floor between them at the island in the kitchen, peering up hopefully at Pop. When the cat saw me, though, it bolted for the porch.

"That cat hates me," I grumbled.

"You have an angry aura," Blondie said. "Sarah." She held out her hand.

I ignored it and went to the coffeepot.

"You're in a pissy mood," Pop commented.

"I had a pissy night."

"How was your date with Shaw?"

"Not much of a date because Dillan sat there and stared at us the whole time and then he accused Shaw of murder."

Pop choked on the bite of toast he took. "He did what?"

Blondie grinned. Today she wore shorts and a T-shirt. The effect was still the same. *Bombshell waiting to explode.* "Yeah, your date is a murder suspect."

"He is not." I sipped my coffee while I considered toast. I wanted eggs, but I wasn't up to making it.

"Tell that to the cops." Blondie grinned when she saw my shock. "Dillan knows what he's doing when he says you need a bodyguard."

"Yeah, right."

"Give him a chance."

"Why?" I demanded.

"Why? Because he's worth it," she said confidently.

I hated the little bite of jealousy that grabbed hold of me. "You speak from experience?"

She tossed her head back, blonde hair cascading over her shoulders. Her laugh was full and raucous. "Nope. My flag doesn't stand at attention for him if you know what I mean."

Pop leaned forward eagerly. "She's a transsexual. I've never met a transsexual person before." He spoke like she was a two-headed dog or something.

"That you know of," Blondie corrected. "I'll bet you've met a few and didn't know it." She winked at me. "Your dad and I have been talking about LGBTQ rights."

"I had no idea. I thought people were straight or gay. There's these in-between areas." Pop shook his head. "What a tangle it must be for some folks. Then you toss these Bible-thumping Christians in the mess and which bathroom can they use, and it gets totally screwed up, excuse my language."

"I think I love you." Blondie grinned at Pop. "Can you adopt me?"

"Good Lord." I went back for a coffee refill. "My father, the gay rights activist."

"There are worse things to be," he pointed out.

"Dillan is good people," Blondie said.

"So is his father," Pop chimed in.

"Stepfather," I corrected.

"And you know his mother is an angel. She helped Lilith after Lilith was attacked," he explained to Blondie. "Olivia sat with Lilith all the times I couldn't get there. She helped us figure out the insurance stuff and the at-home care. There was a lot of surgeries and Olivia was there every time."

"Well, Dillan's no angel, but his mother must be if she can put with him and that bitch stepsister of his." Blondie shook her head sadly. "Sabrina is, well, she's unique."

"We're going there today," Pop told Blondie. "Lilith never wants to go anywhere, but today there's a party at Mark and Olivia's house. Lots of folks from Jean's Place will be there. That's the senior center downtown."

"Dillan probably regrets asking us," I noted.

"No, he probably regrets asking you," Blondie corrected. "I'm sure he'd love to have Grif there."

"I thought I'd call in sick. You can go without me, Pop."

"Olivia wants to see you. She'd be hurt if you didn't show."

He was right, damn it. "Okay. But I won't stay long."

"You don't have to stay long, but you do have to go." Pop leaned back in his chair and crossed his arms on his chest. "And that's that."

169

Blondie nodded emphatically. "I have my orders and you know how Dillan gets if you don't follow orders."

I glimpsed the cat, peering at me from under a chair on the porch. His expression seemed to say, *if I have to suffer, then you have to suffer, too.* "Okay," I said glumly. "But just for a few minutes."

Pop clapped his hand. "Hot dog. Party time."

"Whee. Party," I muttered.

Chapter Eleven

"Big mistake, Pop," I muttered when we entered the Eames backyard.

"Nonsense. This will be fun." He hurried forward to greet Olivia, who spied us and was working her way through a crowd of several dozen people standing in small clumps, chatting.

Pop was snazzy in his pale blue shirt and dark blue jeans. I wore one of my Gypsy Queen uniforms, a dark green skirt with a pale green-and-gold striped blouse. The green matched my eyes, or so Pop said.

We drove to the party in my SUV. "I want a getaway," I argued when Blondie insisted on driving us.

"Dillan won't let you get away," she warned.

"He can try," I countered. "Seriously, is this babysitting necessary?"

"Maybe. Maybe not. Tell you what. I'll follow you. Don't try any funky moves to dodge me. If you do, I'll sic Dillan on you."

I promised solemnly to drive like a church lady and we did just that, going the three miles to the suburbs where Blondie watched me park. She waited until we were at the door, then she waved and drove away.

"You look marvelous." Olivia hugged me gently, her plump, motherly body softly enfolding me. "It's so good to see you both. It's been too long." She turned to

Pop and hugged him, too. They'd spent a great deal of time together when I was first hospitalized. In many ways, Olivia was like family.

"Thank goodness the weather cooperated," she said, leading us to a brick patio in back with a door open to the interior of the house. "The humidity isn't quite as crushing as it was earlier this week. Although we might have storms later. I don't even care if it'll break this damn heat." She waved a hand toward her naturally curly hair, now snow white and as thick as ever. "Well, at least I have some semblance of a hairstyle today."

I always envied her curly hair. Mine was stick-straight with a mind of its own and used to give me fits when I tried to curl it. I finally gave up and went for short, shaggy styles that required minimal maintenance. "I like your house," I said. "This is a nice neighborhood."

She laughed. "It's pure suburbia, isn't it? Every house the same except for paint color. All of us with our half-acre lot, patio out back and barbeque grill. Mark loves to mow, and I hate to fuss with flowers, so I guess it works out fine. What can I get you to drink?" She steered us toward a bar set up near the house, in the shade of a green-and-white striped awning.

Pop got a beer and I got a gin and tonic, mixed by a young man Olivia introduced as 'one of Mark's friends from the station.' I assumed she meant the police station. I sipped my drink, eyeing the mix of people. There were several older people, Pop's age or older, but there were younger people, too. I noticed a couple of African-Americans and three or four Asian people.

"Quite a mix of people," I commented to Olivia.

"Some are Dillan's friends from school, some are Mark's friends from the job, and some are from Jean's Place."

"I see folks I know." Pop waved to two elderly ladies, who beamed at him and held up their wine glasses. "I'll see you later." He headed off, making a beeline for the women.

"Your father is quite the Romeo at Jean's Place," Olivia confided. "Oh, I'm being paged." She waved to some new arrivals bearing plates of cookies. "Wander about and relax. Dillan is here somewhere. I'm sure he'll find you." She bustled away, pausing to laugh and chat with people along the way.

I meandered around the lawn where several tables were set up with umbrellas to shield the occupants from the sun. Even so, it was roasting with temperatures in the nineties and a warm breeze blowing. Dark clouds were starting to pile up in the west and I eyed them nervously. It would be marvelous to have the rain, but I had left the grow lights on, hoping to give a little more incentive to the burgeoning blooms. I would need to run home and dismantle them if it stormed.

I glimpsed Dillan talking to a group of young men, a beer bottle in his hand. Today he wore dark blue shorts, sandals, and a white polo shirt. He saw me, but he made no acknowledgement of my presence. I might have been a shrub for all he noticed me. Apparently, he was still pissed. Well, harsh words were said. I wondered if he felt as lousy about it as I did.

I did another wander around the yard, ending up in the shade where I sat on a brick retaining wall, not far from a bunch of people playing a beanbag toss game. I demurred when someone asked me to join in. I was abysmally inept when it came to anything involving aiming.

Our host, Mark, came over to me. He was a tall, sturdy man, with what we called a farmer's tan: darkly tanned arms and dark legs with white feet in his sandals. His thick white hair was brushed back from his forehead, so disciplined I wondered if he used hair spray.

He introduced himself then said, "I'm glad to finally meet you. Olivia used to talk about what happened to you. She said you were very brave, dealing with the pain."

"She and my father helped me a great deal," I said. "They were there for me the whole time when I recovered."

"Your father is a special guy." He propped one foot up on the planter near my knee. "He's always pushing us to try new things at Jean's Place. Before he came, we were playing cards and hanging out. Now we're taking field trips and going bowling and doing all kinds of stuff."

I followed his gaze to where Pop stood, talking with Olivia and Dillan. Pop was gesturing, one arm outflung and a beer in his other hand. "Yeah, that's Pop. He's an adventurer. I wish sometimes he hadn't gotten saddled with taking care of me. I think after Mom died he might have gone off and traveled." I sipped my drink, smiling at the expression on Dillan's face, a mixture of amusement, affection, and respect.

"I think he did exactly what he wanted to do," Mark said firmly. "He loves you a great deal. There's no place he would want to be than with you." He sipped his drink. "He's proud of you. Proud of what you've accomplished, despite what happened."

"Well, you know what they say," I said lightly. "When life hands you lemons…"

"You weren't handed lemons. You were beaten up by them." He regarded Pop and the others. "Dillan was beaten up, too, until he figured out what he wanted to do in life. I never knew how to manage him."

"Pop and I were more of a team, I guess. He never tried to manage me. My mother did, but she failed miserably. I think fathers and daughters tend to get along better than daughters and mothers."

"It was sure that way in our family. I never was able to connect with Dillan, but my daughter and I always saw eye-to-eye on things. She's a lawyer in St. Louis. Her mother died when Sabrina was little. She was always my little princess." Mark sipped his drink, his face troubled. "She and Dillan got along fine when they were young, but when they were teenagers, they drifted apart. I don't think they talk to each much anymore."

"Life has a way of taking people down different paths," I said inanely.

"He sure as hell went on a bad path. I suppose you know about that."

I nodded in what I hoped was a knowledgeable way. "He alluded to it."

"I couldn't believe it when he joined that damn motorcycle gang. I thought Olivia would die of fear, wondering what crap he was getting into. It was when a friend of his was killed and Dillan almost died from that knife wound that he finally saw the light. Of course, joining the S.W.A.T. squad in L.A. was probably more dangerous than the gang, but I sure was proud of him when he made the team."

Holy Jesus, I thought. S.W.A.T.? No wonder the man had some scars. "I'm sure Olivia is proud of him, too."

He seemed taken aback, as though he'd never considered it.

"I think it's hard for parents to view their children as grown-ups," I said. "We're always their kids and so many parents see the child through a filter of parenthood. It's good sometimes to take a step back and see the adult, separated from the childhood memories." I smiled at Pop, who was chatting now with a portly man holding a champagne glass. "It was so hard on him when I was hospitalized. But now I think he doesn't see his little girl dealing with life, but a woman who's handling it just fine."

Mark regarded me thoughtfully. "You are handling it, aren't you?"

"I have to," I said simply. "It is what it is."

"Don't you wish you could have revenge?"

I considered the melting ice in my glass. "She's dead now. There's no one left to blame."

"What about Shaw Kelleher?" Dillan stepped around Mark to stand next to me.

Mark straightened. "What about him?"

"It's because of him that she hurt you." Dillan took a swallow from the bottle of beer held. "Do you blame him?"

"Not really. I know he's indirectly responsible, but I don't blame him."

"Maybe you should." Dillan regarded me, his face harsh and cold.

I sighed. "Dillan, I know you're pissed off at me

and I'm sorry. But Shaw is a part of my past, a part of my life. You're asking me to—"

"If he's such a good guy, why did he visit Tanya in the hospital?"

"What are you talking about?" I glanced at Mark, who shook his head as if to say *no idea.*

"I got the visitor logs," Dillan said. "Kelleher paid regular visits to her and they weren't an hour or two here and there. He stayed overnight in a visitor suite and she stayed with him." He regarded me steadily. "That's not the behavior of a man who's putting distance between himself and a woman who hurt the woman he loved."

I don't know why, but that hurt. Shaw had visited Tanya. He didn't visit me, but he visited her. "How do you know that? How did you get access to the visitor logs?"

"I know a guy who knows a guy."

I searched for an explanation but couldn't find one. "He insisted that his father help me," I said. "That's not the actions of a man who's guilty."

"Well, otherwise you might have sued him for more money than you're costing him. He bought you off cheap. A house and an allowance are less than what a lawsuit would have cost."

"Dillan," Mark said warningly. "That's rude."

"That's the truth," he snapped.

Olivia and Pop had joined us, standing with Mark, all of them staring at Dillan with varying expressions. Hers was worry. Mark's was anger. And Pop was confused. "What happened?" I asked. "Why are you angry? Why are you being such a shit to me?"

"Lilith." Pop's tone brooked no argument but,

stupid me, I tried.

"What?" I demanded. "He's being pushy."

"Your mother had her faults, but she taught you some manners. You're being rude. We're at a party and we don't disrespect the people there."

I sighed. "I hate when you pull the Mom card."

Pop put an arm around my shoulders and kissed my cheek. "I know. That's why it works."

I went to Olivia. "I'm sorry. Your son is being an asshole and I was rude." I peeked past her to Dillan, who glared at me. Then, slowly, he smiled.

"Yeah," he said grudgingly. "I was."

Olivia looped her arm through Pop's. "Let's let them work out their differences, shall we?"

"Dillan, I think you owe Miss Griffin an apology," Mark said stiffly.

I waved a hand. "He owes me a drink." I tugged on Dillan's arm. "Let's go." We walked away, dodging bean bag tosses that came our way. "I see what Olivia meant about her husband," I murmured, slipping my arm through Dillan's.

"Oh? What did she say?"

"She didn't say it, but I figured he was a tight-assed mean son of a bitch who thought the sun rose and set in his children." I gave Dillan's arm a shake. "His kids."

"Yeah, you got that right."

"I'm amazed she married him."

"You didn't know my father. Now there was a mean son of a bitch. Mark was strict, but he wasn't vicious." He glanced over his shoulder. "I know he loves Mom, so I guess I can't hate him too much."

"Hmm."

We got to the bar and I ordered another drink, this one light on the gin. Dillan led me around the side of the house to a relatively secluded side yard where several empty lawn chairs were in the shade of the neighbor's house. We sat and I was ready to launch into my apology when he said, "What about your Mom?"

"What?"

"Your dad mentioned she had faults."

"Oh. Yeah. She had a gambling problem. We're lucky she didn't get killed or get us killed. She racked up an impressive amount of debt."

"Wow. That's tough."

"We were lucky. An anonymous benefactor paid off her debts after I was attacked. I think people figured poor Pop had enough to deal with without having to face a debt collector." I rattled the ice in my drink before sipping, the glib lie sliding off my tongue. "Now that I've shared my little secret, what about yours?"

"Hmm?" Dillan regarded me guilelessly, his eyes wide and innocent.

"You've had a bee up your butt since before I went out with Shaw last night. Why? What happened?"

"You know, if I had a bee up my butt, I'd be dead."

I leveled a glare at him. "Speak."

He stood, staring at the party in the backyard then turning back to me. "It's my stepsister. Daddy's Little Princess. She's getting an award for something in St. Louis. Mom and Mark are going to the ceremony."

"Why do you dislike her?"

"Because she's a slut," he said flatly. "She's slept her way to the top and relied on men every step of the way. She's fooled Mark all her life. She slept around in high school. She tried to seduce me. When that didn't work, she went after my friends. She's never worked an honest hour in her life."

So much bitterness. So much anger. I imagined his childhood. His own father, drunk and abusive. Olivia and he finally escaped. She married Mark, but Mark had his own standards for what he expected in a boy and Dillan didn't measure up to that. But Sabrina did. Sabrina did no wrong.

I stood, too, and put my arm around his waist. His body was rigid, so full of anger that it was like holding wood or steel. "Thank you. You've shown me how lucky I am in my own father. Pop and I don't always get along, but I know he loves me and respects me. That means a lot."

Dillan drew back to peer into my eyes. "I know how he feels," he said softly.

I wasn't ready for intimacy like that. Years of solitude had made me immune to romance. At least, that's what I told myself. I eased away from him. "Your mother must have been the only person you counted on and when she sided with Mark, I'm sure it hurt. I know how much she loves him. I'm sure she was torn about how to help you."

"You and she have a special relationship, I guess."

"We do. I wasn't supposed to move. If I moved, I might open the scabs. And I was covered with them. It was worst on my right side, but some acid splashed on my left chest and neck. I think those itched the most. I suppose the pain of the other wounds was so intense I couldn't sense the healing, but those smaller wounds itched so bad when they healed. Your mother sat by my bedside and rested her hand over my left hand. Whenever I raised it to let her know the itching was horrible, she'd start to talk."

I closed my eyes briefly, still seeing that hospital room, the monitors and the lights overhead, the tantalizing view out the window of the normal world. The injuries were bad enough, but it was the future that tortured me. How would I live? Who would love me? How would I survive?

"She's a special person," he said. "I wanted to like Mark because I knew he was important to her. But maybe you were right. Maybe I don't know anything about loving people. I sure have screwed things up in my life up to now."

I didn't hear any self-pity. What I heard was honest confusion and I suppose that's what prompted me to speak the way I did. "Dillan, you were right about me. I am afraid of being close to anyone." I chose my words carefully, not sure how to explain it to him. "I was beautiful once. I was the girl that people paused to stare at. I had a beautiful body, a perfect complexion, a happy smile. I was the girl that lit up the room when she came in."

"You still are," he said. "It's something that—"

"Let me finish. I wasn't only scarred. I was changed in a way that never heals. I lost that confidence. I lost my self-assurance. I lost all sense of who I was and who I might be." I saw only sympathy in his dark eyes. "I don't know if a man can truly understand it, but for many women, their self-worth is tied to their appearance. It's taken me years to recognize that I am still beautiful in spite of what was done. I'm afraid if I expose myself to someone, I'll have to face the fact that I'm deluding myself."

"You aren't." He touched my face, his fingers

tracing the line of my jaw. "You aren't deluding yourself. You still light up a room. Only now you're a beautiful woman not a girl. A woman who is far more appealing than that sexy young babe would ever be." He leaned forward and his lips brushed mine. "At least to me."

A rumble of thunder in the distance penetrated the haze that enveloped me. "Damn," I whispered. "Thunder."

"Hmm." Dillan stepped closer to me. Only inches separated us.

"I have to go." I stepped back.

"Why?" He took a step forward, reaching for me.

"The grow lights." I dug my car keys out of my skirt pocket. "I'd better get home and get them disconnected." I turned to gaze around to the backyard. "I don't see Pop or Olivia. I need to tell them I'm going."

Dillan leapt up on the chair. "I see 'em. I'll tell them we're leaving. I'll meet you at the car."

"But you don't have to—"

He was already off, trotting through the crowded yard. I followed at a more sedate pace, dodging people with plates of food to get to the front of the house. By the time I got to my car, parked halfway down the street, Dillan was running to catch up to me.

"Mom is starting to hustle people indoors." He pointed ahead. "My bike's there. I'll follow you. Get going, I think a storm is moving in."

I didn't pause but got behind the wheel and within ten minutes we were back at my house. The sky west of us was an ominous black, with clouds pushing each other around. I parked in the garage as the first raindrops splattered down.

Dillan parked next to me, in Pop's spot. "I'll get the tarps. You unplug the cords." He ran out the door leading to the yard. I was a few steps behind him. He went right, to the storage shed, and I went left to the back stoop. I reached the exterior electric outlet, luckily covered by a small metal canopy. As soon as I pulled out the plug, the rain poured down in buckets, immediately drenching me. I could barely see Dillan as he staggered to me, the bulky tarps cascading over his arms.

"Let's go!" he shouted, heading into Labbie.

We couldn't take any shortcuts with the heavy tarps. We ran along the path and when one tarp slipped out his grasp, I picked it up, dragging it behind me. Just as we got to the center, hail started. Dillan flung a tarp high, draping it over one of the rose arbors. The thud of hailstones on the heavy plastic fabric was like drumbeats. I tried to do the same, but I didn't have enough flexibility to get a good toss.

"Cover the lamps," he yelled. "I'll get the arbors."

I dragged the grow lights together in a group and put them under the metal firepit which I had emptied a few days earlier. I dragged one of the tarps over it then went to help Dillan with the last arbor. I had no idea if they would protect the rose bushes from hail damage, but it was the best we could do.

I stood back to survey the coverage and that's when I saw the blood streaking Dillan's arms. "You're hurt!"

He checked his arm then he pointed to me. "You are, too."

I looked down. My formerly opaque clothing was

almost transparent with the rain, the lightweight linen plastered to my body. The blouse was torn in several spots and there were small dots of blood where the hail cut me. "Let's get inside before we get cut up any worse!" I led the way through the labyrinth, taking a couple of the shortcuts through the yews that I thought he could negotiate.

It was a tight fit but soon we emerged in the back yard. We dashed back to the garage and stood inside, watching the deluge. "I think your mother's barbeque is canceled," I said, talking loudly to be heard above the storm. The hail had abated, but there were still occasional little pea shapes hitting the concrete with solid splats.

"Nah. The party will move inside and the grill will move to the garage. A little rain won't stop Mom." He gave himself a good shake like a dog ridding itself of water.

I laughed and did the same, tousling my hair then lifting and shaking my blouse and skirt. "Thanks for the help. I would never have gotten the arbors covered. Come on inside. We can dry off." I closed the garage door then went to the house door.

"You need to lock that, you know," Dillan said when we entered my PT space.

"I know, but we lost the key and then we never got around to putting on a new lock." I kicked off my shoes and padded across the room to the mudroom. Dillan kicked off his sandals then followed me.

"Hey, guy," I heard him say behind me.

I looked over my shoulder. The cat peered out at us from the powder room, his baleful glare telling me how happy he was to see us.

Dillan squatted and extended his hand. I expected the beast to hiss at him but instead he came forward cautiously and sniffed Dillan's fingers. I sighed. "What are you, the beast-master?"

Dillan rubbed the monster's ears and the animal purred so loud it almost drowned out the sound of the rain. "You gotta know where to rub," he murmured. He gave me with a mischievous grin. "If you know what I mean."

Oh, yes. I did know what he meant. "Grab a beer if you want one," I said. "I'm going to fix a drink, sit on the front porch, and watch the rain."

"Sounds like a plan."

I went to the kitchen and mixed a gin and tonic—heavy on the gin. I spied the blinking light on my answering machine and played the message. "Miss Griffin, I'm Joseph Ewing. I'm the attorney of record for the Blake Kelleher estate. It's urgent that I speak with you as soon as possible. I'm called out of town on personal business, but I hope to be back by the end of the week. Please call my office to set up an appointment." He recited a phone number.

Well, damn. If he wanted to give me dire news about my allowance, I didn't want it to spoil my weekend. I'd call the guy on Monday. I copied the number on a slip of paper and deleted the message.

Dillan and I rounded up some chips and dips and soon were sitting on the front porch, watching the rain, which had shifted to a soothing drizzle. I put my Bluetooth speaker in the window behind us and queued up random tunes on my iPod. The Backstreet Boys crooned in the background.

"Well, we can't sit when that's playing," he said,

setting his beer can on the end table. "Care to dance?" He pulled me into his arms.

We stepped around the porch to "I Want It That Way," with Dillan giving me an occasional spin. He was a good dancer, leading me surely in a modified two-step. His touch was light on my right hand and his left hand, resting on my waist, gently moved me in time to the music. That song gave way to "Islands in the Stream" and he increased our pace, our bodies pressed closely together. I felt the play of the muscles in his thighs, the bunched power in his back where my hand rested.

The Moody Blues were next with "Had To Fall In Love." Dillan pulled me closer and we swayed in time to the music, his leg stepped between mine when he moved us around my small porch. When he slowed then stopped, it seemed the most natural thing in the world to raise my face and have his face lower to mine.

"Hey, Boss." The kiss began tentatively and hesitant, but it changed quickly. Warmth surrounded me, but I shivered, too. My skin, over-sensitive to touch, tingled with erotic sensation. Memories awakened, memories of soft mornings, a male body and my body's response.

I put my arms around him and the kiss deepened. When he pulled away to kiss my neck, I let my head drop back, unmindful of my scars, unmindful of my damp clothing, unmindful of anything but the sensations he awakened. I pushed my hands under his shirt, feeling hard muscle, scars, and skin.

"Before we go too far," he murmured, "do we need to talk about birth control and all that stuff? Because if we do, I might need to inspect the contents of my wallet."

He sounded so bemused I grinned. "I'm not at risk for pregnancy, if that's a worry. I had to have a hysterectomy years ago because of blood poisoning after the attack. And I've been abstinent for years, so I don't think you have to worry about that."

"Whew. I just had a physical and I know I'm okay in that respect." He lowered his head, nuzzling against my neck. "I suggest we move inside before we get to a point where I don't want to stop."

"Maybe we can go to your place. Otherwise Pop might come home and get a surprise."

"Nope. He won't be home tonight." Dillan pulled me against him and I felt the rigid outline of his erection.

"Hmm?"

"I had a chat with Mom. I suggested we might like some privacy. I think your dad might stay overnight at their house tonight."

"In that case—" I pulled his face to mine. I felt the door against my back, his body holding me in place. Years fell away and I forgot my injuries, forgot my scars. I was woman, he was man, and I wanted him— now. "Let's go." I fumbled the door handle, while Dillan pressed kisses against my neck.

"Lilith?"

I looked to my right, at the steps leading to the house. Shaw stood there, watching us.

Chapter Twelve

I was so awash in lust it took a second for the sight to register. "What are you doing here?" I blurted.

"We were meeting today, remember?" He shifted his attention to Dillan, and his mouth tightened. "Apparently you didn't. I thought—"

His face told me what he thought. My first reaction was annoyance. Why now? Why show up here in his Brooks Brothers casual slacks, pale gray shirt, and sockless loafers. Shaw was dressed like an ad from *Vanity Fair* or *Town and Country.* All that was missing was a yacht for him to step onto.

I peeled myself away from Dillan, who kept his hand on my back, steadying me when I swayed. "We discussed perhaps getting together." I struggled to keep my voice calm. "We didn't have any definite plans."

"But—" Shaw took one tentative step closer. "Lilith, we just found each other again after so long. I thought you felt the same."

Dillan's hand on my back spasmed, as though he clenched his fingers. His gaze was fixed on Shaw and Dillan's expression was speculative, evaluating—and cautious.

"Shaw, I'm glad we saw each other again, but you're a part of my past."

Shaw locked eyes with Dillan's. "And he's your

future?"

How did I answer that? I didn't have to worry about it, though. Before I came up with a reply, Dillan said, "Yes, I am."

I couldn't interpret what I saw in Shaw's eyes. Anger, certainly, but also something else, something cold and scheming.

Scheming? I shook my head. Scheming about what?

"I'm sorry I misinterpreted your affection," he said stiffly. "Perhaps we can talk later, in private." Shaw smiled, but it was bitter. "Tomorrow? Perhaps you'll have time for me then?" The stare he directed at Dillan was insulting.

I leaned into Dillan's hand, trying to force him to be still. "I'm busy. I'm giving a speech in St. Louis."

"Really?" He made it sound like an impossibility, as if I were incapable of public speaking. That little twist to his voice irked me, which I suppose is why I did a bit of bragging.

"I'm the keynote speaker for the Vitriolage Victims annual conference. I'll be busy in the morning working on my speech and in the afternoon, we'll go to the conference so I can give my speech. We won't get back until late tomorrow night."

"We?"

"Yes, we," Dillan said flatly.

"I see." Shaw absorbed the information with no visible reaction. "Fine. I'll be in touch, Lilith." He wheeled about and went down the steps, moving quickly but carefully lest he trip on the rough stone.

I watched him go then turned when Dillan said, "I don't trust him."

"Forget him." I leaned against Dillan and he put his arm around my shoulders. "Where were we?" I asked.

Dillan reached past me and opened the front door. "As I recall, we were going inside so we didn't shock the neighbors."

"I don't have many close neighbors," I pointed out.

"Let's say I'd rather not have an audience of any kind." He pulled me into the foyer and closed the door behind me. "Now let's see. I think we were…"

I wrapped my arms around his neck and our lips met. I was unaccustomed to a man with a beard. It was prickly but so masculine. His body was solid and hot, and it seemed like wherever I touched, he was firm. Some parts, like the part where he pressed against my hips, was *very* firm.

We somehow made our way up the stairs without stumbling, shedding a few articles of clothing in my bathroom and on the bedroom floor. By the time we got to the bed, I had on my bra and panties and he wore only his shorts. The scars on his body rippled when he lay next to me where I stretched out on top of the covers.

I traced the scars bisecting his body. "I thought mine were bad," I murmured. "Was this one infected?"

"Yeah, I didn't get to a hospital for a few days after that one." He lay on my left, his head propped up on his bent arm. His gaze swept over my body and I struggled to keep myself still, not covering up like I wanted to do. It wasn't so much the bunched tissue and the scars, but my body, which was no longer supple. I was still slender and shapely, but my breasts had sag to them, and my stomach was no longer firm.

The typical worries of a middle-aged woman, I

decided. It was so long since I even considered myself a female that the realities of aging hadn't bothered me. He shifted his gaze to my face and I forced myself to confess what I had kept hidden, even from Pop. "There are guys who like deformed women," I whispered. "I met a guy once on one of the support forums." I shuddered, remembering the man's obsessed fascination with my injuries. "He kept asking me about my scars and how it felt."

"You're not deformed." Dillan touched my right arm lightly, his fingers brushing over the puckered flesh. "But I am sort of obsessed with your scars." He peered up at me. "I'm afraid I might hurt you."

"I don't know if you will. I've only had sex a few times since the attack." I swallowed, hard. "It wasn't pleasant. I thought he cared about me, but—" I avoided Dillan's perceptive attention. "I suppose he thought I was desperate, so I'd let him do anything he wanted."

Dillan's hand stilled on my arm. "Did he hurt you?" I heard simmering anger in his tone.

"No. I only saw him once or twice." I grimaced. "Once I figured out he was fascinated with my injuries, not me, that killed any attraction. I think he moved on to another woman in the forum. I read later that they got married." I tried a tentative smile. "I suppose one woman's loss is another woman's gain."

"I'm glad you were discriminating." He leaned over and brushed gentle kisses against my arm. That skin couldn't react but everything else in me reacted, including my nipples, which hardened to painful fullness.

"It's only…" I sighed. "I don't want to disappoint you."

He moved closer, his hand gently touching my breast. "You can't disappoint me. You're one of the most beautiful people I know and I don't mean that in a physical sense. That first day, when you told me about the acid attack, you were so matter of fact about it. I've never met anybody who could speak so calmly about something so horrific. And it wasn't a fake calm, either." Dillan cupped my breast, his thumb rubbing over my nipple. "Besides, I'm not normal either. Remember?"

I saw only understanding in his gray eyes. Take a chance? Protect myself? A tiny part of my brain screamed to stop, to move away from him and not let my heart be broken. But a louder voice was saying, *Go ahead. This might be a once in a lifetime chance. You're fifty-five, scarred, and this man doesn't care about any of that. Go for it.*

"Well, I guess you'll fit right in." I slid my hand up his arm.

He pulled me closer. "Let's try me on for size and see if you're right." He lowered his head and our lips touched.

Oh, yeah. He fit.

He fit just fine.

****

It was getting dark when I awoke from a doze. Dillan was gone, his side of the bed empty. I stretched, wincing when some under-used muscles protested. It was years since I'd been loved so thoroughly.

The bedroom door opened, and the cat's head poked through the crack. "Hey, Beast," I murmured.

He eyed me cautiously then came in, muscling open the door and sauntering around the perimeter to one of the windows above the back yard. He sprang up on the sill, glancing at me as though to gauge my reaction. I smelled a faint whiff of tea tree oil coming from the bedraggled bandage on his tail stump.

I waved a languid hand. "Go ahead. I don't care." At that point, I didn't care about anything except enjoying this sated feeling that made me limp.

"I see you've made friends." Dillan entered the room, a tray in his hands. He was barefoot with one of my bath towels wrapped around his middle. "I thought we might like some fuel."

"Fuel? For what?" I propped myself up on my left elbow to regard him.

He waggled his eyebrows. "For whatever might come up, so to speak."

I laughed and scooted over to make room for him on the bed. The tray held a bottle of beer, a glass of wine, some cheese, crackers, and slices of salami. My stomach rumbled, reminding me I hadn't eaten anything since early that morning. "What time is it?" I asked, taking the glass of wine he held out to me.

"About six. It quit raining." Dillan took the bottle of beer then set the tray on the bed. The cat, alert to the possibility of food, craned his neck to peer around the headboard, his nose wrinkling.

Dillan stretched out on the bed, the tray between us. "Here's to thunderstorms," he said, raising his bottle.

We clicked glassware and dug into the food, talking about nothing in particular. At some point the cat padded over the pillow to sit next to Dillan's head, his gaze alternating between the food plate and me. He was surprisingly polite, waiting until I broke off a bite of salami, which I set on the pillowcase next to him.

"You might regret that," Dillan warned. "You don't want to spoil him."

"I think Pop already has." I stretched out my hand and the cat sniffed it then gave my fingers a tentative lick. I rubbed his ears and he purred, a look of blissful contentment on his lopsided face.

"I know how he feels," Dillan said, his hand sliding over my bare hip. "Like I died and went to heaven."

I thought about making a flip response but the warm love in his dark eyes stopped me. I didn't know how to reply. I was out of practice with romance. "Well, you know what they say when somebody asks is this heaven. No, it's Iowa." I gave the cat a tiny taste of Swiss cheese. "I don't know a damn thing about baseball, but I know *Field of Dreams.*"

"You and everybody else in Iowa." Dillan finished his beer and set the bottle on the nightstand. "I'm going out to do a perimeter check."

"A what?" I watched him stand and drop the towel on the floor. His body was lean and muscled, the scars standing out in stark relief against his golden skin.

"Perimeter check. I want to make sure everything's locked up tight." He tugged on his shorts. "Where are my shoes?"

"I think they got left downstairs." I pushed myself upright. "I'll go with you."

"Oh, no you won't." Dillan leaned over and kissed me. "You'll lay here and wait for me to come back. Then we'll pick up where we left off."

"That's bold talk." I slid my hand over his chest and toyed with the snap of his shorts. "Are you sure about that?"

He slapped my hand away. "No distractions. I'm on duty."

"You know, my physical therapist is always telling me to exercise my leg to keep it flexible." I rolled over on my back and extended my right leg. "I might get used to this. I think this is an excellent way to exercise."

He ran his hand over my leg. "Any time, Boss. You holler. After I do a perimeter check." Before I could protest, he was out the door, racing down the hall. "I'll be back in a minute!"

I expected the cat to follow him, but instead Beast sauntered to the end of the bed and plopped down, sticking one leg in the air to begin a vigorous bathing routine. I decided he had the right idea, so I went into the shower.

This afternoon was certainly not what I expected four days ago when Dillan Lyall showed up on my doorstep. Four days? I paused my soaping. Good Lord, what kind of slut was I, to fall into bed with a man I knew for less than a week?

Even as I thought it, I dismissed it. Being with Dillan felt right. I hadn't been asking for a man in my life. Hell, I'd reconciled myself to never having one. Now here he was. We went together so well, not only physically but—

I heard the bathroom door open. "Are you trying to give me a hint?" Dillan called. "Am I stinky?"

"Not at all. I was hoping you'd get in here and help me clean up."

The shower curtain was pulled aside just enough for him to peek in at me. "Your wish is my command, Boss." He shucked off his shorts and stepped in behind me to enfold me in his arms. "Tell me where you need it."

I leaned into his embrace. "Everywhere," I whispered.

****

I slept well that night, which was shocking given how much physical activity I participated in. Sometime around dawn I heard a phone ringing. I awoke and saw Dillan, naked, standing in the bedroom doorway with his mobile phone to his ear. He spoke too softly for me to hear.

When I tried to sit up, I discovered Beast was curled against my backside, his warm body pressed into my legs. I gave up and lay back down.

"Who was that?" I whispered when Dillan rejoined me.

He kissed my cheek. "Nothing. Go to sleep."

I had no trouble taking his advice. When I woke again, it was at first light to see Dillan standing by the bed, fully dressed. "Sleeping Beauty," he whispered, bending over to give me a lingering kiss.

"Where are you going so early?"

"I've got some stuff to take care of before we go to St. Louis."

"St. Louis?" I stretched and yawned. The cat jumped from the bed and padded over to Dillan to rub against his legs.

"You have a speech to give tonight, remember? I'm driving." His dark eyes were unreadable this morning.

I sensed he was hiding something, but I couldn't figure out what. I didn't want to worry. I wanted to bask in the afterglow, so I ignored that slight tug of concern. "I almost forgot. You have that effect on a girl."

He smiled. "That's good to know. I'll be back after lunch and we can take off then. You said you wanted to get there by five o'clock, right? I figured two, maybe three hours of driving with construction and traffic."

"That will work. There's an hour of drinks and hors d'oeuvres then my speech and dancing with some more finger food. We can leave after my speech if you'd like. Don't forget it's a black-tie affair. We can change there." I had no idea if he had a dress suit, but I figured it didn't hurt to let him know I'd be dressed to the nines.

"I'll dust off my tux." He lifted my hand and kissed my palm. "And we will have dancing. I'll see you later."

I watched him go, the cat trotting behind him like a little shadow. It wasn't until I heard his cycle in the distance that I realized I was alone. Didn't I need a bodyguard anymore?

Apparently not. I showered, dressed in capris and a shirt, then made breakfast. The day was cool, with a marvelous northerly breeze. The storm pushed the humidity away and now it was glorious summertime, sunny and pleasant.

As I was eating my toast, Pop returned home. When I asked him where he was the night before, he gave me a smug smile and said he was going to take a nap. The guys from Dillan's work crew showed up so I couldn't quiz him about his whereabouts.

I got them to work tidying up after last night's storm and finishing the mulching in the back. I spent the morning working on my speech and gazing out the window, wondering where Dillan was, wondering what he was thinking, and wondering what the hell I had gotten myself into.

I stopped at noon and went upstairs to inspect my gown for the evening. I never tried to hide my scars when I went to events like this. That would have been hypocritical. Besides, this was one of the few times I felt comfortable showing them. After all, these people knew what it was like.

I pulled the dark green dress from the clothing bag and examined it. It was heavy rayon fabric with a halter neckline, bare shoulders and back, and a long skirt slit up the left side. I went to my dresser and got out my only 'fine' jewelry, a single large emerald on a silver chain, matching earrings, and a diamond-and-emerald bracelet. Shaw gave it to me when we got engaged. Silver, low-heeled shoes rounded out the ensemble.

I tucked the shoes and jewelry into a bag and put everything into the bottom of the clothing bag. I took it downstairs, pausing by Pop's door to knock. "Time to get going," I said. "You can change clothes when we get there." I heard his affirming mumble and I decided he was alert enough.

I made a couple of sandwiches and was sitting down to mine when my mobile phone rang. It was Olivia.

"I apologize for ducking out yesterday," I said as soon as she identified herself. "Dillan and I had to handle some things at the house."

There was a short pause. "Well, that's fine, dear. We understand." Before I could elaborate further, she hurried on. "Would you mind if Mark and I attend your talk? Dillan mentioned it. We're going to St. Louis because Sabrina is receiving an award on Friday. I thought we'd go early and hear your speech. Do you mind?"

I didn't know how to say what I thought needed to be said. "It might not be the kind of event that your husband would be comfortable with. It's for victims and their caregivers. It can be difficult for people who haven't had to deal with people like me. And believe me, some of the victims have far worse injuries than mine."

"I know," she said. "And it may be uncomfortable for him. But it's an important part of who you are and you're an important part of Dillan's life. I think it's time Mark started supporting him."

"Olivia, I think you're misconstruing Dillan's affection," I said hastily. "I mean, yes, he and I have formed a friendship, but I doubt if I'm an important part of his life."

"You are, dear. You just don't know it yet. And he may not know it yet either, now that I think of it. Anyway, you're important to me, and I want to hear you speak. Is that okay?"

What could I say? "Of course, if you'd like to." I gave her directions to the hotel where the conference was being held. "I'll see you there tonight."

"Thank you, Lilith. For everything."

Pop came into the room as I finished the call. "Mark and Olivia are coming tonight," I told him.

"Yeah, she mentioned something yesterday." He sat at the kitchen island, yawning. "I had a late night. I'm not as young as I used to be."

I raised an eyebrow. "You and me both."

He caught my bemused look and burst out

laughing. I heard a car pulling into the driveway and I went to the front door. Dillan stepped out of a dark blue sedan. "Where's your bike?" I asked, joining him at the front porch.

"I borrowed Mark's Dadmobile. I figured it would be more comfortable on the road than your SUV. Are the guys here?"

I jerked a thumb over my shoulder. "In back, finishing up. They're miracle workers. Everything is great."

"I'll have a quick talk with them then we can get going. I put my duds in the trunk, if you want to add yours." Dillan pressed the car keys into my hand then brushed my lips with a quick kiss. "I'm looking forward to a night of dining and dancing."

"It's a pretty low-key affair," I warned.

"That's okay. I'm a low-key kind of guy." He winked and went around the garage to the side gate.

I went back inside and got Pop moving. Dillan rejoined us at the car a few minutes later. "I told the guys to lock up when they leave," he said, settling my bag and Pop's into the trunk. "I figured I'd drive. That way you can review your speech." He glanced at Pop. "And you can nap."

Pop shot him a mock glare. "Are you saying I'm old?"

"I'm saying you're tired. I heard about your partying last night."

Pop sighed. "Well, you're right about that."

"How are Mark and Olivia getting to St. Louis if you're driving their car?" I settled into the front seat.

"They're going with friends and staying overnight at a hotel near where your conference is being held."

"That's convenient."

Dillan backed the car out. "Trust Mom to arrange things. I figured I'd take I-380 south until it changes to Highway 27, right?"

"Yep. It's straight south. Four-lane divided highway all the way. The hotel is on the north side of town, so we don't have to hassle too much with traffic."

"Is this like a national conference or something?"

"This is the North American one. The organization has similar conferences in South America, Asia, India, and other spots." I gazed out my window at the bucolic neighborhood, remembering a couple of the international conferences I'd attended. As a counselor in the support forums, I always wanted advice on how to help others, and these conferences gave me the opportunity to talk to other people in similar situations. "I should warn you. There will be some people there who are badly injured, grotesquely so. It can be hard to be around people like that."

"Yeah, I did some reading. I think I'm ready."

I doubted he was. No one could be ready for such a thing, but I couldn't help that. I opened my computer tablet and reviewed my notes for my speech, glancing now and then at my driver. Dillan seemed preoccupied on the drive, keeping his attention on the road. Was he as surprised as me about last night? What did he feel? Was he glad it happened? Worried about it? Yes, we had fun and it felt great, but—now what?

One day at a time, I reminded myself. A cardinal rule during recovery from a trauma was to take it a day at a time. Don't stumble over the future before it arrives. Enjoy today because it may be all you have.

We got to the hotel and the conference organizers

directed us to a suite where we changed our clothes. When I emerged from the side bedroom, Dillan was standing staring out the window, his hands in his pants pockets. He wore a charcoal gray suit, pale gray shirt, black dress pants, and a black-and-gray striped tie. The overall effect was *studly older guy, ready for a night on the town.*

I handed Pop the emerald bracelet. "Help me with this, would you?"

"He cleans up good," Pop muttered, bending his head to examine the clasp. "I feel like a poor cousin next to him, though."

"You'll be the handsomest seventy-something in the room."

He grinned. "I'll probably be the only seventy-something in the room but that's okay. There you go."

I shifted my wrist, testing the clasp. Dillan turned and his eyes widened. "Wow. That's one hell of a dress." His eyes went to my jewelry. "And some impressive rocks."

"Thank you, sir." I settled the lace shawl I brought over my shoulders. "I believe cocktails are waiting for us."

Dillan stuck out his arm and Pop did the same. Laughing, I looped my arms through both of theirs and we left the suite. When we arrived at the main ballroom, the place was awash in people. I estimated maybe five hundred attendees were there, some with caregivers and some alone. I waved to those I knew and was soon separated from the men when I became embroiled in conversations.

I checked Dillan now and again to make sure he was coping. Pop was steering him toward folks we knew, people Pop had bonded with during my initial recovery. Dillan appeared to be managing fine, but I saw his strained expression now and then when he spoke with some of the victims. I knew how he felt. I was one of the lucky ones.

Someone tapped me on the shoulder. Olivia smiled at me. She wore a black dress with gold embroidery that was stylish and modern. "I'm glad I found you in this crowd." She tucked her arm in mine and we moved to one side, away from the crush of people.

"I'm glad you found me, too. Where's your husband?" I peered around us but didn't see Mark Eames.

"Your father swooped in and grabbed him." Olivia pointed to our right. "He's handling this very well. I don't think I give Mark enough credit. Of course, he admires your father a great deal and I suspect Mark is learning from him. Your father is a special man."

We both watched Pop, who stood with Mark, talking with two men I didn't know. They were badly disfigured, one man wearing dark glasses that rested on what remained of his nose. The other had a hunched posture that told me the acid had eaten through to his bones. Neither Pop nor Mark gave any indication that the men in front of them were injured. They were chatting, drinks in hand, like guys around the water cooler.

"I honestly don't know if Pop even sees their injuries," I commented.

"Oh, he does. He sees it and he accepts it and then he moves on to get to know the person behind the scars. Your father has a unique outlook on life. I don't believe he knows how to hold a grudge." Olivia beamed at me.

"You're like him, you know. The acorn doesn't fall far from the tree."

"Me?" I shook my head. "I can hold a grudge."

"Oh, you can, but you don't. You always see the best a person has to offer. If you can't forgive, at least you don't get bitter. You've made a beautiful life for yourself and you don't even pause to think *what if.* That's a rare talent."

A tone chimed overhead. "Saved by the bell," I said. "I'm up, I think."

Olivia and I wended our way through the crowd to the tables set up in front of the stage and the podium. Dillan already stood by one chair, his hand on the chair back next to it. He smiled when he saw me approaching. "I saved you a seat," he called.

Olivia left me to join Mark at another nearby table where Pop already sat. A young girl in an ill-fitting black dress approached the table where Dillan stood. She leaned heavily on her cane, peering up at him while she asked a question. He pulled out a chair for her on his left. I glimpsed the appalling facial burns that made the right side of her head appear almost melted. She sat awkwardly, fumbling with the cane and having difficulty getting her skirt managed. Dillan helped her, sliding the chair into place.

Dillan said something. She glanced up at him and smiled. For an instant, I thought I could see the young woman she should have been, gazing at a handsome man who was paying attention to her. I saw no hint of pity or disgust on Dillan's face, only interest and concern that she was accommodated.

I believe it was at that moment that I knew I was in love with Dillan.

Chapter Thirteen

I draped my shawl over the chair on Dillan's right. "Save a place for me." I smiled at him and then to the girl on his left.

"Always." He took my hand, resting on his shoulder, and kissed it. "Knock 'em dead, Boss."

I made my way to the short stairs leading up to the stage and the people seated behind the podium. Public speaking held no worries for me but walking in a long dress with swirling skirt did. I moved cautiously until I got to the chairs then I took my seat and awaited my turn.

The conference organizers made a few announcements, then I was introduced, my biography read and my work in the support forums mentioned. I stepped forward to speak, glancing at the few notes I had jotted to remind me what to say.

I spoke about my attack and finding the support forums where people helped me during the darkest time of my recovery. "It wasn't right after being hurt," I said. "No, the big problems came years later, when I discovered how completely my life was derailed. I had to decide whether to be angry about that derailment or try to enjoy the scenery along the detour I was forced to take." Later, it seemed a natural step for me to be a counselor, too, and to help others who were struggling to accept what happened to them.

"It's important to understand that nothing that happened is your fault, but everything that happens from this moment on does belong to you. You can't change the past, but you can shape your future. You have resources and I beg you to take advantage of them. We're fortunate here in this country and on this continent. Vitriolage is seldom the first assault method used, unlike in developing countries where it happens with appalling frequency. We have exceptional medical facilities, an excellent support network, and people who are ready to help those who are victims."

Now came a tricky part in my speech, but I felt strongly that it had to be said. Olivia had made me see this and I wanted others to understand, too. I stared out at the crowd, at the wounded people and the people with them who suffered, too, when they saw their loved ones in pain.

"We have been victims," I said. "We were victims. But we don't have to continue to be victims. We can move past what happened to us and be more than just survivors of vicious attacks. It's hard, I know, but don't dwell on what happened. You are more than a survivor. You are a person with a future ahead of you. You have life ahead of you and your time as a victim is in the past."

I smiled at Dillan and then to Pop, who sat at a nearby table. "Some people will stare at you and pity you or find you disgusting. You're lucky. You have a sure-fire way to know the true character of a person by how they treat you. Find those people who will love and support you. Then go out there and live the best life you can. It's there. You only need to embrace it."

I took a step back and raised my arms, embracing everyone in the room in a metaphorical hug. The applause sounded genuine, which was gratifying, and it lasted longer than I expected. I'd been nervous about denying people their right to be a victim. Some people embraced it, using it as an excuse to avoid the difficulties of living with their injuries. It was a hard lesson to learn and one that took me years to master. If I could share even a bit of that with others, then it wasn't in vain.

I accepted thanks from the people on the stage then I made my way back to the steps. Dillan waited for me and he extended his hand, helping me navigate the steps without tangling in my skirt. He escorted me back to the table and draped my shawl over my shoulders, his hands lingering on my exposed arms.

"Great speech," he said, kissing my cheek before I sat down. "I didn't know you volunteered. That must be tough somctimcs."

"It is hard when you can't convince someone that they can have a somewhat normal life. Your mother helped me so much to understand that. I owe it to her to try to help others."

"Miss Griffen?"

I peered over my shoulder. The young girl who'd been sitting next to Dillan stood there. I held out my hand. "Please, call me Lilith."

"I'm Melanie." She gave my hand a tentative shake. Her hand was badly burned so it was probably painful. "Thank you for such a nice speech. I've read your posts on the forums. It's nice to know you're as real as you seemed."

"Thank you." Music began playing softly, the band

on the far side of the ballroom launching into "Wind Beneath My Wings."

"May I have this dance, Melanie?" Dillan stood and held out his hand.

"Oh. I thought—won't you and Miss Griffen dance?" The girl seemed panicked, as though I might accuse her of stealing Dillan.

"We'll dance later. Right now, I think some fans want to talk to her." He nodded to a group of people headed our way. "Let's take a spin around the dance floor so I don't have to hang around like a dead weight." Dillan gently pulled the girl toward the middle of the room where a few couples were venturing out.

I was soon the center of conversation as people stopped by the table to congratulate me on my speech. I occasionally glimpsed Dillan, who danced with the girl and then with Olivia then another woman I didn't know. The girl, Melanie, danced with some other men before taking a new seat across the room.

I finally slipped away and joined Dillan near the table where appetizers were laid out. "Now that I'm done with my speech, I can eat," I said, piling a plate with cheese, little meatballs, and fruit.

"You find a table and I'll find us something to drink." He handed me his plate and headed for the bar in the corner. I tucked into the food, relaxing now that my stint was finally over. When Dillan returned to the table, his phone rang. He set his glass of beer and my glass of wine on the table and moved off to one side, his hand pressed over his free ear to hear above the crowd noise.

I nibbled on my food and watched him while he listened. His previous preoccupation or worry seemed to have dissipated the farther we went from home. As he spoke on the phone, he visibly relaxed, his shoulders lowering. He smiled, as if the words he was hearing were confirmation of something he'd be waiting for.

He rejoined me, tucking his phone into an interior suit coat pocket. "You look like a man who got good news," I commented.

"I did, in a way." Dillan took a sip of beer and speared a meatball with a toothpick. "The Kelleher funeral was today."

I leaned back in my chair. "My God, I forgot about that. I think Shaw mentioned something about it earlier in the week."

"It was this afternoon. Apparently there was a big crowd of people there. Blake Kelleher was pretty well known." Dillan watched me while he spoke as if waiting for a reaction from me.

I loaded up a cracker with cheese and a dab of spicy mustard. "Why is that good news?"

"Because Shaw Kelleher was there."

"Of course he was. It's his father."

"That means he's not here, disrupting our fun."

I almost choked on the food I was swallowing. "Hmpf?" I managed to croak. "Is that what you were worried about?"

"Yep. I was afraid he might come after us. You saw the way he reacted when he found you and me together."

I washed down my bite with wine. "Jealous and upset. Although why he'd be jealous, I don't know. It's not like I mean anything to him. It's been years since he probably even thought about me."

"It still bugged me. You never know with someone

like him."

"Someone like who? Shaw? He's a rich playboy without a care in the world."

Dillan took another swallow of beer. "Yeah, maybe." The band launched into "Had to Fall in Love with You." "They're playing our song. Come on. I promised you some dancing." He led me out to the dance floor and put his arm around my waist, pulling me against him.

"Wow. What are the odds they'd play that song?"

"Pretty good if you slip the band leader a fifty." Dillan spun us around the dance floor, my skirt swirling around our legs. I relaxed in his arms, knowing he'd watch out for us. It was a heady feeling, to trust someone so completely. I couldn't remember the last time I felt this way.

Had I ever felt this way? I don't think I did with Shaw. He was as self-absorbed as Tanya. In many ways they were so much alike. I suppose that's why Tanya went into the business side of the landscape business. She had no empathic sense at all and a good garden designer needed some connection to people. Neither she nor Shaw seemed able to connect to others except superficially.

What an odd thought. Shaw and I had connected, didn't we? I didn't trust my memories anymore. It was so long ago and so much had happened since then. What was it Dillan said about Shaw visiting Tanya when she was in the hospital? I suppose I shouldn't be surprised. He and Tanya were close all their lives. Still, it was mean of him.

I pushed the bitter thought aside. I would enjoy my evening and I wouldn't let the past intrude. I needed to take my own advice. No matter how long this relationship with Dillan lasted, I would enjoy it.

"We'll probably get back late tonight or early tomorrow," he murmured, his face lowered to mine. "I was thinking maybe you can come over to my place. We can drop your dad off."

"What did you have in mind?"

"Oh, a bit of this and that. I know you'll be busy tomorrow getting ready for the big event on Saturday, so I promise I won't keep you up too late. In fact, I think I can guarantee you'll get a good night's sleep."

"How can you guarantee that?"

"I know a few things that will help you relax so much you'll drop right off and wake up feeling rested and ready to go. I'll be helping out tomorrow, of course."

"You will?"

"You still need a bodyguard."

"I do?"

"Absolutely." He brushed his lips against my earlobe. "I'm on duty for you twenty-four-seven, Boss."

"You're very persuasive."

Dillan swung us in a tight turn. "I know you'll be busy tomorrow night, but I figured on Saturday we can celebrate. I'm a hell of a grill master, so I'll barbeque something. It may not be as fancy as some meals you've had lately."

"Well, you know me. I'm a wine-in-a-box kind of girl."

"Are you? I get the feeling you might like the finer things in life." His eyes flickered to my emerald earrings and necklace.

"Who doesn't like a few nice things?"

I couldn't interpret his odd expression. Worry? Confusion? Disappointment? I didn't have a chance to evaluate it. The song ended and Pop immediately claimed me for a dance, then another old friend tapped me on the shoulder.

Before I knew it, two hours had passed, and Pop came over to me where I stood talking with some people. "I hate to cut the party short, but we need to take off if we're going home tonight," he said when I broke away from the conversation. "It's almost nine now and it'll take us most of three hours. Unless you want to try to get a room tonight." His eyes twinkled with amusement.

It was tempting, but I had a ton of work to get through on Friday, so I shook my head. "You're right. Where's Dillan?"

"He went to pack up our clothes. We can drive in our finery, right?'

I didn't want to spend three hours in a backless dress, but Pop seemed anxious, so I agreed. I made my good-byes to the conferences organizers and soon we were waiting in front of the hotel for the valet to bring the car.

I shivered in the chilly night air. "Who would think July in Iowa would be this cool?" I murmured, rubbing my arms.

Dillan took off his suit coat and held it open. "Help yourself."

I slid into the coat gratefully. It was still warm from his body and it smelled faintly of aftershave or cologne. When he moved ahead to hand a tip to the valet, I saw his gun, clipped to his belt at his waist. I almost said something but decided against it. I got into the front passenger seat and settled back to relax.

When I leaned my head against the headrest, my dangling earring snagged, tugging at my lobe. I unclasped them and the necklace, dropping them into the inner pocket on Dillan's coat.

"That's some expensive jewelry," Dillan commented.

I covered my mouth to hide a yawn. "Shaw gave it to me. I don't have much opportunity to wear it. It matches my dress."

We were quiet for a time, each of us busy with our own thoughts. "I suppose you got used to living the rich life with him," Dillan said.

I nodded, but he probably couldn't see me in the dark. "Yeah, I did. Shaw liked to live large."

"Do you miss it?"

"No, not really. I was only with him a short time. It wasn't like I had time to get accustomed to it."

"From the way he's been acting, you might have that chance now."

It took a minute for me to figure out what Dillan meant. "What? That's silly."

"Is it?" He kept his eyes on the road, his gaze traveling back and forth to check the sides. This was deer country and Lord knows one might jump out at any time. "Yesterday Kelleher sounded like he had other thoughts."

I waved a hand tiredly. "I can't figure out what Shaw is thinking. Why would he ask me to go to the funeral with him?"

"So he can start to introduce you around to his people," Pop said from the back seat.

"What?"

"If you're serious about a woman, you take her to a family function, like a wedding or a funeral." Pop's face was mostly hidden in the darkness but I got a sense of his bemusement. "I think Dillan's right. Shaw is hoping to pick up where you left off."

"Well, that's stupid. A person doesn't waltz back into someone's life after decades of being absent and expect to be welcomed with open arms." The idea was laughable.

Except no one was laughing. Dillan seemed tense again, his hands rigid on the steering wheel. He was like a ghost, his gray shirt blending with the shadows. I caught glimpses of his expression in oncoming headlights. His mouth was set in a harsh line and his eyebrows were drawn together, like he was perplexed or angry.

Angry about what? It made no sense. So what if Shaw was paying attention to me? It was probably because of what happened to his father. The old man was found at my house and that brought Shaw back into my circle, so to speak.

Why was Kelleher at my house? I hadn't even thought about that for days. Why would someone dump a body in my labyrinth? Did Tanya do it? No, she couldn't have. She didn't have the strength to drag a dead weight, excuse the expression, through the labyrinth.

Of course, Hunter said Kelleher was somewhat conscious. Perhaps he was given a psychotropic drug, one that made him pliable and mobile. I had a passing knowledge of such things, gleaned from too many hospital visits and discussions with psychologists and pain managers.

Dillan's gaze went to the rear-view mirror then his side mirror. I glanced back. A car was approaching quickly, the headlights startling bright on the black, two-lane highway that stretched behind us. Other traffic, on the opposite side, was sparse, with only one or two cars in the distance, far ahead of us.

"He's going too fast," I said. "What if a deer comes out of nowhere and—"

The car reached us, began to pass, and then it swerved. Dillan reacted immediately, jerking the wheel. Our car bounced to the right, the front tire going onto the rumble strip and making a startling sound, as intended.

The passing car seemed to swerve left then it cut in front of us, like the driver was trying to pass and misjudged the distance. I grabbed onto the door handle when Dillan slammed on the brakes. For one instant I thought we'd avoid an impact, then the rear of the car in front of us crashed into our hood. The collision spun us dizzily, our car twirling to the right. The passing car slammed on its brakes, too and we spun into it, the impact crunching into the back half of our car.

"Pop!" I screamed. I was tangled up with my seat belt, which had tightened so much it almost strangled me. I tried to twist, to see into the back but I didn't have enough range of motion. I kept my arm up, vaguely aware that the air bag might deploy when I least expected it. I had no idea what might make it activate but I didn't want to take any chances.

Our car swerved again, the rear sliding crazily toward the ditch. I grabbed on to the console when we tilted, our headlights shining up into the night. Dillan gunned the motor and the car righted itself, bouncing back onto the pavement.

The passing car gunned the motor, too, its wheels spinning and black smoke streaming off the tires. Then it was gone, the engine screaming when it sped away down the road. It vanished almost immediately. Either the driver shut the lights off or it left the road, because all was blackness ahead of us.

I twisted on the seat, reaching for Pop and that's when the side air bag did deploy, jamming me hard against the seat belt. The pain was excruciating, the sharp impact slamming against my wounded right side. I must have passed out because the next thing I was aware of was Dillan, pounding on my window. "You have to get out!" he yelled. "There's a gas leak!"

My right arm was useless. When I tried to move it, the pain almost made me faint again. I twisted again in the damn seat belt, finally getting it released. I fumbled for the door latch and found it, but nothing happened when I pulled up on it. "It's stuck." My voice didn't work very good. "Stuck!" I said louder.

He disappeared only to reappear around the other side of the car. The driver's door was open. Dillan leaned in, grabbing the armrest part of the console and pushing it lower so the seat was relatively flat. "Come out this way." He held out his hand.

I peered blearily at him. "I don't think I can." Everything hurt—my arm, my back, my neck.

"You have to. Come on, Lilith."

I tried to peer behind me. "Get Pop."

"He's out. We need to get you out. Damn it, Lilith, move!"

The fear in his voice galvanized me. Dillan didn't get scared. He shot guns and did S.W.A.T. stuff. If he was scared, then I should be scared, too. I stuffed my small beaded evening bag into one of the suit coat pockets then I grabbed a handful of my heavy skirt and dragged it upward, pulling it above my waist so I wouldn't be hindered by it. I cautiously scooted backward, digging my heels into the seat to push myself. I didn't dare pause. If I did, the pain as my injured right side scraped against the seat would have made me stop.

It felt like it took forever, one tortuous inch at a time. "I've got you," Dillan said. His hands went under my arms and he dragged me out the rest of the way until I swayed on the pavement. He kept an arm around me, half-dragging and half-directing me away from the wreckage of the car to the side of the road where several cars were parked.

"Where's Pop?" I stumbled forward, but Dillan caught me before I fell flat on my face.

"You're hurt. Come on, you can sit over here."

I batted away his hands. "Where's Pop?" My vision blurred, and I swiped at my eyes. When I looked at my fingers, they were bloody. I didn't have time to care about that now. I needed to find my father and—

I spied him, stretched out on the side of the road. A man knelt next to Pop, whose head was propped up on a rolled-up blanket or towel. The headlights from a car illuminated the scene. Pop seemed shrunken, his face abnormally pale. Maybe it was the lighting. I prayed it was.

I took a step toward him, and my right leg gave out. I began to fall but Dillan caught me, lifting me and carrying me to the cars. One of the people there opened a door and Dillan lowered me so I could sit near Pop.

"What happened to him?" I bent over as far as I dared, but a wave of dizziness made me gasp and I grabbed hold of the open car door to keep from falling out.

"You're hurt, Lilith." Dillan knelt in front of me. "You have a gash on your head and God knows what other injuries. Hang on. Let me get my phone." He pulled open the suit coat I wore and reached into an inner pocket. Then he spread the jacket open even wider. "Lilith, you're hurt. You're bleeding."

"I'm fine." I tried to gaze past him at Pop. "What happened to him? Is he okay?"

"I'm fine." Pop peered up at me. "Just some chest pains, that's all. Nothing to worry about."

"Oh, my God, you're having a heart attack." I tried to stand. "We have to get him to a hospital. Where's an ambulance? Did anybody call the police?" My head whipped right and left, assessing our location. Cornfields dissolved into darkness and the highway stretched out on both sides of us with no towns in sight. "We have to get him to a hospital."

"Ambulance is on the way," Pop said. "You sit down. You're making me nervous. You let Dillan take care of you."

"But you're—" I gripped the edges of the car door. Everything was freezing all of a sudden. Sweat beaded on my forehead and I shivered. "We need to get him help." I swallowed hard, exhausted and shaking. "I'm so tired. Why am I tired?" The world spun around me. "Damn. I think I'm fainting."

"You're in shock," Dillan said from a long way away. "Lay down. Get a blanket. We need to keep her warm!"

Exceptional idea, I thought.

Something wrapped around me. Then I heard loud noises. A siren. I lay on a pallet of some kind. Someone shone a light into my eyes. I answered some questions. I think. Then I was moving again. I tried to tell them to take care of Pop, but I couldn't talk.

I think I dozed off. When I woke up, I was warm. I lay on something soft and there were dim lights around me. Noises, too. Beeps and sighs. I tried to sit up, but I was weighted down. Dillan stood with his back to me. He had on his suit coat again. I guess that meant I wasn't wearing it. He was talking to a man in a uniform. A policeman of some kind.

"I screwed up." Dillan's voice was thick with self-recrimination. "I let down my guard."

"Not your fault," the other man said. "There's no way you'd know."

"It was a bad driver," I said. "You couldn't guard against that."

"We woke you up. I'm sorry." Dillan leaned over and touched my cheek. "You go back to sleep."

I tried to grab his hand, but my arms were tangled up with tubes and wires. Damn. I was in a hospital bed. "It's not your fault. You're a good driver. That guy was an asshole."

"That guy tried to run us off the road. I should have paid closer attention. I screwed up."

"No, you didn't." I tried to look around the room. "I'm in a hospital, aren't I? Where's my father?"

"Right here," a weak voice said from my right.

I turned my head. Pop lay in a bed not far away,

"Where are we?"

"In a hospital on the Missouri border. It was the

closest hospital to the crash scene." Dillan touched my hand, which was taped up with a tube going into it.

"Missouri? I can't be here." I pushed against the bed, trying to get upright. "I need to get home. I have stuff to do. I have to—"

"You have to heal." Dillan put his hand on my shoulder and gently pressed me down. "I'll be back tomorrow to pick you up and take you home. Until then, all you need to do is rest."

"But—"

"Lilith." Pop's voice was weak but firm. "Listen to the man."

"Don't worry." Dillan bent over me, his face close to mine, lines of worry and exhaustion around his eyes. "We'll make sure everything is ready for Saturday. For now, though, you need to rest. You have a concussion, a cracked rib, and several gashes that need to start healing."

"Gashes? Where?" I lifted the sheet covering me to check. "What the—where's my clothes?"

"I owe you a dress." Dillan kissed my cheek. "Sleep now. I'll be back. I got your other clothes from the car, so you won't have to go home naked. That would be a sight, wouldn't it?" He tried to sound light-hearted, but there was pain in his dark eyes.

"Where are you—" I tried to take his hand when he straightened, but he got away from me. "I don't understand." I yawned and felt the weight returning, dragging me back to sleep. "You have to explain."

"Tomorrow. I'll explain tomorrow." His voice was already far away.

"I'm holding you to that," I warned. "It's not negotiable."

I heard his soft laugh. "Okay, Boss."

Chapter Fourteen

It took longer than I wanted to escape from the hospital. First there were tests to run, then Pop had to meet with a cardiac person, then I had to work with an occupational therapist to make sure my mild concussion wouldn't cause problems. Consequently, we didn't get home until late afternoon on Friday. It was a good thing that the drive was only an hour or so long. Otherwise, Dillan and I might have come to blows during the journey.

My injuries weren't that bad. Just the concussion, two fractured ribs, one cut on my face and one on my side where, apparently, I ran into a nail file while sliding along the seat. Dillan promised to give his mom hell about that until I slapped him on the arm and told him to shut up.

Dillan drove us home in my car. He'd already been to the house to feed the cat and check with the work crew. While he was there, Swanny showed up for my appointment and Dillan sent him on his way. I wasn't in any shape for physical therapy with two banged-up ribs. I made a mental note to give my trusty PT a call later.

"I'm sure it was deliberate," Dillan said while he drove us home. "That car came out of nowhere. I think the driver was waiting for us."

"But why?" I twisted to view Pop, stretched out in

the back seat. "Are you okay? You're sure?"

He waved a hand. "Those pills the doc gave me are working wonders. I'll be up and around in no time."

"No, you won't," Dillan said. "You're supposed to rest. That means no heavy lifting, no running around, and no partying until dawn."

"You're no fun," Pop muttered. "It wasn't a heart attack. It was a heart event. That's what the doctor called it."

I rolled my eyes. "It was close enough for government work. We have an appointment to see your doctor on Monday and I'm going with you. Until then, you're relaxing." I turned back to Dillan. "Why do you think someone would want to hurt us?"

"Think about it. That car wasn't behind us until we passed that intersection. Then it came tearing out as soon as we went by. It was running us down."

"But nobody knew we'd be on this road." I tried to rationalize the whole thing. "You think somebody hung around, waiting for us to pass, and then they sprang out to hurt us?"

"Shaw Kelleher knew."

"What? That's ridiculous. You said yourself he was at his father's funeral. How could he be halfway to St. Louis?"

"He disappeared immediately after the funeral." Dillan said it flatly, his eyes focused on the road ahead.

"Disappeared?" Pop asked. "What's that mean? Poof, burst of smoke or something?"

I'm glad Pop asked the question and not me. I was getting the feeling that Shaw was a tricky subject for Dillan.

"What I mean is the police are searching for him

and they can't find him." Dillan's fingers flexed on the steering wheel. I imagined them around Shaw's throat. It was easy to imagine.

"Why are they looking for him? Is he in trouble or something?"

I couldn't mistake the flinty glint of anger in Dillan's dark gray eyes. "He's wanted for questioning in the murder of his father and Tanya Sidero."

The idea was so ludicrous I would have laughed if my bandaged ribs allowed it. Once again, Pop unknowingly came to my rescue. He laughed out loud. "Shaw? Wanted for murder? In what world? He's a rich, useless nobody, not some criminal mastermind. Sorry, Lilith, but he is."

"Don't apologize to me." Despite my words, I was miffed, as though making fun of Shaw was making fun of me by association. "He's right, Dillan. Shaw doesn't have the personality or the mindset to murder somebody."

"Oh, really? How do you know what it takes?"

Well, he had a point there, but his condescending tone grated on my already grated nerves. "Okay, maybe I'm not an ex-cop or I don't teach Criminal Whatever, but I know Shaw Kelleher. Or, rather, I *did* know him. He doesn't have the—the—I don't know, the spine to murder somebody."

"You'd be surprised what people are capable of."

I saw this argument was going nowhere, so I switched gears. "Why would he kill them?"

"That's easy," Pop piped up. "Personal gain if his father dies."

"Maybe," I conceded. "But he's already working for his father. What else does he get if his father dies?

And Tanya? Why kill her? For that matter, why would anyone kill her? I had the best motive, as the police so quickly pointed out." I thought about my poor roses. "That bitch," I muttered.

"If there's a motive, the police will find it," Dillan said.

"You're confusing them with the Mounties, who always get their man." I glared at the outside world, which mocked me by being sunny and beautiful, the cornfields shimmering in the July heat.

"That still doesn't explain why Shaw would want to hurt Lilith," Pop said.

"Maybe it wasn't Lilith he was after. Maybe it was me."

"You? Why?" I examined Dillan's face, which revealed nothing. "You think he's jealous? You think that's why?" I leaned back in my seat, wincing when my injured ribs made themselves felt. "That's crazy."

"Why?"

Luckily, I spotted that minefield before I stepped in it. I deftly avoided any pitfalls about my feelings for Dillan and focused instead on Shaw. "Because Shaw knows he means nothing to me. Why would he be jealous of you?"

Dillan sighed with feigned patience. "Why do you think he knows that he means nothing to you?"

"Because I've—"

"You went out to dinner with him. You told him to come over to your house on the Fourth."

"I did not. I said I was busy and maybe we—"

"I saw how he acted when he saw us together."

"When you were together? When?" Pop leaned forward, peering between the two front seats. "What did he see?"

"Nothing," I snapped.

"He saw us kissing," Dillan said.

"Whoa. It must have been pretty hot and heavy for him to get bent out of shape and come after us to run us off the road."

"You aren't helping, Pop." I gave him a gentle shove. "Sit down and shut up."

"Was it hot and heavy? I'm not saying that's a terrible thing, but you might want to take it inside if you're doing—" I managed to turn around and skewer my father with a baleful glare. "Just a suggestion," he finished lamely.

"All I'm saying is I didn't like the way he stared at us when he saw us on the Fourth," Dillan said. "I've seen guys like that, guys who thought they had a woman in their back pocket and then found out they were wrong."

"Where have you seen that? In that gang you were with?" I regretted the words as soon as I said them, but it was too late.

"I suppose Mom told you about that."

"A gang?" Pop leaned forward again. "What kind of gang? A motorcycle gang? Hell's Angels? Is that where you met Sarah? She said that when she was a he, he was in a gang of some kind."

Dillan peered at Pop in the rear-view mirror. "He wasn't in the chapter I was in, but yeah, that's where we met."

"They have chapters? It's like the Masons or something like that? Wow, I didn't know they were that organized." Pop sat back then leaned forward again. "Did you pay dues? Did you have a membership card?"

"No, no, and I think Kelleher is still in love with you," Dillan snapped.

I tossed up my hands. "Shaw wasn't actually in love with me twenty-five years ago. Why would he be in love with me now?"

"Are you still in love with him?" Dillan didn't look at me directly.

"Why are you even asking that?" I demanded.

"You keep defending him. You keep finding reasons why he couldn't be involved in anything bad."

"It's because he's an old friend. It's because I know him. Shaw isn't capable of what you're talking about. Pop was right. Shaw doesn't have the nerve to do anything like murder someone."

Dillan was silent for a long moment. "I think you're wrong. I think your feelings for him are clouding your judgment."

"Fine. Think that. I don't care." I stared resolutely out my window at the inoffensive scenery rolling past.

We were silent the rest of the way home. When Dillan pulled into the driveway, he said, "I talked to Detective Hunter before I came to pick you up. No matter what you think, he thinks there might still be a threat against you, so he'll have two officers stationed here until they find Kelleher."

"Stationed here? What does that mean?"

"I'm sure they can give you the details." Dillan opened the garage door with a tap on my remote opener. His cycle was parked behind Pop's pickup truck inside. "They followed us home."

"They did what?" I checked my side-view mirror. A dark sedan was parking at the curb. "What about you? Aren't you—will you—are you still on duty?"

Dillan shut off the car. "Nope. The police are handling it now. You don't need me." He stared at me, challenging me.

Well, shit. Nothing like putting a girl on the spot. "Fine. I'll talk to them." I flung open my door and managed to exit the car without falling on my face. The bulky plastic hospital bag did get snagged on the under-seat adjustment gadget, but I got it unhooked without tearing it, which was a miracle.

"Lily, honey, you should—"

I slammed the door on whatever Pop was trying to say. I stomped from the garage to meet the two men walking to me. They were young, one with blond hair and one with dark hair, and they wore jeans and short-sleeved shirts. I thought they were more like college kids than cops, like the crew Dillan had hired to help out. The two introduced themselves as Officer This and Officer That, but I barely heard them. I was acutely aware of Dillan, talking to Pop in the garage.

"…the way. We know you have an event tomorrow and…" Office That was talking, businesslike and eager.

"Dillan, wait," Pop said.

I didn't wait to see what was going on. I began walking toward the front door. After a hesitation, the two officers went with me. "I need you to be inconspicuous," I said, keeping my back to the garage behind me. "I'll have people here in the morning doing the judging for the garden competition then the garden is open to the public in the afternoon."

"We know about…"

I heard Dillan's cycle start. I unlocked the front door and went inside. "Good." I interrupted whatever the policeman was saying. "Thank you for helping. Let me know if you need anything." I slung the hospital bag on the living room couch and stomped into the kitchen.

"Lily?"

Pop entered the house behind me. I left the policemen to him and stalked into the mudroom and from there to the back yard. The hell with Dillan Lyall. I don't know what pissed me off most—that Dillan didn't believe me when I told him I didn't care about Shaw, or that Dillan thought Shaw loved me. Good God, wouldn't I know it if someone was in love with me? Why would Dillan think that? I'd seen Shaw three times in a week and hadn't been alone with him any one of those times. What was Dillan reading into those perfectly innocent encounters?

I sucked in a deep breath, not as deep as I wanted because of my damn cracked ribs. My head was pounding from the stitches on my forehead, my body was bruised, and I was so angry I couldn't see straight. Not a good start to the evening before my Event. I tried another breath and inhaled thyme and rosemary. My racing heart slowed, and the sweetness of my garden seeped into my senses.

I needed a circuit in Labbie to calm down. I went to the labyrinth, my hands brushing the sides and releasing the scent from the yews. I forced myself to pace evenly, deliberately. Go left then walk twenty paces, watching the path below my feet which was uneven. Left again, small steps for twenty-two paces, looping back to the start.

As always, disorientation began when I lost track of back and front, conscious only of the walls of green that kept me on the path. Go right and now the long walk, looping around the outside perimeter. The arbors of climbing roses on the outside were vibrantly red, showed me a glimpse of the outside world through their vines. The fragrance was heady in the summer heat. Go right and loop back inside then right again for the long interior loop, the green walls fragrant and soft against my hands. Left and walk. Right and walk. Right and walk around the inner circle, tantalizing snippets of it seen through the climbing rose arbors, these whites and pinks, scattered throughout the yews.

The rhythm of the labyrinth calmed my over-heated brain. By the time I reached the center after five minutes of slow and steady movement, I had found my own center again. Appropriately enough, I found the blue roses on the inside were blooming. I would dismantle the grow lights and they would be perfect for the judging tomorrow. I breathed a sigh of relief, not only about that but about my new-found perspective on what had happened.

This was probably a massive misunderstanding. Once the police found Shaw, it would be straightened out. He had probably left town on business. After all, his father just died and now he was in charge of the family finances. Didn't he say he was in Minneapolis earlier in the week? Perhaps he needed to make another trip.

I retraced my steps. Once it was cleared up, Dillan would see how ludicrous it was to even think that Shaw cared for me or I cared for him. Dillan was being over-protective. Olivia told me how seriously he took his job when he was a cop. It was the same thing when he acted as bodyguard. Dillan lost sight of practical things in his need to be thorough.

I emerged from the labyrinth, relaxed and

refreshed. I wandered around the back yard, taking in the work the guys had done. It was amazing. The flower beds were raked and tidy, the 'wild' area was in some semblance of tame, and fresh gravel filled in the bare spots on my paths.

Pop came out as I was finishing my inspection. "There's another call on the machine from that lawyer. You'd better give him a call back first thing on Monday. He sounds anxious."

"I'm not anxious to talk to him," I said. "I think he'll give us news we don't want to hear."

"We'll figure it out, honey. Don't worry." He stared at the yard. "Those boys did a damn outstanding job. We never would have gotten this much done."

"I know." I glanced at the house. "What about the babysitters?"

"They're taking turns. One will stay inside while the other one walks around the yard every hour or so. Apparently, Shaw is a person of interest." Pop surrounded the word with air quotes. "They aren't too worried about him showing up here, or that's the feeling I got. I think they're staying here more as a just-in-case. You know—dotting an I and crossing a T. If you ask me, they're both young and don't know what they're doing, but I guess I'm old and jaded."

"I still think it's silly." I walked with him back to the house. "Once they find Shaw and talk to him, they'll realize it's a mistake."

Pop held the door for me to go into the porch. "I don't know, Lily. There was always something about Shaw that bugged me."

I headed for my chair, but the cat was already there. I changed direction and went to the couch. "You never said anything."

He shrugged. "You know how it is. I didn't want to rain on your parade. Do you want something to eat?"

I leaned back cautiously. "I don't think so. I'll eat a cracker or two before I go to bed. I think I'll go up early tonight. I didn't sleep much last night in the hospital."

"Or the night before?" He chuckled and went into the kitchen.

The night before, when Dillan stayed overnight here. I closed my eyes, remembering. The warmth of him, his strength, the gentle way he took care not to hurt me when we tumbled around. I missed him already.

"Mpfm?"

The cat sat at my feet, head tilted to one side.

"Sure. Come on." I patted the couch next to me. The critter jumped up, padded the cushion, then sank down. "I wonder if I'm supposed to put goop on your tail?" I ran a hand over his head and he purred softly. "Dillan handled that, but I guess I need to do it now." I sighed. "I got used to having him here."

The cat peered up at me and I imaged a thought bubble over his head. *I liked having him here, too.*

Well, we'd get it straightened out in the next day or two. I had to get through the Garden Showcase first. Then I'd deal with Dillan. It was just a big snafu.

Isn't it odd how you plan and anticipate something for months, the way I did with the Showcase? I began planning in the winter, deciding on color schemes for the annual plants, figuring out texture in spots, choosing the right gravel color to top-dress the paths. You spend hours, days, weeks and finally the day comes. And then, suddenly—BOOM—it's over.

That's how it felt to me that Saturday. I blinked and it was done. Three groups of three judges came through the garden in the morning, one group at nine, one at ten, and the last at eleven. I know that representatives from big nurseries were interspersed in the judging groups, so I had hopes that they would notice my blue roses. I'd send thank-you letters to the judges after the event, so perhaps I could parlay that brief contact into a contract to acquire my roses for their growing programs.

The two cops proved to be useful. One of the officers sat on the front porch, pretending to be with the Showcase committee and he inspected the credentials of each group before the other officer escorted them to the back garden and watched them, covertly, while the judges prowled around.

As instructed, I stayed away and let my garden speak for itself. I lurked on the porch and upstairs, where I tried to eavesdrop on the judges while they examined the space. I didn't get any meaningful tidbits, although it appeared the second group of judges were more active, making many notes on their clipboards and lingering in the middle of Labbie to examine the roses. While it would be nice to get an award from the official judges, it was the People's Choice Award I truly coveted. That one would easily translate into clients.

When the last judges left, I went into the labyrinth and strung netting over the rose arbors to ensure the public wouldn't be snagged by any thorns and to ensure that the over-eager public wouldn't snag my roses. It was a chore to drag the nets and position them. I remembered Dillan when he manhandled the heavy tarps and I wished, not for the first time, that he was there.

At noon, when the garden was open to the public, the officer at the front took tickets from people who had pre-purchased them while Pop sold tickets to anyone who wanted one. I made Pop promise he'd stay seated and not exert himself. He was supposed to rest, I reminded him. He waved a hand and promised. The officer with him gave me a nod and I knew he'd keep an eye on my errant father.

I was kept busy moving people through the garden, directing traffic. The other officer also pitched in, helping anyone who had a walker, cane, or wheelchair. A slender young black girl, probably twelve or thirteen, appeared and declared she'd been sent by her uncle to make sure nobody messed with my flowers. She dragged out one of my lawn chairs and positioned herself at the labyrinth entrance, fixing people with a steely gaze when they tried to push past her.

"Only six at a time every ten minutes," she declared, checking her stopwatch and making notes on the tally sheet balanced on her knee. Her fierce presence ensured that the labyrinth didn't get overcrowded and I noticed her eagle-eyed assessment of anyone coming out. If anyone was going to pick flowers, they wouldn't do it on her watch.

Activity began to wind down by three o'clock, an hour before the official close of the tour. The heat of the day was settling in. The southerly breeze kept the air moving, but it stilled later in the afternoon and the humidity rose. I was chatting with a group of visitors, handing out business cards, when my cell phone thumped me from the pocket of my skirt. I excused myself and ducked onto the back porch.

I didn't see a phone number on the phone display. Instead it said *Private*. Hmm. "Hello?"

"Miss Griffen, it's Detective Hunter." His voice sounded faint and dispersed, like he was in a wind tunnel or something.

"I wasn't sure who it was. There isn't a phone number showing."

"Yes, we block the number for official business. I wanted to let you know that the search for Shaw Kelleher has been called off."

"I beg your pardon?" I wasn't sure I heard right.

"Yes, he's no longer needed for questioning. We're pursuing a different line of investigation."

"Oh, I see. Does that mean the police officers will be leaving?" I spied the backyard guy, the blond, walking around the perimeter. He seemed bored and I didn't blame him. I suppose for a cop this was grunt work.

"Officers? Oh, yes. They won't be needed. I wanted to let you know that Mr. Kelleher has been cleared of suspicion."

"Okay, thanks for letting me know." I ended the call and went to the front porch, where Pop and Officer That were chatting with new arrivals. I didn't see an opportunity to tell the policeman about my call, but I figured they'd get the word eventually. I didn't mind them hanging around a bit longer.

The final hour wrapped up and Pop came to find me where I stood in the back, giving my labyrinth guarder a twenty-dollar bill for her help. "Call me if you need me to help again." She pocketed the money and handed me her tally sheets.

"I will. Thank your uncle for me."

The girl turned to survey my yard. "He does decent work," she said grudgingly. "Real decent work." With a cavalier wave, she took off to meet her friends at the nearby swimming pool. I remembered summer days when my bike was my transportation and all I had to do was meet friends at the pool. I envied her the freedom.

"I'm taking our till to the bank." Pop brandished a deposit pouch. "I'm glad I remembered where I put this thing. It's been months since they handed them out."

I was glad he remembered, too. I'd forgotten completely about our fiscal responsibility part of this Showcase. "I think it went well. I handed out a bunch of business cards." I surveyed the garden, which didn't seem too much the worse for wear.

"We had a few hundred people come through. I'll bet we'll get some business out of it. I'm stopping by Jean's Place on my way home. Tonight's all-you-can-eat barbeque and I'd hate to miss out on that."

"You take it easy," I warned. "Come home early. You're still supposed to be getting some rest."

Pop waved away my worries. "I'm fine. I'll be back before you know it." He headed for the garage, bank pouch tucked under his arm.

The blond police officer came toward me, phone to his ear. When he reached me, he tucked it back into his shirt pocket. "I just got word. I'm being reassigned. There's an accident out on the Interstate and I need to get out there. Detective Hunter said we're not needed here anymore, but we'll leave Officer Alexander here in front for another hour or so in case any stragglers come by."

"Yes, I talked to Hunter a while ago." I went with him to the front where he conferred with his partner. I waved to Pop when he drove away then watched Officer Blond get into his car.

"Do you need a refill on your water?" I asked Officer Alexander.

"No, I'm fine, ma'am. I'll be here for another hour then a squad will be by to pick me up."

"In that case, I'm going inside to relax. It's been a busy day."

He smiled, which made him look even more boyish than before. "It sure has been. You go ahead and put your feet up. I'll make sure nobody bothers you."

That sounded like an excellent idea. I considered changing out of my Gypsy Queen uniform, but decided I was too tired to climb the stairs to my room. Instead, I went into the house and fixed myself a gin and tonic, then wandered to the back porch. Beast emerged from his hiding place under my chair and soon we were dozing on the couch, the cat draped over my legs. The overhead fan augmented the light breeze coming in, and I felt months of worry and stress blow away with it.

I don't know how long I lay there, stretched out without a care in the world. The ice in my glass had melted quite a bit, though, and dusk was starting when I heard my name. "Lilith?"

I twisted to see the side gate. Shaw came in, dressed like the epitome of "rich man on a summer day" in his crisp khaki shorts, snug knit shirt and polished loafers.

At that moment, my phone rang. I sat up and Beast headed for the kitchen. "Shaw, what are you doing here?" I peeked at the phone. *Dillan Lyall.* "I need to take this call." Then I thought better of it. If Dillan knew I was talking to Shaw, it might be a very short phone call.

"I have some business papers for you to sign." Shaw came around to the porch door. "Do you have time?"

"Sure, come in." My phone rang again. "Excuse me, I need to answer this." I unlocked the door then went to the kitchen, phone pressed against my ear. "Hey."

"Before you hang up on me, I wanted to apologize. Mom reminded me how you always give people the benefit of the doubt. I shouldn't have jumped on you for being nice."

"Well, thank you." I decided to be magnanimous. "I'm sorry, too."

"Listen, I'm at Nelson's Market, up the street. I thought I'd get a couple of steaks and we can grill and celebrate. I need to return your jewelry, too. It was in the pocket of my coat."

"I forgot about that." I glanced at the porch. Shaw stood there, watching me, a file folder in one hand. "I'm kind of busy now. How about in half an hour or so?"

"Okay. I'm sorry your faith in Kelleher wasn't justified."

"What do you mean?"

"I thought you knew." Dillan sounded pissed off. "Damn, I didn't want to be the one to tell you. He's in custody."

"What?"

"They caught him going west, heading for Omaha. They're bringing him back to the station now. He was driving the family car. They tracked the license plates."

I turned. Shaw smiled at me. "I think you're

wrong," I said, my voice suddenly shaky.

Shaw took a step toward me. "Hang up the phone, Lilith. We need to talk."

Chapter Fifteen

"There must be some kind of mistake," I said into the phone.

"Hang up the phone, Lilith." Shaw moved from the shadows of the porch. Something in the set of his mouth, something in the way he tilted his head to one side to regard me worried me. Why did I ever think he was handsome?

His pale blue eyes had a flat, impersonal expression. I had seen that before. The realization hit me so hard it was like an ice bath. Shaw used to regard some of the partygoers at his house with exactly the same expression, like they were beneath his notice. He and Tanya both made fun of some of the hangers-on who were always around him, lured by his money and his largesse.

The thought surfaced and disappeared, but the aftereffect remained. I took a step back. "I'm busy, Shaw. I'll be with you in a minute." I pressed the phone toward my face like a lifeline.

"Shaw? He's there? That's impossible." Dillan sounded stunned.

"No, it's not," I said patiently.

"Listen to me, Lilith. I know you might not believe this, but he's dangerous. The police have solid proof that he murdered his father and probably murdered

Tanya. You need to get away from him."

"We need to talk." Shaw reached for the phone. *How did he get so close to me?*

I shifted position, phone still close to my ear. "What are you—"

"Try to put as much distance between—"

Shaw made a grab for the phone. I dodged him and stuffed it into my skirt pocket. "There. I hung it up. What's this about, Shaw?" I fought to try to think of something calming to say, something to diffuse the rage simmering in him. In the meantime, Dillan's words were cycling through my brain.

Solid proof that he murdered his father. "How did the funeral go yesterday?" I asked inanely. "I'm sure there were quite a few people there. Your father was quite a community figure."

"It was a funeral. I suppose it was fine." Shaw slammed the folder on the kitchen island. "I need you to sign some papers."

"What kind of papers?"

"Did you talk to the lawyer?"

The words made no sense. "What lawyer?"

"Our family lawyer." Shaw flipped open the file folder. Inside was a sheaf of papers, bulky and legal looking.

"No. A person has called but he had to leave town." I noticed a nervous twitch above Shaw's eye when I said that. "He said he had personal business."

"In Minneapolis. Yes. Does that mean you never talked about Father's will?"

I moved, one painful inch at a time, putting more of the island between me and him. "I haven't had time."

Shaw's hand splayed over the pages. "Then you

don't know."

"I know you're acting oddly and I'm not sure what to think." I was starting to get pissed off. "Why were the police searching for you?"

His hand flexed, wrinkling the top page of the stapled batch of papers. "Father thought the world of you. Did you know that?"

"That's news to me. I thought he detested me. You said yourself that he threatened to cut you off if you married me."

Shaw frowned. "Why would you think that? He was happy we'd get married. He thought you would help straighten me out."

"But you said—" My phone thumped in my pocket. "Hold on." I pulled out the phone. As I expected, it was Dillan. "I think there's been a mistake," I said before Dillan could speak.

"Hang up the phone, Lilith. We need to get these papers signed." Shaw made a grab for the phone, but the kitchen island separated us.

I kept it between me and him while I tried to listen to Dillan. "...positive proof. You need to leave the house now and..." I saw Shaw's thunderous expression. I immediately lowered the phone, flipping it over on the countertop. "There. I'm paying attention."

"I'll leave as soon as you sign them." Shaw tried a smile, but it was obviously strained. "Then you and your boyfriend can get back to whatever you're doing. It's obvious you're not going to love me."

The words were so stupid they didn't make sense. I stared at him. "Love you? Why would I?"

I think I must have stunned him. Shaw froze, as though the words didn't compute. Then he shook his head, pushing off an unwanted thought. "It doesn't matter now. Sign the papers."

I snatched the stack of papers and dragged some over to me, where I stood opposite him. I saw the title on the page. *Transfer of Ownership of Kelleher Properties and—* "What is this?"

"Father left a large part of his estate to you. I need it and you have to sign it over to me."

"That's insane. Why would he do that?" My phone buzzed again, banging against the laminate countertop. Before I could answer it, Shaw jumped up, diving over the island. He threw the phone against the fridge. "I told you to hang up. I need your attention." He spoke in short bursts, measuring the words before speaking.

My phone was shattered, lying in pieces on the floor. What kind of strength did it take to do something like that? "What's wrong?" I stepped back, grabbing on to the sink for support when my knees began to tremble.

I glimpsed Beast, behind Shaw. He was poised on the doorway to the porch, his gaze alternating between the phone and us. His cat curiosity was at work, unsure how to proceed: object on floor. Inspect. Angry humans. Avoid.

Shaw whirled, obviously worried about what I saw. I grabbed Dillan's epi-pen from the counter and jammed it into my pocket. I don't know why. Did I think I needed a weapon? The idea was crazy. Shaw wouldn't hurt me.

"That's one ugly cat." Shaw glared at the animal as though daring it to move. The cat glared in return, his tattered ears laid back. He took a cautious step forward and Shaw lunged, aiming a kick at the animal's side.

I didn't even stop to think. I grabbed a fork from the drying rack in the sink and stabbed Shaw in the back, near the top of his shoulder, as hard as I could. "That's my cat, asshole!" I shouted. "You leave him alone!"

Shaw whirled and that's when the gun came into view. He must have had it in his pocket. It was small, but it also looked deadly. It was so close to me. It was too close to me. I froze.

My paralysis was shattered when the cat took off running, skittering through the kitchen and going into the mudroom. I caught a glimpse of Shaw's enraged face and I followed the cat, careening through the room, bouncing off the counters until I got to the back door. I threw it open and the cat and I fell outside. He took off with a bounding run toward the labyrinth and I went right, to the garage, reasoning that if I got there, I'd go through it to the front of the house and the policeman who was, hopefully, still there.

I made it halfway there when I was jerked back so hard my blouse tore, buttons popping off the front when it twisted around my torso. "I wanted to do this the nice way, the right way." Shaw wrapped one arm around my neck and dragged me back against his body. "You stupid bitch."

Something cold pressed against my neck. I knew what it was. The gun. I couldn't see it but I'm sure that's what it was. I gasped, struggling weakly. He was taller than me and I sagged in his arms until he shifted his grip. Then I kicked back as hard as I could, connecting with his shin or at least a part of it. He released me, and I pitched forward, barely keeping my balance and heading for the garage door.

It was locked. Son of a bitch. We locked it in case any of the visitors that afternoon might try it. I didn't pause but kept running, heading for the side of the garage. The gate was locked, but I squeezed past it, scraping my way through the shrubs forming the boundary of my property. I didn't pause to see if he was following. I pushed through the greenery and rounded the front of the house.

Good God. A man was in the middle of the driveway. There was blood. It trickled down the concrete in a thin line. For one terrified instant I thought it was Dillan. Then I saw the man's hair was dark, not gray. It was the cop.

I stumbled, slamming into the garage door, but I didn't stop. I knew I didn't dare. I raced past him and got to the front door, praying that Shaw had followed me and not doubled back. I went inside and sprang up the steps. I don't know why. I don't think I was actually thinking at that point. I was in pure panic mode, running to get away. I was beyond fear. I'd heard that cliché before, but now I knew how it felt.

I ran along the hall to my bedroom. Where to hide? The closet? Under the bed? Stupid options. I ran to the window and peered into the back yard. Where was Shaw? Was he out there, searching for me?

The neighbors. Didn't they hear a gunshot or whatever it was that made that poor policeman bleed on my driveway? Stupid me. No, of course not. I had warned the neighbors about the Showcase and the increased traffic, pedestrian and vehicular, on the street. They went out boating for the day.

I heard Shaw below. "You can't get away, Lilith. I'll kill you if I have to. That's not the best way to handle this. If I kill you, the estate will go into probate and I'll have time to put back the money I borrowed."

Put back what money? Borrowed? What the hell was he talking about?

"If you would sign away the property, then it'll be done. I'll take control of the business and you can go back to your stupid, boring life." The voice was closer. He was at the bottom of the steps.

He was insane. Didn't he know the police were looking for him? I spun around my room frantically. Why the hell did I do this? Why did I come upstairs? I was trapped. I peered at the garden. The awning was right below me. Should I—

I didn't pause. I opened the window. We'd replaced the old double-hung windows years ago with sliders that provided more ventilation and easier maintenance. It was a simple matter to pop out the screen. I tossed it as far away as I could. It landed on Labbie, balancing precariously before dropping from sight.

The opening was easily big enough for me. I balanced in the window for a second then let go, sliding along the shingles of the outer wall of the house to the awning's metal framework. Amazingly enough, it held my weight. I sat on the heavy canvas fabric and scooted forward. I felt a telltale shiver when the frame began to pull away from the house. To the right, about four feet ahead of me, was a flower bed of annuals. I launched myself toward it just as the whole awning collapsed with a screech of tearing metal.

So much for a covert escape. I staggered to my feet. My skirt was torn up the side, tangling around my legs. I grabbed two pieces of fabric and tied it around my waist. My blouse flapped open, exposing my camisole which was also torn, but at least not in my way.

I heard Shaw in the house, door slamming and heavy footsteps. He'd be here in a minute. Where to go? Back to the front? Run up the street? I was poised to run that way when I glimpsed movement on the far side of the yard, near the porch. I froze. Had Shaw come out that way?

The figure in the shadow straightened and gestured frantically. I almost fainted. Dillan. I ran to him, glancing to my left at the house as I passed the windows. "How did you get here?" I whispered. "I didn't hear your—"

"I left it at the top of the hill. Where is he?"

"I think he's inside. I jumped out the window." I pointed to my bedroom.

Dillan glanced up then at me. "You're lucky you didn't break your neck."

"He has a gun."

"I do, too." Dillan raised his hand and I saw his weapon.

"Why is he doing this? None of this makes sense. Why would he come after me?"

"Let's worry about that later. For now, we need to stay safe."

"Good point."

"I called for backup. They'll be here soon. All you have to do is stay out of his way."

"Me? What about you?"

"I'll distract him. You make your way to the front of the house but stay in the trees." He nodded over his shoulder at the trees lining the property on this side.

"Are you kidding? I'm coming with you."

"No. It'll distract me. I'll be too worried about you."

"And I'll worry about you." I pulled his face to mine and kissed him as hard as I could. "Shut up and follow me." I headed for Labbie.

"Lilith!"

I ignored his hissed gasp, making a beeline for the labyrinth entrance.

"Lilith, stop." Dillan came after me, catching up to me a few steps inside Labbie. "This is a dead end."

"No, it only seems that way. Come on." I ran into the labyrinth, moving surely along the path.

"Damn it." Dillan breathed out a curse behind me. "This isn't a smart idea."

I didn't waste time arguing. The greenery that comprised the labyrinth distorted sound, voices and noises bouncing around in odd directions. I couldn't count on that to tell me where Shaw was.

I rounded the corner and came to the first 'thin' spot, one of my shortcuts. "Through here."

"I know you're in here." Shaw's taunting voice seemed to come from directly behind us.

Dillan whirled but I grabbed his arm. "Come on," I whispered. "He's not that close."

"Lilith, I'll just meet you in the center." Shaw sounded delighted at the prospect, not worried. "This was another stupid move, one of many you've made."

I emerged on the other side of the wall, Dillan popping out a second later. "He doesn't know I'm here." Dillan's face was pressed near mine, his breath warm on my ear.

"Go through here." I pushed him, tugging branches

to one side.

"You first."

"Go." I pushed him forward. I followed and when I emerged, I went a few steps to the right. I knew every inch of this place. I had walked it thousands of times. I knew every bump, every rock, every branch. I visualized it in my mind, overlaying a map of the space with our location. The turns were tight and Shaw didn't know his way. He'd move slowly. "Shaw? Why do you think you can get away with this? What happened with Tanya?"

Dillan grabbed me and put his hand over my mouth. I peered up at him. "Trust me," I mumbled. I went to the left, heading for the next thin spot where we could make our way through, going back to the outside. If we played it right, we'd be leaving the labyrinth just as Shaw entered the center. I needed to slow him down, though.

Dillan cautiously moved his hand. Shaw's voice came to us, fainter than before. "Tanya knew I went to Minnesota. She helped me."

That made me pause. "Minnesota?" I muttered.

Dillan pulled on my arm. "Keep moving," he breathed.

I went a few more steps. "Through here," I whispered. *He's right there.* I jabbed a finger toward the yews far to the right while I mouthed the words. *We'll be behind him. He'll go around the corner.* I made a circuit in the air. *We'll go straight through the next row.*

Dillan nodded his understanding. He raised his gun, moving forward to peer between the branches, using the gun to push them aside. The dense shrubbery made for slow going, especially for someone as tall and broad-shouldered as he was. The nearby rose arbor was still covered with netting and stretchy plastic "Caution" tape to warn visitors about the thorns.

I saw Dillan through the shrubbery, a faint outline of his dark green shirt and the lighter fabric of his brown shorts. He was almost through this row of yews. I prayed he was timing it right, that Shaw would be so focused on the path ahead he wouldn't notice anyone behind him.

I started into the yews, the fragrant needles biting into my exposed arms and legs. One of the vines from the arbor had infringed on the yews and I was momentarily hung up on a large thorn that snagged my blouse. I heard pounding footsteps. I twisted, trying to get away from the rose bush.

Shaw rounded the corner. I ripped the blouse and stumbled, almost falling onto the pavers. I didn't have time to dig through the shrubbery. He'd shoot me before I could get through, or else he'd follow me through and shoot both Dillan and me. That reasoning took less than a second for me to process.

I took off at a run, Shaw a few yards behind me. This was the long part of the labyrinth, the outside loop. I caught tantalizing glimpses of the garden through parts of the foliage. I hesitated once, considering making a break for it, but a glance behind me told me Shaw was so close I'd be dead before I went two steps.

I ran, skidding around the corner and coming to another thin spot. I poked through, working my way back to the outer edges but Shaw caught up to me. He grabbed my right arm, his hand clamping around my scarred skin.

I screamed, pain mingling with fear. He flung me against the yew wall, my skin abraded by scratchy needles and branches. Shaw pressed an arm against my upper chest almost suffocating me. Suffocating. Like Tanya. His gun dug into my stomach. "I'll shoot you," he whispered, his face so close to mine I saw the small beard hairs he'd missed when he shaved that morning. "If you think burns are bad, wait until you try to recover from a gut wound."

"What do you want?" I gasped, struggling to breathe with his body pressing me into the trunk of one of the small trees. I was twisted at an odd angle, part of my back supported by the tree but my left side dangling free. I tried to raise my arm to push him away, but he moved closer, his entire body leaning on mine. My arm came as high as my thigh and that's when I felt the epi-pen in my pocket.

"I want my life back." Shaw glared at me, his eyes boring into me. "My father ruined my life. I want it back."

It made no sense. None of this made sense. That didn't matter now. What mattered was I was going to die. The pen probably wouldn't harm Shaw but I might be able to startle him. I fumbled it from the pocket and dug off the safety top with my fingernail.

"I don't understand." My voice came out in a croak and my vision was beginning to blur. I waved my left hand feebly, searching for his leg.

Shaw shifted his stance, his right leg coming forward so he had more leverage. "I thought if I killed my father I'd get the money. But he left most of it to you."

"Killing…me…won't…help," I gasped.

Shaw's smile was cold and bitter, distorting his handsome features into a caricature, like a handsome prince made into a monster. "It will make me feel one hell of a lot of better." The hand holding the gun shifted, moving upward.

I drove the epi-pen into the side of his leg and pressed the plunger. I had no idea what the effect might be on someone who didn't need it, but if nothing else, I was hoping for surprise. When I leaned into it to push the pen in further, I saw Beast crouching behind Shaw, obviously unsure which way to run. He had probably come into the labyrinth to hide only to be caught between running human beings who threatened him.

Shaw reeled back, his eyes wide and mouth open. For a second he didn't move then he gasped, drawing in a huge lungful of air. Okay. I had my answer. Whatever drug was in the pen obviously had an effect. I vaguely remembered reading about it, something about blood pressure, I think. It was doing a number on Shaw, whose face reddened while he struggled to breathe. His foot landed on Beast's front paw and the cat yowled and twisted, kicking out with his back foot to dig his claws into Shaw's leg, bare in his khaki shorts.

I dropped the pen and barreled into Shaw, dumping him back into the rose arbor. Shaw fell with his arms flailing, his gun flying off to the right. The netting tangled him while the vines enfolded him. He let out a scream when the thorns dug into his arms, twisting to escape them. That only made it worse and his screams changed to terror when thorns tore his face and sank into his neck and upper body.

I whirled, searching for a spot in the yew wall. Before I could, Dillan ran around the curve and almost ran into me. "Where were you?" I yelled.

"I went left instead of right. I got mixed up." Dillan reached for Shaw, but I pulled his hand back.

"Be careful. The thorns."

Dillan tucked his gun into the holster at his back and tore the netting free of the pins holding it place. He looped the netting around Shaw's upper body and dragged Shaw from the vines, manhandling him to the ground. Shaw struggled to get up and Dillan leaned over and hit him so hard I heard bone crunch.

"Ow." Dillan straightened, shaking his hand.

I sagged back against the yews then slid to the ground. "My hero." Something jabbed me in the butt. I shifted position and found the epi-pen. "I owe you a pen."

"I'll add it to my landscaping bill. Are you okay?"

"Yeah. I wish I understood what the hell is going on, though."

Shaw stirred, arms pushing at the netting.

"You need to bring the police in here," Dillan said.

I crawled to my knees and went to a thin spot. "No problem. Don't go anywhere until I get back."

Dillan grinned. "You're the boss."

Chapter Sixteen

"That's why I called the police." Joseph Ewing, the Kelleher attorney, regarded me, Pop, and Detective Hunter over the expanse of his desk. "I was concerned about Shaw Kelleher and what he might do."

It was Monday afternoon. I spent most of Saturday night at the police station, repeating my story over and over again. I spent Sunday recovering, sleeping most of the day only to wake and discover I lost the official damn Showcase competition by only a couple of votes. Stupid fussy judges.

I did, however, come in second in the public opinion competition, which was pretty darn good. Pop and I decided that Three Sisters won only because of the sympathy vote due to Tanya's death. And two of the nursery growers contacted me about my roses. There was potential there, I was sure.

I wasn't so sure about the potential with Dillan. I don't know where he was. He went with me on Saturday to the police station, but he vanished shortly after that. I thought he'd call on Sunday, but he didn't. Then Detective Hunter came over on Monday and insisted we talk to the lawyer, and here we were, sitting in an office downtown with a bunch of documents in front of us.

"Mr. Ewing called me on Wednesday evening,

before he left town, when he couldn't get in touch with you," Hunter said to me.

Wednesday night. The night Dillan and I slept together. I kept my face coolly interested but inside I was tumbling. Why hadn't Dillan called? What was going on?

"That's when we began to consider Kelleher as a viable suspect in our investigation. He'd always been a suspect, of course."

"Of course?" Pop asked.

"The next of kin is often anxious to inherit." Hunter nodded to Ewing.

The lawyer smiled sadly. He reminded me of a minister I once knew who used to visit me in the hospital. White-haired, quiet-mannered, and almost preternaturally calm. I suppose lawyers and ministers took in many secrets and had to maintain a smooth façade. "Kelleher Senior told me that he had discussed the will with you," he said to me. "When Shaw Kelleher came to me after his father's death, he knew the provisions in the will. I didn't discuss details with him. I wouldn't do that until I could talk to you. But he knew. I'm not sure how he knew, but he did."

"Knew what?" I prompted.

"Blake Kelleher left you the bulk of his estate."

I stared at the lawyer. I'm sure I appeared as stunned as Pop did. "Why would Blake Kelleher leave me money? The agreement we had was that his heirs would continue the payments after his death."

The man folded his hands over the stack of papers on his desk. "Well, that's the problem. He didn't have an heir."

"What are you talking about? Shaw is his heir."

"Not anymore."

"But—but—" Words failed me. "Why would he do that?"

"Months ago, Mr. Kelleher removed Shaw from his will and stipulated that you become the main beneficiary. Well, you and several charities that support people who are victims of acid attacks, the way you were."

"I don't understand. Shaw has always been his father's heir."

"Let's put it this way. Shaw proved to be a disappointment in more ways than one. Mr. Kelleher saw no reason to reward his son simply because of biology. However, he did feel an obligation to you. Your stipend will be increased and in addition, he stipulated that you receive a cash settlement of twenty-five thousand dollars."

"Twenty-five thousand? Why? How—why?"

"It's a thousand dollars for every year since the attack. In addition, you have access to another one hundred thousand dollars in a trust fund, to use as you see fit. He wanted to do this years ago, but his son negotiated that initial contract with you and it couldn't be changed. Mr. Kelleher wanted a fund set up for you that would help you long into the future. He was a fair man and an honest man. That's more than I can for his son."

"What?" I couldn't keep track of what was happening. It was too much coming too fast.

The lawyer and Hunter exchanged a look. "Shaw Kelleher embezzled from his father's companies," Hunter said. "His mother covered up for him by paying for his errors from her own trust fund. When she died, it started to unravel."

"But—but—"

"I became suspicious when Blake Kelleher's attorney contacted me and told me he was unable to get in touch with you because he'd been called out of town on urgent family matters," Hunter said. "Mr. Ewing told me he'd talked to Shaw Kelleher on Sunday afternoon."

"Then my daughter was attacked in Minneapolis," Ewing said. His hands, clasped in front of him on the desk, tightened.

"Attacked?" Pop and I exchanged startled glances.

"Shaw told me he went to Minneapolis on Monday," I said.

"We were keeping an eye on him. When he left town, we checked with the police. Mr. Ewing's daughter was attacked on Monday night."

"Is she okay?" Pop asked. "What happened?"

"She was mugged coming home from her office. The person who attacked her hurt her badly. She was in the hospital for several days." Ewing's lips thinned into a bitter line. "The police here faxed a picture of Shaw Kelleher to the authorities and she positively identified him as her attacker."

"But why? That doesn't make sense." I shook my head. "I think I'm saying that a lot lately."

"It pulled Mr. Ewing away. That would give Shaw time to get close to you and hopefully have you transfer ownership of the properties to him."

"But I didn't have ownership," I protested. "I hadn't talked to Mr. Ewing yet."

"Shaw wasn't sure about that. He thought that when his father came to see you, that his father told you about the will. Shaw had papers drawn up that would immediately transfer ownership of the trust fund to him as well as control of the other business interests. He already had buyers lined up."

"But he said he wanted to replace the money," I said. "He said that when he attacked me in the labyrinth."

Ewing shook his head. "He wanted the money so he could leave the country. He was planning to sell his disposable goods, take the ready cash, and flee."

"We found a one-way ticket to Thailand, his passport, and almost two-hundred-thousand in bearer bonds that he removed from the company safe. If you signed over the rest of the assets, he would have had almost a half-million in disposable cash. A man can live like a king on that kind of money in Asia." Hunter cleared his throat. "When we interrogated him, he told us that he planned to seduce you and you'd sign over everything to him. He had a low opinion of your, um, intelligence." The tips of his ears reddened.

I shook my head. "What an asshole. He assumed that I'd be so happy to have him back again that I'd do anything he asked. It's been twenty-five years—why would he think that? Do I really appear that desperate? That stupid?"

All the men in the room were silent, exchanging worried looks.

"Rhetorical question, guys," I snapped. "I'm not putting anybody on the spot here."

"Perhaps this will help clear up some of the confusion." The lawyer slid a sealed envelope across the desk to me. "Mr. Kelleher asked that I give this to you when we spoke. I believe it will explain a great deal of what happened."

I opened the stiff, thick envelope and unfolded the sheets of paper. It was typed on an old-fashioned typewriter, some of the letters fainter than the others where the key didn't strike as hard. I suppose the old man typed it himself. I gave him grudging credit for that. Nowadays it was so easy to leave an electronic trail. The old days of typewriters allowed for some privacy.

Miss Griffen—Lilith:

This is a letter from a dead man. I want to set the record straight and I want to protect you if I can from my psychopathic son. I have covered up for him and lied for him all my life. I refuse to do so at my death.

Shaw has always been deeply disturbed, from the time he was a small child. We could not have pets because of his treatment of them. His mother made excuses, but his behavior was reprehensible. He gravitated to the weak and the vulnerable and he took pleasure in making those creatures suffer.

I suppose he told you about the 'private boarding school' where he and Tanya spent their formative years. It was a psychiatric hospital for juvenile delinquents. They spent almost their entire childhood years there, undergoing different treatments, none of which served to instill any sense of empathy in either of them. On the contrary, I think it bonded them more closely to each other. They weren't tied by normal emotions of love or sympathy, but by a common desire to do whatever they wanted, regardless of the cost.

They convinced their doctors that they had their illness under control and for his college years and young adulthood, Shaw was an ideal son—or so I thought. His mother helped him cover up his 'indiscretions'. I didn't find out until later about the women he abused and abandoned, about the terrible perversions he and Tanya practiced on unsuspecting men and women.

Initially I hoped that being with someone like you—someone loving and kind—would show Shaw what life could be like. But I soon knew that he would ruin you the way he ruined so many others. I tried to warn your father and solicit his help in breaking up your relationship with Shaw. I did everything I could to encourage you to leave him, arranging for an audition, offering your father money. Nothing worked.

God forgive me, I was ashamed of him and afraid to put the light on what he had done and what he was capable of. I was afraid of the impact on my business dealings and my reputation. I should have warned you. I knew what Tanya was capable of doing. She should have stayed locked up, along with my son. I blame myself for not protecting you.

I have details about his illegal business dealings, his vicious attacks on unsuspecting victims, and other behaviors that will result in an investigation and probable jail time for him and Tanya. I've left the document with my lawyer and he was instructed to give it to the police in the event of my death. I will not continue to protect Shaw. He must accept the consequences of his actions and the world must be protected from him. Prison is the only way to do that. Shaw has proven that he cannot be 'cured.'

I've made certain that no funds will be available to Shaw to construct a viable defense. I am leaving the majority of my estate to Vitriolage Victims, but I have *directed my attorney to divert a sizable portion of my estate directly to you. I will not have you suffer any more for my lack of courage. It will not recompense you for the last twenty-five years, but I hope it will make your remaining years more enjoyable.*

Please give my best wishes to your father and tell him from me that he raised a remarkable daughter. I wished at one time that I might call you daughter, too.

Blake Kelleher

I lowered the letter, little memories of my time with Shaw making my hands tremble. The way he and Tanya always acted like co-conspirators, with so many secrets. What Tanya said, her casual dismissal, when she disfigured me: *I wanted to hurt her. I didn't think it would be that bad.* The disregard Shaw had for anyone's grief or pain. The way he treated me when I didn't feel well. He was always disinterested, so removed from anyone.

So many memories surfaced, now making sense. "Shaw never loved me. He did it to try to fool his father. I was a convenient tool." I think, somewhere in the back of mind, I had known that, but now it was spelled out for me. I handed Pop the letter and stood, making my way to the office window to stare at the prosaic street outside. "Shaw was the better actor, not me," I whispered.

The room was silent behind me. I heard the letter passed from person to person. Finally, Pop came to stand beside me. "You've always said you were lucky." He put his arm around my shoulders. "If you married him, he might have killed you."

Tears rolled down my cheeks. "You're right." I dabbed at my face, sniffing loudly then turned. "What about Tanya?"

Hunter leaned forward, setting the Kelleher letter on Ewing's desk. "She screwed up. She told you what Shaw was thinking about doing."

"She did?" I went back to my seat and Pop followed, sticking close to me.

"That's what he said. What do you remember about the conversation?"

Good Lord, that happened a lifetime ago, didn't it? I thought about it. "She said something about anything between me and Shaw would be temporary. I remember thinking she must have been crazy to think there'd be anything all. And she said something about him lying to her." I shook my head. "I don't remember it that clearly. Maybe Olivia does. She heard most of it."

"We talked to her and she did write out some of what she heard. She's a cop's wife," Hunter added when he saw my surprised expression.

A cop's wife. Like Dillan's wife? That thought surfaced, leaving me so surprised I lost my train of thought.

"I never liked that girl," Pop declared. "I always thought she was mean."

I banished thoughts of Dillan's wife and refocused on the here and now. "Shaw said something in the labyrinth. He said she knew about Minnesota."

"He had her call Mr. Ewing's daughter and delay her at her office. That's why she left late and that's why she was alone." Hunter glanced at Pop. "You're right, you know. Your daughter is lucky. Even if she signed over the property, Shaw Kelleher probably would have killed her. We're in possession of the documentation Blake Kelleher mentioned in that letter. Shaw is vicious, cold-hearted, and ruthless with a well-developed antisocial personality disorder."

"A sociopath," Pop muttered.

"Actually, he's probably a psychopath," Hunter corrected. "Neither term is clearly defined, but a sociopath is usually created by his environment and a psychopath is usually born that way. From what Kelleher says in that letter, his son has always been that way and we have no reason to believe his family or environment might have caused him to act that way." He shrugged. "That's for his defense to decide, I suppose."

"His defense?" I never thought about that. I assumed that Shaw would be locked up and somebody would throw away the key.

"There'll be a trial. You and Dillan Lyall will need to testify. Mr. Ewing may have to testify as well, at least about facts that aren't covered by attorney-client privilege. It will be months before that happens, though. I'm sure there will be numerous medical tests and delays."

"Maybe he'll go to some fancy spa like Tanya did." Pop glowered at the letter on the desk. "Money talks."

"He doesn't have any," Ewing said. "His father made sure of that." He regarded me. "I realize this is a great deal of information to absorb. I'm ready to help however I can. Blake Kelleher was a friend of mine and I know he'd want me to do what I can to assist you. It probably doesn't feel like it now, but you're a lucky woman. What happened to you years ago is a travesty, but I hope you'll accept what Blake wanted for you in the spirit in which he intended it."

"I'm sure I'll have questions. Is that all you need me for now? Do I have to sign anything or do anything?"

"Yes, there are several documents for you to sign. I'll have my secretary come in as a notary public." Ewing looked at Hunter. "Would you serve as witness?"

"Sure. Glad to do it."

Ewing pressed a button on the phone console on his desk and soon a man entered with a fat folder. What followed was an hour of 'sign here' and 'initial there' with explanations of everything as it was presented to me. I absorbed about half of what was said, my brain still reeling from the past two hours.

Pop and I finally left with assurances from Hunter that he would stay in touch. As we shook hands outside the lawyer's office, he said, "Oh, by the way. I talked to Lyall. He mentioned he still had some jewelry of yours. He asked me to give it to you." He reached in a pocket and pulled out a baggie containing the jewelry I'd worn at the conference speech.

"Oh. I thought I'd call and—I thought he might—I mean, I forgot about it." I stuffed the bag into my purse. "Thanks."

"He, uh, was wondering, I think, if you might need him for some garden work." Hunter smiled blandly. "I think he wasn't sure if he should, you know, come back." He and Pop regarded me with polite, questioning eyes.

"Well, of course," I stammered. "I mean, I didn't pay him yet. And I'm sure there's some work to do and, well, you know, work. To do."

"Good to know. If I see him, I'll tell him. You

folks take care now. I'll be in touch." Hunter headed down the street to a dark sedan parked at the curb.

I drove Pop and me home, each of us deep in thought. "I don't want the money," I said. "I don't need it. We have everything we need and with the bumped-up allowance, we have more than enough."

"Maybe some traveling? Reconstructive surgery? They've improved the techniques in the last few years."

I shook my head. "Why? I've lived most of my life like this. Why change now? Besides, I can't stand the thought of another hospital stay." I shuddered.

"I can't say I blame you." Pop tapped the bulky portfolio of papers on the seat between us. "Maybe…"

"What?"

"What about a scholarship? That kid who worked in the yard talked about how hard it was to get scholarships. Maybe something like that."

I nodded eagerly. "Yes. That's perfect."

"And you can work with Dillan on it. He probably has some ideas about what kind of scholarships might be useful."

"Sure. Maybe."

Pop glanced at me. "Just give him a call. Chat about it."

"Hmm."

He whupped me upside the head.

"Ow." I rubbed my noggin.

"I didn't raise a stupid girl. Call him."

"Yeah, yeah." I held up a hand when he tried to talk. "I've got too much to think about, Pop. Give it a rest."

He sighed. "Okay."

I knew that wasn't the end of it, but at least he

dropped it for the moment. We got home and I took the papers out to the porch to review. Beast wandered out to sit next to me on the couch.

Pop came out on the porch. "See what we got." He hefted a large gold trophy in the shape of a trowel.

"Where'd that come from? We didn't win the competition."

"A guy dropped it off." Pop came out and handed me the award. It was surprisingly heavy, with a solid wooden base.

"What guy?" I peered at the plaque affixed to the base with tiny little screws. *Best Boss Around.* "What the heck?" I looked up to quiz Pop, but he wasn't in the doorway.

Dillan stood there. "The guys figured you needed a trophy."

I swallowed hard. "They did?"

"Yeah."

Beast jumped down and went to Dillan with an enquiring *mff?* Dillan leaned over to rub the cat's ears. He had scratches on his arms from the thorn bushes. His dark gray shirt matched the gray in his hair and goatee and his dark gray jeans matched his eyes. I was suddenly overheated even though the night had cooled.

I tore my eyes away from him. "Did you know about this?" I lifted the documents resting on my lap.

He straightened and leaned in the doorway, arms crossed. "I heard something about it. I guess you're rich now."

"I suppose so." I couldn't quite decipher his tone of voice.

"I guess you'll be hiring a real landscape crew. You won't need amateurs." He stepped out onto the porch.

"Maybe." I shuffled some papers around on my lap.

"I know a guy who knows your garden pretty good." Dillan moved closer. The cat took this as an invitation. Beast went to the porch door and pawed at it. "Can he go out?"

"Sure." I waggled a finger at the cat. "Leave the birds alone," I warned. "This is a no kill zone."

Beast flicked the stump of his tail at my words as though to say, *yeah, right, go ahead, try to stop me*. Dillan opened the screen door, but the cat changed his mind, sniffing the outside world then whirling about and stalking back to sit and regard me.

"What about mice?" Dillan leaned over and picked up the papers resting next to me on the couch.

It was hard to breathe. I think my heart was beating double-time. "Mice are negotiable," I said.

"You're willing to negotiate?" he asked, putting the papers on the coffee table.

"Sometimes."

Beast jumped on my lap. He settled down, positioning most of his body on my left leg. I touched his head and he peered at me over his shoulder, a satisfied smirk on his piratical face. "You've found your spot, haven't you?" I whispered.

"He's not the only one." Dillan sank on the couch beside me on the left. Beast sighed contentedly when Dillan's thigh pressed against mine and the cat's body slid toward him.

"You're right," I said. "I think we've found what we were looking for." I stroked the cat's head.

"There's one thing I need to know. I can't figure it

out."

I focused on the cat, not sure I wanted to hear. "What?"

"Why the hell were you and Shaw Kelleher ever together in the first place?"

"Oh." I let out a breath I didn't know I was holding. "I'm not sure I ever really loved him." I shook my head. "I was almost thirty and my friends were getting married. I wanted to get married, and Shaw was there, and he was rich, so I guess I talked myself into loving him."

"That makes more sense than you being in love with him. I can't believe you were ever that superficial."

"Yeah, well, when you're young, you can do some pretty stupid things."

"Yeah, no kidding." Dillan put his arm around me.

I leaned on him. I wasn't sure what to say so I blurted the first thing I thought of. "You know, I think I do need you."

"To do what? Gardening?"

"I don't know. But I guess I'll figure out something."

He smiled. "That's why you're the boss."

"Am I your boss?" I asked, looking up at him.

"You bet." He lowered his head and our lips met. "Always."

A word about the author…

J L Wilson writes mysteries with a touch of romance—and romance with a touch of gray. She has a few dozen mysteries out there to keep you entertained.

Do you want to know who's the Beauty and who's the Beast in this book? Go to her website to find out! Just click on Who's Who.

www.jayellwilson.com

Thank you for purchasing
this publication of The Wild Rose Press, Inc.

For questions or more information
contact us at
info@thewildrosepress.com.

The Wild Rose Press, Inc.
www.thewildrosepress.com